We hope you enjoy this book. Please return or renew it by the due date.

You can renew it at www.norfolk.gov.uk/libraries or by using our free library app.

Otherwise you can phone 0344 800 8020 - please have your library card and PIN ready.

You can sign up for email reminders too.

NORFOLK ITEM

30129 085 993 690

NORFOLK COUNTY COUNCIL
LIBRARY AND INFORMATION SERV

D1334084

BY A. E. WARREN

Tomorrow's Ancestors

Subject Twenty-One
The Hidden Base

SUBJECT TWENTY ONE

A. E. WARREN

1 3 5 7 9 10 8 6 4 2

Del Rey
20 Vauxhall Bridge Road
London SW1V 2SA

Del Rey is part of the Penguin Random House group of companies
whose addresses can be found at global.penguinrandomhouse.com.

Penguin
Random House
UK

First published by Del Rey in 2021

www.penguin.co.uk

A CIP catalogue record for this book is available from
the British Library.

ISBN 9781529101348

Typeset in 10/14.5 pt ITC Galliard Std
by Integra Software Services Pvt. Ltd, Pondicherry

Printed and bound in Great Britain by Clays Ltd, Elcograf S.p.A.

The authorised representative in the EEA is Penguin Random House
Ireland, Morrison Chambers, 32 Nassau Street, Dublin D02 YH68.

Penguin Random House is committed to a sustainable future for
our business, our readers and our planet. This book is made from
Forest Stewardship Council® certified paper.

For Lee, with love

'The measure of a man is what he does with power.'

Plato

CHAPTER 1

Elise stared at the Museum of Evolution's heavy side door as it closed behind her. It was unassuming in design, unlike the grandiose entrance at the front of the building, but it still held her attention. She had finally been offered a job that she wanted, her first and only chance to escape the daily eleven-hour shifts fixing handles onto the ends of brooms and coaxing splinters out of the palms of her hands. She would have agreed to start that day, but as she was expected to live at the museum during the week, she had matters to settle at home first.

Reasoning that she couldn't continue to stare at a closed door, no matter how fond she had recently become of it, she bent over her backpack and dug out her favourite grey hooded top. Pulling it on over her shirt, she zipped it all the way to her chin. She drew the hood over her cropped brown hair and pushed her thumbs through the holes in the sleeves that she had created years ago. Her actions were carried out with intention; she never dithered outside her home. 'Purpose and Productivity' was Thymine Base's motto and she always adhered to it, in public anyway.

Straightening, she slung her bag over her shoulders. The straps had been tightened so it sat high on her back, the best position to allow her to run. She then set off at a steady pace towards her parents' house.

As Elise navigated the small, winding paths, she watched the sun preparing to set over the low roofs. The sleeping quarters were dug into the ground and only the kitchens nudged their way above the surface to catch the natural light. Each building was angled to maximise its exposure and to take advantage of natural windbreaks; there was no symmetry or aesthetic considerations in their positioning. To the untrained eye, the effect was of children dropping their building blocks and abandoning them as they fell.

This was Elise's favourite time of day. It was when she felt that she might just keep on running, past the circular boundary line marked by dense ferns and into the unknown. It was an idle thought, though, one she teased herself with at the production centre to pass the time. People like Elise didn't get to leave; they weren't important enough to warrant the supplies needed to make the journey to another base.

Pushing the thought away, she allowed herself to be soothed by the noise of her feet steadily hitting the soft rubber pathway. Ignoring the splashes from the small puddles that had formed after the brief autumn shower, she allowed her mind to drift.

She had only told her parents about the interview that morning, to limit their time to object. Weighing her options, she reasoned that her only way to win them over was the extra tickets. She guessed that her mum would understand her reasons for wanting to work at the museum but would try to persuade her to stay. Her dad would just ban her from taking the job. The tickets would make them both think again.

As Elise rounded the corner to join the narrow path that led to her house, she slowed to a brisk walk to cool down. Although it was a short run, it was all uphill. Shielding her eyes from the sun, she turned to look down over the only base she had ever known. The grass and wildflower-covered roofs of the distant houses blended so well with the landscape that she could barely pick them out. The only indications that this was a settlement were the public buildings in the centre of the valley that were allowed two or three floors of indulgence. No higher, though, as the natural slopes of the valley had to conceal the settlement from afar. From only half a mile away, Thymine did not exist; it was just another valley in a vast, unpopulated landscape.

There were only eight Sapien families who lived off this tendril of the pathway. Each of their low-slung homes was made of panels of recycled material from old car tyres, plastics and glass. These were then covered in packed earth and vegetation where possible. The houses were unevenly settled around a small stream. This positioning near the water was arbitrary, though, as it no longer held any practical purpose. Despite being so clear that you could see the round pebbles resting on its bed, none of the locals would drink or swim in it. The fear of reinfection was too great. Instead, each house had its small tank replenished every day with treated water that tasted so sharp it was only drunk out of necessity, not refreshment.

Elise's home was at the far end of the lane. They had a little bit more land to the side of the house, which her mum and dad used to grow vegetables. Their neighbours were amused by the family's insistence on growing some of their own food, one of the many reasons they were shunned. The neighbours couldn't fathom why anyone would spend their spare time doing something so unnecessary as growing fruit and vegetables. All of their staple food was evenly distributed by the most advanced species of human, the Potiors. Tickets would buy the rest. Free time was for relaxing, to prepare for the next day, not for unnecessary digging.

As Elise neared her home, she saw her mum, Sofi, kneeling next to one of the borders of spring onions with a small trowel. She was still, and her grip on the trowel was so loose that it was almost falling from her hand. Staring into the forest edge, she looked lost in her thoughts. As Elise approached, Sofi turned. She smiled and motioned her to go inside the house.

Elise followed her into the small kitchen, the centre of their home. There were no cupboards in which to tidy anything away and, consequently, all of their pans, utensils and plates either hung from hooks on the walls or were displayed on narrow shelves. Even the carving knives were strung along the edge of the highest shelf like macabre bunting. It was Elise's father, Aiden, who insisted on this open cupboard policy; he would arrange the heaviest pans so they were the easiest to grab from the walls. Sofi and Elise did their best to soften this severe display by dotting the room with small, hand-tied bunches of seasonal flowers; this week it was cornflowers. They would even drape ivy along the shelves, careful not to cover the pan and knife handles.

It wasn't until they closed the door that Sofi spoke. 'So how'd it go?'

Her mother leant against the door with both hands behind her, her cheeks rosy from the chafing wind.

'I was interviewed by two Medius and they offered me the job, is the shortened version.'

'Do you want it?'

'Course I do,' Elise said, half smiling, trying to soften the impact of her words. 'Can you imagine what it might be like? Getting to work with all those species of animal that have been brought back again? I can help "restore what should never have come to pass",' she recited before noticing Sofi's frown. 'And if I do well with Twenty-One, they might even let me be a Keeper one day.'

Sofi's frown deepened.

'I want to help out with the extra tickets, too,' Elise added.

'Change can bring you down as well as up, Elise. Don't think that because something's different it's also better. And don't pretend that you wouldn't do it for half the tickets.'

Elise knew this was true.

'Your dad is out with Nathan collecting seeds, but he should be back soon. I would save the long version for when he's home and we'll talk it through as a family.'

Sofi pushed herself away from the door and walked over to the sink to wash her hands. As she passed Elise, she rubbed her shoulder, but the gesture didn't have its usual settling effect. Elise knew if her mum wasn't convinced, there was no chance of persuading her dad. She pulled out a seat at the kitchen table her uncle had made before she was born. Tracing her fingers across the underside, she found the familiar grooves where he had carved his name and glanced at Sofi's turned back. Deemed an adult from the age of fourteen, she knew she didn't technically need her parents' permission, but she didn't want to cause a rift in the family either. If she just left, her dad might not let her see her younger brother, Nathan, when she came home to visit. If her dad even let her visit.

Knowing she would have to wait for him to return, she picked up the household screen filled with the news articles her parents read every day. Resting her forehead against one of her hands, she read the first headline: 'No Sapien Dies of Starvation for Over 50 Years'. Elise scanned the article that confirmed this achievement had happened for the first time in recorded history. It went on to contrast this with the Pre-Pandemic figures of 20,000 Sapiens dying every year from starvation. The reporters always contrasted the Pre- and Post-Pandemic figures. As usual, the article had a sobering effect on Elise as she thought of all those who had died even before the Pandemic that had nearly wiped out her species. She could never escape the Sapiens' legacy. Her previous elation dissipated and she felt drained of energy, as if she could lay her head on the table and fall straight to sleep.

Making an effort to rouse herself, she flicked over to the next article: 'Only Two Violent Crimes Recorded in Thymine Base in the Past Year'. There was only one outcome for anyone committing these offences. Expelled from the base, they would die within days without supplies. Elise didn't bother to read further. The reporters never described what the 'violent crimes' were and she didn't want to know the Pre-Pandemic figures; it would only depress her further.

'Can the Medius and Potior choose enhanced genetic traits to help them know what we're thinking?' Elise said, flicking over to the next article as she considered whether she had ever thought about committing a violent crime.

Sofi turned abruptly from the sink, water dripping from her hands onto the floor. 'What happened? What did you say in that interview?'

Elise wasn't surprised by Sofi's tone; she was used to her mum leaping to the worst conclusion. She didn't want to upset her, though, so she used her most soothing voice. 'Don't worry, I didn't say or even think anything wrong. I just said what they wanted to hear, as you've always told me to.' Once her mum had been appeased, Elise held out the screen. 'It was just this article I was thinking about.'

Sofi pulled out a chair from the table and perched on it, considering Elise's question. 'As far as I know, there's nothing they could do except teach them how to read body language and the like. But not the mind. That's always safe. As long as you keep the face still at all times and—'

'Never, ever, react,' Elise finished for her.

Sofi leant forwards and put her hand on her daughter's knee. 'I know you think your dad and I over-worry, but if you take this job you must be careful. While you're in the museum compound you'll be monitored at all times. Everyone is. Think carefully about whether it's worth the risk.' Sofi squeezed Elise's knee and leant closer. 'This life might be stifling, but it's safe. At the museum you might as well be one of the displays.'

Elise jumped when the door burst open and banged against the wall. Her younger brother, Nathan, ran in, followed closely by their dad, Aiden.

Nathan went directly to Elise and signed, 'We bought pumpkin seeds and are going to try and grow them.' He was grinning. 'Dad said they should grow bigger than my head, maybe even bigger than my body if they get enough sunlight and water.'

Smiling back at Nathan, Elise pulled out a chair so he could sit next to her. She lifted her hands to sign to her brother.

'Maybe we can go out and plant them together before it gets dark. All four of us.'

She turned to Aiden, who was leaning against the kitchen dresser with his arms folded over his chest. It was only when he was at home that he stood straight and his size could be fully comprehended. When he was outside, he had a tendency to stoop and almost fold in on himself. Elise could see that he had already guessed her news and there was no chance of this day ending with a normal family activity.

'So I got the job,' Elise signed.

'I didn't doubt you would, but you know you can't take it,' Aiden signed. Before she could respond, he changed the subject. 'Did you run back from the museum? What was your time?'

'Forty-two minutes.'

Normally she would be a little concerned about telling him this, but today it had become trivial.

Aiden rubbed his eyes. 'You can't let your fitness levels slip any further. You have to concentrate on it over the next few weeks.' He pushed himself away from the dresser. 'You never know when you'll have to get out of a situation and your body could easily let you down if you don't keep up your training. I'll come up with a new programme and we can start work on it tomorrow.'

Turning, he reached for the skipping rope hanging from a hook by the front door.

When Elise had been younger, she had willingly complied with her dad's relentless regimes and training, eager to please him and win his approval. Then, slowly, as she had spent more time away from home, first at school and then at work, she had come to realise that there were no dangers out there for her to contend with. No plain-clothed officials came knocking at the door in the middle of the night. No one ever threatened her or her family. She could walk through Thymine Base at four in the morning and anyone she met would wish her a good day and make a pleasant comment about watching the sunrise. It was the thought of her dad extending his suffocating hold over her that she feared, not Thymine.

'My new job starts tomorrow.'

Aiden bristled. 'I suppose they'll want you to live at the museum as well, eh? Don't want to live with your mum and dad any more? How about your brother?'

Elise winced and turned to Nathan. 'I'll be home every Sunday and we can spend all afternoon together. Do whatever you want, I promise.'

'*You can't work in the Museum of Evolution.* I won't hear any more about it,' Aiden signed, more forcefully than usual.

He picked up the skipping rope and held it out to Elise expectantly. She didn't move to take it, gently putting her hand on Nathan's arm when he started to reach for it, never taking her eyes from their father. Sofi started rearranging the jam jars on the lowest shelf in the room, her small way of trying to defuse the situation. The clinking of the glass containers was the only noise for a full minute.

Sighing, he put down the skipping rope and continued slowly as if explaining something to a small child. 'You'll be one of the few Sapiens in the museum compound. This means that you'll be watched more than if you were working with, say, two hundred Sapiens in a production centre. The best place to hide a knife is in a cutlery drawer. Same applies to you.'

Elise had heard a similar speech nearly every day of her life; it was difficult to hide her frustration. 'I don't need to be hidden;

this level of secrecy and protection isn't needed. The Rising ended nearly twenty years ago. You've said yourself that we have to move on, be grateful for what we have and not pine after what could've been. I can't live with this paranoia any more.' Aiden lifted his hands to respond, but she quickly continued. 'They won't be interested in me anyway. I've passed all the neuropsychological tests and nothing was flagged: no feelings of resentment, no exceptionally high IQ, no borderline personality disorders or sociopathic tendencies. I'm completely mundane.'

'You know why I'm doing this; we've already lost too many people in this family.'

'That was twenty years ago, before I was even born.'

'Okay, Nathan, I think it's time for bed. Go and get ready and I'll come and check on you in a minute,' Sofi signed, clearly trying to brighten her face.

Elise could see that Nathan was thinking about protesting, but after glancing at his mum, he decided against it. Instead he turned to Elise and signed, 'Have you got a new job?'

'Maybe,' she signed back, 'but I'll tell you about it in the morning.'

Elise leant over and hugged him close.

'I'll see you in the morning, I promise,' she signed, nudging him towards his bedroom.

Once the door had closed, Sofi went over to Aiden and reached for his hand, giving it a little tug to get his attention. 'I think we have to remember that Elise isn't a child any more; she hasn't been for years.' She paused to see if her words were having any effect. 'We can help her with decisions, but we shouldn't make them for her. No good will come from that.' She squeezed his hand. 'Everything is settled; it's not like before.'

Elise turned to Aiden again and tried to keep control of her voice. It was better to reason with his smudged view of the base than try and convince him that her excitement about working in the museum was a valid reason for taking the job.

'You can't protect me forever, Dad. And there isn't much to protect anyway. I'd get to see more of Thymine as well, not just the Outer Circle. And at the museum I'll just fade into the background as I always do; you know I'll keep my mouth shut.'

'It's not what you say; it's what you accidentally do that I'm more concerned about.'

Elise decided to ignore this comment. 'You know we need the extra tickets. We've hardly any Medi-stamps.'

She was starting to feel desperate. This was her only opportunity to live somewhere else. Even if she married, her husband would move into her parents' house, just as Aiden had moved into Sofi's family home, which they had shared with Elise's grandparents until they passed away. No Sapien started afresh in their own home; it was deemed unnecessary and sometimes four or five generations would live together.

'I'll be spending all my time with Twenty-One anyway, so I'll barely see anyone. I'm allowed to come home every Sunday, so next Sunday, which is only five days away, I'll tell you about everything that has happened and if you don't think it's safe I'll quit straight away and say that I can't keep working there as I'm terrified of Twenty-One.'

Elise stopped to draw a breath and was about to continue when Sofi interjected. 'We do need the extra tickets. We've hardly any Medi-stamps. What will we do if one of us gets really sick? And you know she's smart enough to stay on her guard.

She doesn't ever lose her temper. Like she said, she passed the tests. They won't be interested in her now. They've more important things to worry about than a Sapien girl from the Outer Circle.'

Aiden turned to Elise and she met his gaze. 'Five days and then you come straight back here and we discuss how it's going. Agreed?'

Elise nodded at Aiden and leant in to hug him quickly, pleased she could leave with some sort of permission.

When she pulled away, he held on to her by both shoulders. 'Just be careful out there; you know I'm just trying to protect you. If they find out what you can do, they will want it for themselves; they always do. We've already lost your aunt and uncle.'

Awake by six the next morning, Elise calculated that she had only had four hours' sleep. For the moment, the adrenaline would have to keep her going. She was sitting at the kitchen table nursing a mug of hot water and fresh lime juice when Sofi padded in.

'I think we're going to need more than lime juice this morning to get us going; I didn't sleep well either,' she said, heading to the kitchen dresser.

She reached up to the highest shelf to pull down the old, battered biscuit tin where they kept their ground coffee. This was a rare occasion as coffee cost five tickets, half the price of a Medistamp.

Elise smiled with anticipation as Sofi measured the coffee and brewed it on the electric hob, all the while making small talk about the local news. Elise would normally only half listen, but this morning she savoured these familiarities.

Sofi poured the coffee into two mugs and brought them over to the table. 'I just remembered what I didn't tell you last night. I was so caught up with your news it slipped my mind.' She took a sip from her mug. 'The Thinckles won this month's lottery. There was so much squawking coming from their house I was finding it hard to pretend I couldn't hear what was going on. I had to act surprised when Deeta bustled down the path to tell me. She was bursting with it, and I think she's already started to walk with a little extra swagger.' Sofi paused and stared into her mug. 'I shouldn't be so cruel, though; I know it means everything to her.'

Elise rolled her eyes. 'You're not being mean, Mum. Everyone knows that Deeta Thinckle has all the sense of a teaspoon. I can't believe how patient you are with her. Nobody else is.' Elise looked at her mum to see if her words had registered. 'So has she chosen her traits yet?'

The monthly lottery was the only access the Sapiens had to genetic engineering. Three altered traits made you a Medius; ten would make you a Potior. Sapiens were born without any tweaking, stuck with whatever shuffled genes they inherited from their parents.

'No, not yet. She mentioned height and IQ, of course, the two classics.' Sofi paused. 'The conversation ground to a halt, though, when she mentioned the genetic trait for luck. It was a bit awkward. She thought that if the child were lucky then they'd get access to more engineering in the future and they could become a Potior. You'd think her child becoming Medius would be enough.'

Sofi sighed. 'It reminded me of when you ask someone what they'd do if they had one wish. And then they ask for more wishes.

I decided not to tell her that there isn't any genetic coding for luck; she already thinks I'm a know-it-all. Anyway, I'm sure she'll work it out soon enough when she sees that it's not on the list.'

Draining her coffee mug, Sofi placed it firmly on the table. 'Right, I'd better get you some supplies. We don't want you relying on those Nutri-tabs or you'll end up with scurvy locked up in that compound. It's the real stuff for you, Elise, and no quibbles either.'

Elise didn't protest. Instead, she stood and stretched. 'I'm going to head over to Holly's now, if that's okay? I'll be back before you all leave, though.'

Sofi grabbed Elise's arm as she turned to find her hooded jacket. 'Don't mind your dad, now. You know his bark is worse than his bite.'

Elise just nodded and swallowed the rest of her coffee, along with everything else she wanted to say.

Setting off with her head up, Elise tried to savour her last moments outside for the next few days. Elise's closest friend, Holly, worked as a teaching assistant at the local Sapien junior school and Elise knew she could catch her before she left her home if she ran fast enough.

When she arrived, Elise tapped on Holly's window rather than the front door, more out of habit than necessity. The recycled glass was thick and mottled with small bubbles of air caught in its surface. It was designed to let in light without losing heat, rather than provide a clear view of the outside world; it was like staring through the bottom of a bottle.

Elise could hear Holly through the open window, trying to push a stuck drawer back into its rightful place. She was clearly frustrated with the task, based on the amount of shoving and harrumphing.

'I'll be at the front in two minutes,' Holly called out when she heard the three taps on the window.

Smiling to herself, Elise pictured petite Holly waging war with a drawer as she trotted round to the front door. Sitting on their usual bench, she tried not to shiver as the wind whipped around her head; it was always more blustery at the lip of the valley. She had only just sat when Holly poked her head around the door.

'Who won?' Elise enquired.

'I may've lost the first round, but it's all "Purpose and Productivity" here,' Holly said, rolling her eyes.

Holly had always resented living in Thymine, where manufacturing was the usual employment for Sapiens. Most weeks, she would tell Elise that she wished she had been born in Guanine Base, where the universities were. Its motto was 'Education and Enlightenment'. If she had been born there, she could have worked as a librarian's assistant. Instead, the local junior school was the closest thing Thymine Base offered to Sapiens, and it was a poor second for Holly.

'How come you're here so early? Everything alright?' Holly said, sliding onto the bench next to Elise.

'Everything's pretty good,' Elise said, smiling. 'I got the job as the Companion. What's even more shocking is that Dad's agreed to me taking it. Didn't stop him from acting as if we were still living through the Rising, though.'

'That again! Your folks are always stuck in the past.' Brushing them aside, Holly grinned. 'What's more important is you're actually going to get out of the production centres and whatever else they've lined up for you.' She paused as she scanned Elise's face. 'What's with the lack of smiling joy, though? Do you not want it?'

'No, no, I do. You know I've always wanted to be a Keeper there and this'll hopefully be my stepping stone. I just don't know what to expect of the Medius is all. I only ever really see them on the pathways. And there was our teacher, of course, but that's not the same as actually working with them.' Elise leant forwards and lowered her voice. 'You do, though, and they're fine with you, aren't they?'

Elise watched Holly twist her earring stud between her fingers, a habit she had developed in the last couple of years. Elise didn't try to hurry her.

'Well, yes . . . but I work at a school and most of the Midders there are pretty harmless,' Holly finally answered. 'You don't get asked to work with eight-year-olds if you've had your warrior gene tweaked, do you? The Midders can be a bit full of themselves, especially the ones with increased IQs. But they know I'm pretty smart too. One or two of them even ask my opinion on how to handle some of the more withdrawn kids. Only when there's no one around to hear them, though.'

Holly pushed some of the loose soil with the toe of her boot and leant forwards with her arms on her knees. 'But the point is that you're not going to work in some Outer Circle nursery. You'll be going into the belly of the beast.' She paused. 'Well, perhaps not the belly, but definitely the oesophagus of the beast. All of the Midders there will have high-grade engineering. No enhanced basket-weaving skills there.'

Elise leant back, accepting Holly's point. Genetic engineering was tiered so that some skills were more expensive. IQ, immune system and body conditioning were at the top. The sex of a child, eye and hair colour, and the more passive traits, such as an enhanced ability to nurture, were at the lower end.

Holly smiled at Elise's look of concern and playfully nudged her elbow. 'Don't worry about it, Elise; they won't even notice that you're there. You'll probably be made to feel on par with a door handle: a functional necessity, but hardly worth having a conversation with.'

'That's fine by me, as long as they occasionally pop into the cage to notice the outstanding work I'm doing with Twenty-One.'

'Elise, don't *say* that. Are you actually going to be caged up with it every day?'

'I imagine so. We're hardly going to be setting off on twilight strolls round the museum grounds. Who knows what I'll be doing? We never hear of them or get to see them. It might just be a stuffed display that I have to dust every day and wheel around on a trolley.'

'Caged all day with it? Bleugh.' Holly shuddered. 'Well, that's just given me the spinal cord shivers. You no longer have my congratulations. I take them back.' Holly grinned at Elise and gave her a gentle shove. 'So when do you start?'

'In about two hours.' Elise smiled at Holly and stood. She started to brush the back of her trousers. 'So I'd better get home before I miss Nathan. I'll be back on Sunday, though, if you're around?'

Holly grinned. 'Of course I'll be around. I'm not going to miss hearing your daring tales of life in a cage, not talking to anyone. Wouldn't miss it for all the tickets in the world.'

Holly paused as she scanned Elise's face. 'You've probably had enough unwelcome advice from your folks, but it's my honorary right as best friend to chuck in my ticket's worth. Don't get too pally with the Midders. One or two of them might pretend to be your friend, but they're not. They see the Potiors as the way forward and us as a backwards step on the road to perfection. Any niceties on their part are no more than charity. They don't actually give a stuff about us.'

Elise arrived at her parents' house with only ten minutes before they left for work. She suspected that Sofi had spoken with Aiden; he was clearly resigned to her leaving. Sofi had prepared a canvas bag with some limes, olives, spinach leaves and peeled carrots, which Elise was under strict instructions to eat every day. There was no more mention of her reconsidering her decision.

Goodbyes were said and everyone agreed that it was only a few days until they would see one another again. Elise made sure she spent a long time saying goodbye to Nathan; she wanted him to know how much she would miss him. No one mentioned that this was Elise's first time away from home for more than one night.

When they had left, the house was quiet. Elise found herself clattering around to fill the place with noise. She unpacked and repacked her bag, an unnecessary but occupying task. With nothing left to do, she sat at the kitchen table and wondered when she would next be completely alone.

CHAPTER 2

* *

The Museum of Evolution opened daily at ten to the general public. Elise had tried the handle of her new favourite side door but it remained firmly closed, quickly going down in her estimation. As she was early, she decided to wait at the main entrance instead. Settling on the top step, she rested her chin on her knees. From this position, she had a clear view over the gardens.

The outside of the museum could have been mistaken for base offices if it weren't for the glass-domed roof and landscaped islands of plants encircling the building. These floating gardens were surrounded by shallow water that lapped at their edges. Each distinct zone was of a differing size and shape, all large enough to be walked around by several visitors at once. Suspended wooden walkways crossed over each teal-coloured expanse and linked the plots. Visitors passing over these swaying bridges on their way to the next island could stop and admire the occasional plant popping its head above the surface of the water.

Although undoubtedly delightful, like everything designed by the Potiors, there was also method in the layout. It wasn't until the visitor was standing at the top of the museum entrance steps that the final picture could be grasped: the gardens were designed as an atlas. Each continent was shaped with its own indigenous plants. The wooden bridges crossed the oceans, allowing visitors to explore each country, or view the smaller islands represented by just a cluster of plants.

A Medius teacher was standing next to a clutch of palm trees in the southwest corner of the map. He was gesturing and pointing in different directions, using the time before the museum opened as an opportunity to lecture the Sapien children who were gathered around him. Too far away to hear what he was saying, Elise could still make an accurate guess. Each year that she had been in school, she had been brought here by her teachers and had received the same prescribed tour. Even as a baby in nursery school, she'd had to attend. The order of the displays, the emphasis, and even the explanatory tone never changed. Sixteen tours in total.

Most of her classmates had decided to leave school at fourteen; the call of adulthood and independence was too irresistible. Despite the financial pressures, Elise's parents had made sure she stayed in school as long as a Sapien was allowed, till she was sixteen. It was dangerous to teach Sapiens beyond that age; history had shown that they could not be trusted with too much knowledge. It was better if they contributed through work, not ideas.

Looks of mild bewilderment crossed the children's faces. One little boy was crying. Elise guessed that the teacher was relaying the Sapiens' intentional destruction of the rainforest. They would then move on to the consequent extinction of multiple species that relied on its habitat for survival. This was just one of the *Seven Routes to Extinction*; a short film containing the more graphic images usually accompanied this part of the tour. Restoring the habitat of Zone 3, which was once known as Europe, was one of the reasons they lived in four tightly populated bases, hundreds of miles apart from one another. They couldn't be allowed to spread out as they did before.

Grabbing her bag, Elise stood when she heard the bolts at the back of the doors stubbornly slide open. Metal ground against metal. Elise waited until she heard the bolts lock into place behind the surface of the doors. Both of the twelve-foot gates swung inwards at the same time without a glimpse or clue as to who was opening them. The effect was unearthly. Elise took a deep breath before forcing her feet to carry her inside.

She was the first of the visitors to climb the black marble staircase that led into the reception hall. The stairway was intentionally confined and Elise never failed to give a small gasp when she emerged into the main room, despite visiting most weekends in her free time. Following the claustrophobic staircase, the brightness of the glass atrium made her blink rapidly. Her other senses took over as she became attuned to the calls and songs of animals long ago lost to the outside world. Once her eyes adjusted, she peered into the distance, searching for any boundaries or walls, anything that indicated the parameters of the expanse. There were none, though, not to the human eye. Everything was landscaped to give the suggestion of a never-ending continuance; deep stretches of trees and gently rolling hills in the distant corners hinted at what lay beyond. Compounding the effect was a glass ceiling so high that the entire central atrium appeared open to the sky.

Walkways spiralled in every direction to viewing platforms. From them, visitors could safely observe woolly mammoths, leopards, giraffes, dodos, bottlenose dolphins, giant sloths and other previously extinct animals grazing in their differing habitats. Species were separated into individually designed pods, which replicated the environments they had previously thrived in. But there were no physical boundaries between the pods that could be seen; an uninterrupted vista was held in place by the invisible barriers between sections. The woolly mammoths were in a herd in the snow-covered tundra. Next to them, the sabretooth tigers prowled through grassland. The pod below held the leopards, lounging in low branches as they watched for prey. Salt and freshwater pools teeming with fish of all sizes and shapes were dotted around. All the animals' instinctive needs were accommodated and they were either kept alone or in packs to mirror their habits in the wild. Each animal was free to roam in its own meticulously designed captivity.

The Potiors, as the new guardians of the planet, had set themselves the task of reversing the devastation inflicted on the environment by the Sapiens. One of the key projects was systematically reversing the order of extinction, starting with the most recently lost species such as zebras and baboons, then working backwards, through humpback whales, dire wolves and bush-antlered deer.

They had not managed to bring back all extinct animals, only the ones where near intact genomes could be mapped and copied in a process that evolved from cloning. The animals they were unable to revive, due to the deterioration of the DNA samples, were displayed as life-sized models in the rooms leading off the arboretum, so realistic that they were warm to the touch. Teams of Medius biologists, archaeologists and palaeontologists travelled across all of the zones searching for remains to further expand the collection.

A sparkling sign above the reception desk, which Elise thought at odds with the natural vista, confirmed that the Potiors had reached 40,000 years of reversal. The majority of species lost in the past 40,000 years had been successfully copied and now roamed the museum.

Refraining from taking any of the enticing walkways, Elise instead presented herself at the reception desk. Glancing at the receptionist, Elise could tell she was a Medius from her appearance, even before she took in her name's three syllables on the badge pinned to her lapel: 'Katheryn – The Art of Impart'. Names were strictly controlled, two syllables for a Sapien and three for a Medius – no departures and no exceptions.

Elise didn't often get to look at a Medius so directly. Not that Katheryn looked so very different from Elise, just more polished. Any Sapien imperfections sanded away. Admiring Katheryn's thick, blonde hair, which fell in gentle waves, Elise absent-mindedly reached for her own hair. It felt coarse between her fingertips and she thought there was glitter in it from the sign above her head.

Following Katheryn's instructions, Elise placed her bag in one of the lockers and stood in the middle of the foyer, waiting to be collected. Her attention flicked to the slightest waft of air that was circling her head. Smaller than a bluebottle fly and just as mobile, the camera had been drawn to her slightly raised heartbeat. The trick was to continue as normal. If it thought it was recording covertly, it would move on quicker. The cameras were there to protect the citizens, heralded as the reason that violent crimes were so low. Elise, therefore, continued to absent-mindedly pick the glitter off her sleeve while she waited.

Satisfied, the camera drifted over to a group of school children. Their frustration at not being able to run off and explore while their teacher signed them in had drawn the camera's attention. Elise was certain that she was now outside its range and interest.

A short, bustling woman approached, clutching her screen tightly, and Elise straightened up, ready to be introduced. She wasn't sure if the woman was a Sapien or Medius; her manner projected Medius, but her underwhelming appearance suggested Sapien. Elise would have to wait to hear her name.

'Right, Elise Thanton, I presume?' Elise opened her mouth to respond, but was cut off. 'ID first.'

Elise had known this was coming and had already started to unbutton the shirtsleeve covering her right arm. Rolling the sleeve up, she angled her wrist so that the woman could read the black tattoo markings more easily.

'Elise Thanton, 17 February 2250, Thymine Base, Sapien,' the woman said, glancing between Elise's wrist and the small screen she held in her hand.

When Elise pulled her sleeve back, she paused for a second and let her finger linger over the tattoo, imagining her arm without it. Like all Sapiens and Medius, she'd had the tattoo done on her fourteenth birthday. For Elise, the tattoo was confirmation that she would never be a child again. For a Medius, it was confirmation that they would never be mistaken for a Sapien again.

'Right, now that's over, I shall begin. I am Har-ri-et Thimble from the Worker Profiling Department and I am in charge of your induction.' Harriet made a point of emphasising the three syllables of her name, clearly concerned with there being no confusion. 'Each new recruit, even the Cleaners and Companions, must be given the initial tour. This ensures that everyone who works here is able to answer basic questions posed by a member of the public. We cannot be held out as an institution of education if our own staff are found lacking.'

Harriet never once lifted her eyes as she addressed Elise; she stared anywhere except at her face. 'Of course, you will not be expected or required to go into much detail. Answer briefly and then point them in the right direction for the exhibition rooms. One of the museum Hosts will then take over.'

Harriet was wearing a fuchsia-pink blouse which had a large bow at the collar and frills at the end of the sleeves. The bow had caught some of Harriet's breakfast, a crusty stain she was seemingly oblivious to. Guessing it was the remnants of runny egg, Elise tried not to stare; it made her stomach churn.

'We shall start in some of the back rooms as they give a concise view of evolutionary history. The central atrium,' Harriet made a sweeping gesture with her arm that Elise had to jerk backwards to dodge, 'is more for the schoolchildren.'

Sniffing, Harriet headed across the foyer. She didn't check to see if Elise was following. Instead, she briskly stepped onto a concealed moving walkway rolling towards an arch in the far corner. Elise could see writing over the archway but couldn't make out the words. Harriet drifted away from Elise as if she were the mechanised one, not the walkway. Cautiously stepping forwards, Elise hoped that she had picked the right place to join the hidden travelator. Relieved that her left leg started to move forwards, she pulled her other leg up as well.

Elise caught up with Harriet, whose back was still turned; she was pleased that Harriet hadn't witnessed her less than graceful ascent. They could have continued to walk along the travelator, but Harriet seemed content to let it convey them at a grindingly slow pace.

Turning around, Harriet pulled herself up to her full height and opened her mouth. It was a false start, though. Her eyes darted down to her screen again. Then, with a faraway look and grandeur in her tone, she began. 'It is only through observing and accepting our past that we can begin to comprehend our future. This is the reason that the Museum of Evolution was built.'

Harriet furtively glanced at her screen again and returned to addressing the cypress tree over Elise's shoulder. 'As you are hopefully aware, we are of the mammal class.'

Harriet raised an eyebrow, only continuing after Elise had nodded. 'There are many subcategories of mammal. Humans are part of the Great Ape family, along with chimpanzees, gorillas and orangutans. We share ninety-seven per cent of our DNA with orangutans.'

Despite her annoyance at Harriet's pompous style, Elise was interested in the potted history. As they silently drifted through the savannah, Elise carefully listened to Harriet's speech while taking the opportunity to watch the mammoths grazing in the pod over her shoulder. It certainly beat her introductory tour at the production centre, which had comprised being shown where the toilets were, followed by the emergency stop button for if someone's hand became caught in the machinery.

'Before the Pandemic, Zone 4 was called Africa. It was here, between six and seven million years ago, that what would become the human evolutionary line split off from the chimpanzee.'

Elise tried to let this sink in; she had not been taught about it in such depth. Her anthropology and history classes had centred on the destruction that Sapiens had previously caused, and the methods the Potiors were using to rectify this.

'Over the course of the following millions of years there were many branches of our predecessors. Many trials . . . and many failures. It wasn't until two million years ago that anything distinctly human emerged.'

Neatly hopping off the end of the travelator, Harriet started to walk through the arch they had been moving towards. She didn't turn to see if Elise was following. Glancing up, Elise could see that there was only one word above the archway: 'Humans'. Elise took a few seconds to stare behind her at the open savannahs before following Harriet.

They entered a small room where all the walls and the floor were painted black. There were ten lifelike models of humans of varying heights. Each one was lit by a single spotlight, which gave the impression of complete isolation. There was nothing to provide the context of time or place. Elise thought that the ones closest to her appeared similar to tall apes standing on two feet rather than on all fours. However, towards the far right, she could see that the figures were strikingly similar to herself and Harriet.

Each of the models was set wide apart from the next one, with ample room for the viewer to walk around them. Harriet began to weave between them and Elise followed. She found it disconcerting that as Harriet moved out of one spotlight, she would disappear for a few seconds before reappearing close to another model. Harriet was not the sort of person Elise wanted to lose track of.

Harriet stopped directly below one of the spotlights, which cast long shadows down her face. 'Of course, you would have come to a similar room during your schooling, but I don't honestly know how much of it really sinks in with you Saps.'

She gave Elise a sideways look to see if she had provoked a reaction, but Elise just continued to stare passively over Harriet's head, her features unmoved.

Harriet linked both her hands behind her back and gently rocked backwards and forwards on her feet. 'Did you know that before the Pandemic the Saps didn't even really teach anthropology in schools? It was seen as a specialist subject that might be chosen at university along with floristry or economics. They were so basic. So misguided as to what an education should consist of.'

Elise bit the inside of her lip. She decided to concentrate on the stain on Harriet's bow, which was gently rocking in and out of the light. Evidence that for all her pomp and glory, Harriet still occasionally missed her mouth while eating.

With a sigh, Harriet set off again towards the far end of the room, her screen clasped to her chest. 'At the time that the Saps started to categorise and class animals, plants and fungi, they decided to use a dead language, Latin, to do so. We are currently discussing a clear reclassification into modern language, but this system is so entrenched that it is still in place today. One day, we will have a complete rebirth and eradicate all those redundant Sapien classifications and idiosyncrasies. The Potiors have to prioritise their work, though, and for the moment they have far more pressing matters. Until then, we must do our best with what we have.'

With Elise duly following, Harriet continued circling the models. 'Each animal, including ourselves, is given a two-part name in Latin. The first word describes the umbrella group they belong to and the second word describes their species.'

Harriet stopped dead and Elise only narrowly avoided bumping into her. 'To be human is not a species; it is instead an umbrella term. You are a Homo sapiens, so your umbrella group is Homo, which means man in Latin, and your species is sapiens, which translates to wise. Put into the right order it makes . . .'

'Wise man.'

'Correct. The Sapiens who invented the categorisation system decided to refer to themselves as the wise species of human, which is remarkable to say the least.' Harriet paused. 'I, on the other hand, am a Homo medius. My umbrella group is also human, but my species is Medius . . . rather than Sapiens.' Harriett sniffed. 'But I digress. It was only around four hundred years ago that modern-day Sapiens began to realise that they were not some stand-alone animal, unrelated to any other. Despite much wrangling and denial, they eventually had to accept that they used to have other brother and sister species within their umbrella group of human. It is not the case that there was a linear development from the first descendent who split from the chimpanzee through to us.'

Harriet stopped again in front of one of the models and Elise only just managed to avoid another collision.

'Two hundred thousand years ago, when modern-day Sapiens first existed, there were also at least eight other types of human stretched across Zones 1, 3 and 4. All existed at the same time as the Sapiens and all became extinct shortly after crossing paths with them.'

Harriet stared pointedly at Elise's collarbone, refusing to meet her eye.

Realising that Harriet disliked being shorter than her, Elise casually straightened up and scanned the models. She was drawn to one named 'Upright Man'. According to the sign on his plinth, he had lived until at least 250,000 years ago. He had a pronounced brow ridge that jutted from his forehead. His nose was not dissimilar to Elise's, but the area around his mouth pushed his lips forwards and this feature dominated his face. His face was more human than ape, but he certainly wouldn't be mistaken for a Sapien.

Apart from this, his body was similar to hers and she was surprised that they were the same height. Elise had thought he would be shorter, as she equated height with the development from chimpanzees through to Potiors. Clearly, Harriet did too, and Elise wondered why her parents hadn't chosen to tweak her height gene if she came from such short stock.

Harriet looked over at what had caught Elise's attention. 'Ah, Upright Man. He is considered one of the most successful species of human. His remains have been found from Zone 4 all the way to Zone 1, which used to be called Asia. They were also the first to control fire and invented many different types of tool. Most importantly, they survived for nearly two million years, up until a few hundred thousand years ago. Which, coincidentally – or perhaps not so coincidentally – is around the first time the remains of Saps were found in their region.'

Elise ignored Harriet's pointed comment and waited for her to continue.

'I doubt that Saps or perhaps even Medius will last another 1.6 million years to match Upright Man's record. But I do think that the Potiors have a good chance,' Harriet said in a considered tone, moving over to another model that was nearly half her size.

'This little fellow,' Harriet said, patting him on the head, 'is Flores Man, who was named after the small island in Zone 1 he was found on. He survived up until fifty thousand years ago, just as the Wise Men were passing through the area.'

Elise received another pointed look that she avoided by staring intently at Flores Man.

Harriet surreptitiously glanced at her screen. 'He is short of stature as this conserved his energy. He lived on a single small island, which was not rich with food. He did, however, hunt miniature elephants with teeny weeny spears, which I advise everyone to go and see as they are just darling.'

She chuckled.

Glancing down at her screen again, Harriet returned to her serious tone. 'All of these other species of man died out well before the Saps kept any written records of their history. Until two hundred years ago, Saps had been the only living human species for forty thousand years.'

Harriet swiped a page on her screen. 'And, of course, that may have remained unchanged if there hadn't been the Pandemic. The combination of the virus and resulting food crisis wiped out ninety-five per cent of the Saps. It was only when they were on the verge of extinction that the Saps began to seriously experiment with genetic engineering. They had previously only dabbled, but it was now imperative that the next generation be in peak condition for survival. All restrictions were lifted, enhancements began and scientists were free to see where their innovations could take them.'

Elise lowered her head. She knew how this story finished.

'Their experimentations with genetic engineering led firstly to my species, which is, of course, Homo medius or "Man in the Middle". Then, Homo medius paved the way for Homo potior or "Superior Man". Both are two separate human species and both have left Saps somewhat out in the cold.'

Egg-stained shirt, egg-stained shirt, Elise repeated, staring at the floor.

'Now, don't look so worried, Elise. Us Medius and Potior have no desire to drive the Sapiens to extinction. Even though some may argue it would be a fitting end to a species who eradicated countless others . . . we have no need to assert our superiority through indiscriminate killings and genocide. Our superiority is clear for everyone to see. Instead, we believe that with both order and benevolence, all species of man can live in harmony.'

Harriet clipped Elise with her screen as she turned and walked over to one of the jet-black walls. 'Now, if you follow me, I will take you through to the private viewing gallery, which isn't open to the public. You might even get your first glimpse of Twenty-One. Formal introductions will take place tomorrow, though.'

Harriet touched the black wall. Elise watched as a panel swung in a full circle and opened into a second large room. She would never have guessed that the panel could rotate and she tried to remember its location.

'There are doors like these all over the museum. They help employees move quickly around without clogging up the travel-ators and spoiling the views. You just have to know where to find them,' Harriet explained.

Passing through the door, Elise entered a large concrete room. The thick, solid walls gave it the feeling of a bunker. Although disorientated, Elise was certain that they were not below ground. The room had a functional air, as if nothing was allowed inside unless it held a purpose. Clusters of people in white coats huddled around a few whirring machines. Noticing that it was cooler, Elise buttoned up her light jacket.

As they walked into the centre of the room, Elise's attention was fixed on a glass screen running along the length of the main wall. She desperately wanted to go over to the viewing platform but knew that she would have to wait to be invited. A few people next to the platform stood out, as they weren't wearing white coats. Something made her look at them again and she caught her breath.

Elise saw Potiors on the screens all the time – as the base leaders, they were everywhere – but having one in the same room was different. Not wanting to be caught staring, she purposefully gazed towards the other end of the viewing platform, but she couldn't resist taking surreptitious glances.

Everything about the Potior was impressive. His height was the first striking thing; even from across the room, Elise knew that he would tower over her. He managed to be broad but appear lean at the same time. Standing casually, he rested his weight on his right leg and his large hands moved animatedly as he talked. There was an intensity Elise had not seen in anyone before and she soon found herself unable to pull her gaze away; she wanted to soak up every detail.

As if he had heard what she was thinking, he glanced over. A look of recognition crossed his face and he held his hand up to the people he was with, abruptly ending their conversation. To Elise's alarm, he walked towards her. She panicked, as it wasn't clear why he had taken an interest. What could he want? She shoved her clammy hands into her pockets, unsure what to do with her arms.

As he approached, she could not help but watch his movements with fascination. All of his muscles stretched and snapped back into place. The way he walked reminded Elise of the lions she had seen downstairs, every stride intentional and exuding confidence. He did not rush; there was no need. He knew everyone would wait for him. When he had almost reached her, Elise stepped towards him, hands still firmly jammed in her pockets.

Without acknowledging her or stopping, he swept past.

Elise turned, unable to pull her attention away. The Medius who had interviewed her, Samuel, was standing a little way behind her, quietly watching. He had barely spoken to her during the interview and instead chosen to gaze out of the window while she tentatively answered the questions posed by the other Medius from the Worker Profiling Department. Mortified, Elise realised that it was Samuel that the Potior had noticed and not her.

A trickle of shame spread through her, gathering pace. She had forgotten who she was and how little she meant to a Potior; that she had been so susceptible to his appeal made her feel worse. Straightening, she breathed in deeply before retreating behind the fixed, passive expression which she always found refuge in.

Oblivious to Elise's feelings of shame, Harriet sighed a little as she openly stared at the Potior. An inane smile crossed her face as her eyes attentively followed his every move. It was the first time Elise had seen Harriet smile and she wished that she hadn't.

'How is Seventeen progressing?' the Potior said to Samuel.

'Very well, very well indeed. The pregnancy is progressing with few concerns. The child is now viable and we expect labour to begin in the region of ten to fifteen weeks.'

'Excellent. Good work, Samuel. Let me know as soon as it starts. We do not want the crew to miss a minute of it for the screening. Labour should take several hours, but we cannot be certain, this being the first one in forty thousand years.'

Elise was struck by the colour of the Potior's eyes. They were an impossible shade of violet, bright, clear and alert. Although unquestionably beautiful, there was a wax-like quality to his face that Elise did not feel entirely comfortable with. His skin was flawless, without a line, mark or even enlarged pore to show the human qualities she was so used to.

'I have a full medical team on standby,' responded Samuel, who had taken his glasses off to wipe them with the edge of his sleeve.

The Potior raised his eyes to the ceiling and then stared down at Samuel. 'That is reassuring to hear, but we want to avoid any medical intervention, if possible. Nature must prevail this time.'

Samuel's head snapped up, startling Elise. Putting his glasses back on, he seemed lost in thought. 'No medical assistance? Surely we would not want to risk losing her?'

The Potior smiled and put his hand on Samuel's shoulder. 'I do so admire your protective qualities, Samuel; it is what makes you perfect for your role. Unfortunately, I have some difficult decisions to make and to do so I have to consider the picture as a whole.' The Potior paused while he searched Samuel's face. 'In this case, the priority is a natural delivery. We need to study the process. Take her to theatre if we are going to lose her or the offspring, but only as a last resort.'

The Potior squeezed Samuel's shoulder. 'Only intervene if you are losing them. This order comes right from the top.'

Samuel met the Potior's gaze and nodded.

The Potior turned to Elise for the first time, his hand still on Samuel's shoulder. Avoiding his gaze, she did not move at all.

She even held her breath, which she realised didn't present the composed air she was hoping for.

His gaze roamed over Elise. He didn't look away from her, even though his question was directed at Samuel. 'Is this the new Companion?'

'We hope so. She will be trained over the next few days, but she is already fluent in sign language. Apparently her brother is deaf, so she has grown up using it at home.'

Elise was not surprised to hear Harriet titter next to her. She was annoyed at Samuel for mentioning her brother, whom she always tried to shield from this kind of unwanted attention.

'That is a pity . . . probably a genetic issue,' the Potior surmised as he turned from Elise and let his gaze range over the room. 'Well, at least we won't have to teach her to sign, which is an improvement on the last one.'

Turning to Elise, the Potior spoke loudly, as if she were the one who was deaf. 'How are you finding your introductory tour?'

Despite the unnecessary volume, the smile and warmth that radiated from him overwhelmed her. She had to work to regain her composure. 'Very interesting, sir. I've always wanted to work in the museum.'

'Excellent,' he said, smiling at her but still not lowering his voice. 'You Companions do a very valuable job. You are essential to the workings of this particular project. If you have any problems at all, then please do not hesitate to speak to Samuel about them.'

Elise looked up at the Potior and smiled broadly. She had barely registered what he had said, but it didn't matter. All she knew was that his unquestionably sincere tone made her feel as though she were the centre of his world.

Samuel, who was quietly watching this exchange, continued to push the hair from his forehead. Stopping midway, he let it fall.

'Something's wrong,' he said to the Potior.

Elise jumped when the swing doors on the opposite side of the room slammed open. A pudgy cleaner burst inside, his little spectacles knocked to one side of his face. Sweat was pouring down his cheeks and Elise thought he was going to throw up.

'*One of the tigers!* One of the sabre-tooth tigers has gotten out of its pod and the school children just entered the museum!' he shouted, before collapsing against a wall.

The shovel and brush he was still carrying clattered to the floor as his legs buckled.

Without saying a word, the Potior sprinted towards the doors, closely followed by Samuel. Without thinking, Elise turned and ran after them.

CHAPTER 3

* *

Racing through the swinging doors, Elise tried to skid to a halt; her feet slid on the slick, metal walkway as she desperately tried to stop herself from hitting the handrail or, worse, falling under it. She was twenty feet above the ground.

The Potior and Samuel weren't stopping, though. Without hesitation, the Potior gracefully leapt upwards, his left foot lightly touching the metal handrail as he jumped over the side. Samuel, who had chosen to vault the bar in one fluid motion, closely followed.

'Don't!' Elise shouted, clasping the handrail, her knuckles turning white as she helplessly watched them drop.

With a thud, they landed in crouched positions and pushed off, speeding across the grassland.

Acutely aware of her limitations, Elise sprinted to the staircase at the end of the walkway. All she could think about was the school children, who were completely unaware of the danger. What if it had been her brother? She had to help in whatever little way she could. Noisily clattering down the steel stairs, she pounded after them once she reached the ground, where she was able to pick up her pace. Her strong legs pushed her forwards, used to the strain. Controlling her breathing, she fixed her attention on the two men. The savannah blurred as they pulled farther away.

The crunching of the dry grass snapped her attention back to her surroundings. She was running into the centre of a pod. With growing fear, she realised that she had no idea what animal it contained. No longer able to see the two men, she ran faster as she went up a gentle incline. Glancing behind her, she expected to see people from the room she had run from coming to help, but with growing horror, she realised she was the only one. As she passed over the ridge, Elise slowed to a standstill and took in the scene below.

The Potior was sprinting in a large arc around the side of a clutch of oblivious gazelles. Her eyes flicked over to Samuel, who was nimbly pulling himself up through the branches of a leafy tree. The gazelles, realising they were not alone, scattered in panic. Anticipating their change in direction, the Potior arced around and herded them back into one group.

A flash of orange burst out from the undergrowth.

A smaller gazelle skittered away from the giant paw. Without pausing, the tiger pushed off after his prey, his body surfacing from its hiding place. First came his two canines: wider than two of Elise's fingers and as long as her forearm, curling round on the outside of his mouth. Thickly muscled shoulders followed, which made even the Potior look fragile. Finally came his extended body, powerful back legs and flicking tail, which helped balance him as he effortlessly changed direction. The sabre-tooth's protruding canines reclaimed Elise's attention. She guessed he had claws to match.

Standing at the top of the ridge, Elise realised with a jolt how exposed she was. He was four times her size with teeth so big they had to hang down on the outside of his mouth. If the tiger decided to switch his attention to her, there was nothing she could do. She had no weapon. She had no giant, flesh-tearing teeth or claws and she couldn't outrun him. The only vulnerable part was his eyes and she would have to get past those canines first. She couldn't even retrace her steps to the safety of the building behind; it might be the fatal move that caught his attention. Mouth dry, all she could do was stay still and watch.

The Potior swerved to cut off the gazelles' path to the other side of the pod. The tiger was closing on them from behind. Taking the path of least resistance, the gazelles sprang off in the direction of the tree. The tiger's powerful back legs dug into the earth and he quickly pushed off in the same direction, dirt spraying up behind him.

Closing in, he tried again to catch the same small gazelle. His thick front paw, claws extended, curled around its sweat-soaked hind leg. There would have been no escape this second time – if Samuel hadn't intervened. Dropping from the tree branch, he landed flat on the tiger's back, his weight momentarily pushing him to the ground.

The tiger froze, stunned at being demoted to prey. Then instinct kicked in. He let out a roar as the gazelle scrabbled away. Only briefly incapacitated, the tiger started to push back onto his paws.

Realising that Samuel couldn't hold the tiger by himself, Elise moved towards them, only stopping when the Potior reached the sabre-tooth. In one fluid movement, the Potior's strong arms locked around the tiger's neck and he curled his legs around both of the front paws, human handcuffs. Frustrated, the tiger doubled his efforts, thrashing and jerking to free himself. The Potior held on tight, not letting go of his debilitating lock; Elise was sure he was laughing.

Her eyes flicked to Samuel, who was having less success lying across the tiger's back legs. She desperately scanned the edges of the pod to see if the Rangers were on their way. Nothing.

Clenching her teeth, she sprinted over to the writhing bundle of limbs, her mind screaming at her to turn around.

'What can I do?' she shouted when she was halfway there.

'Look in my jacket pocket!' Samuel shouted at her without turning around. 'There's a sedative pen!'

Elise slid to a stop next to Samuel. Crouching, she reached into the open pocket and pulled out the pen. Noticing her approach, the tiger panicked and redoubled his efforts. Turning, twisting, he was making every attempt to get free. His gums were pulled back, saliva strung between his teeth. Elise gagged at the stench of his breath.

She stared at the pen, turning it in her hands. 'I don't know how to use it!'

In slow motion, she watched in horror as one of the tiger's back legs broke free from Samuel's grip and swiped at her. Without thinking she whipped her arm around and out of the way. No hesitation, perfectly calculated to avoid contact.

A look of confusion crossed Samuel's face. Elise knew she had made a mistake. She shouldn't have been able to move that quickly.

Just as Samuel seemed to regain control, a second set of claws swiped at Elise. Gritting her teeth, she forced herself to stay still. She braced as a single claw sliced through her shirt and raked along her arm. Nothing could have prepared her for the pain that followed its path, though. Trying not to scream, she bit into the side of her mouth until she tasted blood. Her eyes lost focus and she squeezed them shut.

Without pausing, Samuel locked his limbs around the tiger's legs, gaining complete control. His attention diverted, Elise opened her eyes and twisted towards the tiger's hind leg. She jabbed the pen deep into the thick fur and pushed the button.

Nothing happened.

Panicking, Elise scrabbled backwards, not knowing what she should do.

The Potior flipped his grip on the tiger's head so that his right arm curled underneath its chin. His left arm snaked around the back of the animal's head. He was serious, no longer enjoying the thrill. Elise realised that he was preparing to break the tiger's neck. The Potior shifted his weight to gain enough force to deliver the killing twist and Elise turned away, unable to watch.

It didn't come, though. There was no sound of snapping bone.

She glanced back. The tiger had begun to weaken as the sedative took hold. Slowly, Samuel and the Potior eased their pressure until the sabre-tooth was still. They only let go once he was immobile and quietly snuffling, his once fierce eyes staring blindly ahead.

Nursing her arm, Elise looked up and froze. Samuel and the Potior were staring down at her.

Samuel was the first to speak. Glancing at the tiger, he addressed the Potior. 'I will arrange his transportation back to the correct pod and work out how this happened. The barriers have never failed in the whole time I've been here. It needs to be properly investigated.'

'Thank the stars that you were able to hold him with one arm to administer the sedative.' The Potior pushed himself back onto his feet. 'I thought I was going to have to break his neck. We cannot afford to lose any of the exhibitions at this stage.'

Shrugging, Samuel looked up at the Potior. 'Well, after he clawed her I had no choice but to just grab the pen and use it.' Elise could only stare as Samuel mimed the action of using the sedative pen. 'We can't afford to lose a Companion at this stage either.'

'But why did she follow us anyway? What could she possibly have thought she could do to help?' the Potior said, pacing up and down behind the tiger.

Elise forgot the pain in her arm. They were going to dismiss her. She was going to have to return to her parents' home and then straight back to the production centre tomorrow. They would never let her work at the museum again. All because she didn't know how it worked around here. She had only wanted to help. The thought made her head swim. She dug her fingernails into the palm of her hand to prevent her features from conveying her distress. She stared at the ground and waited for the final blow.

'It's her first day,' Samuel said as he stood in front of Elise. 'I am her direct Overseer. She obviously felt it was her duty to follow me at all times.'

The Potior stared at the top of Elise's bowed head before speaking. 'Yes, well, that level of loyalty is commendable, but the sooner she is installed with Twenty-One the better.' He glanced over at the building they had come from. 'As you said, our top priority must be knowing how the barrier came down in the first place.' His eyes briefly returned to Samuel. 'Take care of the Companion. I will let you know if I find anything.'

Without saying anything further, the Potior sprinted to the metal walkway. Elise watched as he leapt twelve feet into the air and pulled himself over the edge of the railing.

'Now he's just showing off,' Samuel muttered, picking up his glasses from the grass and inspecting them for damage.

Elise stared in wonder; she had only just begun to understand the full spectrum of the Potior's abilities. She wanted to know more. Still fixed on the walkway, Elise grimaced when Harriet clapped as the Potior passed through the doors.

'That was very foolish, but thank you,' Samuel said to Elise, bending the frame of his glasses back into the correct position.

Relief washed over her as she realised they would let her stay and she looked at Samuel properly for the first time. She guessed that he was only a couple of years older than her, although it was difficult to tell with a Medius. He was handsome like most Medius men, but there was a difference in his approach. It took Elise a moment but then she realised what it was; he didn't seem to care about his appearance. He obviously hadn't recently shaved, and his hair wasn't styled, flopping over his forehead. As Elise watched him, he absent-mindedly pushed it from his eyes. After a few moments in its new position, the thick, brown lock gradually slipped down his forehead again and the whole process was repeated. He was in perpetual motion.

Distracted by her throbbing arm, Elise knew she would have to do something about it or it would become infected. Carefully peeling off her shirt, she winced as the material pulled on the already congealing blood. She was grateful for the small T-shirt she had on underneath her shirt, which spared them an awkward moment.

The wound ran nearly the length of her forearm. Gritting her teeth, she pulled it open with her finger; she was pleased to see that it wasn't deep and hadn't cut through the muscle. She knew it would scar, but infection was her main concern.

'Do you think they'd let me leave the compound to buy some honey?' Elise said.

'Why would you need honey right now?' Samuel said, rubbing his thumb against his jawline. Elise listened to the scratching noise of stubble and adjusted his estimated age by a few years. He pushed his hair back from his forehead again and, without meeting her gaze, continued, 'We need to get you to the medical centre anyway, for that laceration; it looks pretty bad.'

'No. No medical centre. I just need to clean it out and put some dressings on with some honey is all. Should be fine then and not get infected.'

Since she was a little girl, her mother had coached her on the basic properties of plants. Elise and her parents relied mainly on natural remedies so that they could save their Medi-stamps for if disaster struck. Their neighbours would also go to Sofi for a decoction or compress if they were low on Medi-stamps. Even though Medi-stamps lasted five years before expiring, it was imperative that reserves were kept for emergency surgery or treatment; no amount of sage and dock leaves would help remove a burst appendix.

'Don't be silly. You need a nurse to assess that cut. Why would you . . . ?' A look of realisation passed over his face. 'Of course, how stupid of me.'

He crouched next to Elise. 'You don't have to use your Medi-stamps. This happened while you were working, so the museum will take care of it.'

Elise was wary of the suggestion. She had heard stories of production centre workers accepting similar assistance. They were then ordered to repay the Medi-stamps when they tried to change jobs.

Samuel had anticipated her next question. 'You won't have to pay them back either. I promise on the long-dead stars that form part of every one of us.'

Elise didn't hold much store in Samuel's promises, even if they were made in the presence of the stars. He had lied so smoothly to the Potior about being the one who administered the sedative. She peered at the cut on her arm; the throbbing was intensifying. Weighing her options, she realised that the risk of not being able to work if it became infected was too great. She resigned herself to trusting what Samuel was saying, an unappealing proposition, but the only option.

'Okay, if you're sure I won't have to pay anything back. We can't afford to lose Medi-stamps just for a cut.'

'Come on then,' Samuel said, standing. 'I don't think you should leave it much longer.'

Elise pushed herself onto her feet, cradling her arm, and followed Samuel, who was striding briskly in the direction of the viewing platform. Elise trotted behind and marvelled at the way he walked, full of energy, with elbows and legs darting off in different directions. It was as if his limbs belonged to different people, each with their own idea of where he should be going. Watching his energetic walk, Elise wondered how someone who could run so gracefully had still not mastered the art of walking in a straight line.

'I know a shortcut this way,' Samuel shouted over his shoulder.

'You don't have to come with me,' Elise said as she tried to keep up. 'I'm sure you've got other things to do now one of the barriers has failed.'

'Yes, it's very concerning. Honestly, it's never happened before; it shouldn't even be possible.' Samuel's brow wrinkled. 'Even to manually override it, you would need two authority codes.' He picked up his pace before turning to check she was still following. 'I will walk you over there at the very least.'

Instead of climbing back up the metal staircase, Samuel took them through a door on the ground floor. Elise was pleased that she wouldn't have to walk past the people in white coats covered in savannah dirt and dripping blood onto the polished concrete floor; her first day was already going badly without the additional humiliation.

'This is the corridor that leads to Twenty-One and Seventeen's . . . residencies,' Samuel finished weakly.

Elise raised an eyebrow as she passed the two heavy steel doors. Both had electronic readers at the side of them that scanned the identification of the person entering, although Elise was more interested in the thick metal bars which slid across the doors. Electronic and manual security; not even the sabre-tooth tigers had both.

'It is just through here,' Samuel said, diverting Elise's attention from her new office. She was trying to take note of which way she was going, but was starting to feel light-headed. After two further turns she was lost.

When they finally entered a small waiting room, a nurse came out to greet them as soon as they sat.

'Samuel, where've you been? You haven't dropped by for a couple of weeks,' the young woman said reproachfully, smiling down at him. She tucked a loose strand of her vivid red hair behind one ear and widened her eyes. She was practically purring and rubbing up against his leg. 'Not since we . . . umm.' She stopped and glanced at Elise, her eyes darting to her arm. A look of concern crossed her face and she became paler, if that was possible. 'Ah, I see this is not a social call. You'd better come with me.' She took Elise by the elbow. 'Are you waiting, Samuel?'

'Well, ah, I can't really, Georgina. I have to go and check on something important.' He pushed his hand through his hair. 'And I know you will take excellent care of her.' He glanced around the room as if he had forgotten where the exit was. 'Well, I'll see you both soon. Bye now!'

He was gone before Elise could ask where she should go afterwards.

'Sorry about that; I'm not his type, but I just love to mentally frisk him.' Georgina smiled at Elise, her bright red lipstick revealing even white teeth. 'He's just so bumbly; I can't resist teasing.'

Georgina led Elise to a small elevated bed in the next room. 'Now, pop yourself up and tell me what happened.'

Georgina pulled a small stool with wheels over for herself.

Elise duly climbed onto the bed, feet dangling, unable to reach the floor. She lowered her gaze so she wasn't looking directly at Georgina.

'Now, now. I won't have any of that etiquette stuff they drill into you Sapiens,' Georgina said. 'This is my medical centre and

I want a normal patient–nurse relationship with you. I can't help people if they're too scared to tell me what's wrong. So we'll try again. Was it a lion, tiger, very angry house cat or none of the above?'

Elise couldn't help but smile back. 'Pretty angry sabre-tooth tiger.'

It was Georgina's turn to lower her eyes as she peered at Elise's arm. 'Well, I'm glad that the tigers still feel obliged to make the odd swipe between their carefully prepared meals; instinct is still winning for the moment,' she said, closely inspecting Elise's arm.

Trying not to wince, Elise closed her eyes as Georgina pushed and pulled at the cut. She felt fresh blood seep out of one end and trickle down her arm.

After Georgina had finished, she straightened. 'It didn't tear the muscle, which is the good news, but without proper treatment you will end up with a noteworthy scar. I'm guessing that you just want the story and not the scarring to go with it. So will you let me seal it up for you?'

'Will I have to pay for it, even in the future? If I do, then please just clean it out for me; we can't afford to use our Medi-stamps.'

Georgina squeezed Elise's other hand. 'Don't worry; I wouldn't be working here if this was some sort of Medi-stamp racket to pull one over the Sapiens. It's all included and no one has ever been asked to repay, even when they've left on bad terms.'

Reassured, Elise nodded.

She settled on the bed and tried to prepare for what was coming. She'd never had medical treatment for such a minor ailment. Other than the mandatory vaccinations, her mother had always managed to patch her up.

With one push, Georgina rolled across to the other side of the room on her wheeled stool, legs not touching the floor. She seemed to get an almost childlike pleasure from careering across the room. Still on her stool, she pushed back to Elise with a trolley in tow.

'So I'm firstly going to use local anaesthetic,' Georgina said, laying a soft pad on Elise's forehead.

Georgina fiddled with the controls of the machine on the trolley as Elise braced.

Suddenly, she felt nothing from her arm. No pain, no aching, not even the temperature of the room. It was as if her arm were no longer there. She tried to wiggle her fingers. Nothing. Elise didn't like the sensation.

'Now for the cleaning,' Georgina updated her, holding the cut apart and inserting a clear hose into it.

Georgina ran the hose up and down the inside of the cut, watching what travelled down the clear pipe. The suction grew louder as Georgina pushed the instrument deeper into the wound.

'Interesting collection you have here. I think we've recovered a small bit of tiger fur, a sizeable amount of savannah dirt and a remarkable amount of grit,' Georgina said, moving the hose up and down one more time.

Elise's stomach turned as the sucking sound reached a crescendo. For the finale, a slurping sound joined in. Georgina was no longer carefully handling her cut and was instead rummaging around like it was her handbag and she had lost something.

'And now for the magic!' Georgina said, brandishing a pronged instrument.

Elise felt faint as she wondered what Georgina was going to do with it.

Georgina carefully put both sides of the cut between the two points and pinched. Pulling the cut together, Georgina moved farther down her arm in one smooth motion. The laceration sealed. There was only a neat, pink scar and a little swelling.

'I can live with that. Thank you so much,' Elise said, preparing to hop off the bed.

'We're not finished. That would be considered a hideous disfigurement if you were a Medius,' Georgina called out, freewheeling to a cupboard in the far corner. 'I am nothing if not a perfectionist.'

Elise could hear her rooting around the shelves, glass bottles clinking.

'There you are,' Georgina muttered before pushing herself back over to the bed.

She was cradling a small crystal vial in the palm of her hand.

'Now, this is special,' Georgina said, lifting the stopper which extended all the way through the vial.

She uncorked the jar. It contained a glistening, golden syrup. There were thousands of flecks of light in the liquid that radiated and pulsed with its own life.

'It's beautiful,' Elise said.

'It is indeed. Dermadew can mend and reverse just about any deterioration to skin tissue. Some of the wealthier Medius ladies even use it to attain that flawless sheen that the Potiors have. It's not cheap either; a pot like this would cost fifty Medi-stamps.'

Georgina scraped a thin layer of the Dermadew over the length of the scar. She then placed a thin gauze bandage over the top, which she stuck down at the edges.

'I want to give it a chance to soak in, so no picking at it. Come back in a few days' time and we'll see how it is.'

The feeling came back into Elise's arm after the pad was peeled from her forehead. Stretching, she rotated her wrist at the same time. She clenched her hand into a fist and was pleased that everything felt back to normal. Without Georgina's help, it would have taken two weeks to progress this far.

Grabbing her shirt, Elise hopped off the bed and turned to thank Georgina.

'You have the magic touch,' she said, waving her arm to show how good it felt.

'Well, it's more the tools than real skill on my part. And I'm always happy to help when the need is genuine. So if you have any further encounters, be sure to come straight over.'

Elise nodded, smiling as she left. Her mind darted back to Holly's advice about befriending Medius and her mood dampened. It sunk farther when she opened the waiting-room door to see Harriet perched on one of the chairs.

'There you are! I was so worried!' Harriet exclaimed. 'I don't know what I was going to tell the Head of Worker Profiling if I couldn't find you. We can't just have you aimlessly wandering the building. That would never do. There is a prescribed tour that *must* be adhered to.'

Elise nodded. Harriet was clearly flustered, but Elise didn't feel sorry for her.

'Yes, well, perhaps we should see the canteen and your sleeping quarters next. Then you can have some food. What with all the excitement, you have missed the dinner hour, but we can get you something from one of the service machines. The last thing I need after today's events is you passing out on me.'

Harriet bustled off down the corridor and Elise followed, careful to walk a few steps behind. Tired of always narrowly missing collisions with the woman, Elise had decided to give her a larger turning circle.

There was a new spring in Harriet's step. 'Wasn't Fintorian spectacular?'

Elise had no idea what or who Fintorian was, but she was sure that she would soon find out. Harriet tended to fill silence.

'His lightning instincts, his gracefulness, his speed, his . . . his . . . prowess!' Harriet finished with a flourish.

Elise narrowed it down to either the Potior or the sabre-tooth tiger.

'He has only been with us for nine months, one week and four days, and already the museum has a new lease of life. His vision is breathtaking; he wants us to be the most influential Museum of Evolution in Zone 3. Maybe even the world!' Harriet said, her voice rising in excitement.

'Where'd he transfer from?' Elise asked, eager to hear about the other bases.

'His last post was in Cytosine Base, but he has travelled all around.'

Elise had always been interested in Cytosine, which specialised in the sciences: 'Ingenuity and Innovation'. It was one of the closest bases to Thymine at only 150 miles away. She had heard it was perched at the edge of a cliff overlooking a canyon. The residents lived in a network of caves dug into the ground that could only be accessed via the sheer cliff face.

Elise tried not to smile as she watched Harriet perform a little skip as she continued. 'Apparently he is over ninety years old and has some of the highest-grade engineering.'

Harriet glanced around her. 'But that is a private matter, of course.'

Elise considered this. Fintorian hadn't looked much older than twenty-five, certainly not over thirty. Regeneration of this nature was the highest level of biological engineering available. If used correctly and combined with other key traits, it was theorised that this would make the recipient practically immortal, as long as they had access to the medical care that could repair most unexpected, traumatic injuries. The Potiors hadn't been around long enough to know for sure, but with every decade they lived through it was becoming more likely.

'We don't have time to go around a sample pod, but I think that you already get the gist after today's activities,' Harriet said, frowning. 'What you were thinking is beyond me. Scuttling after a Potior and a Medius that way . . .'

It grieved Elise that Harriet was right; she should never have run after them. She had barely helped and, even then, Samuel had taken credit for her actions. She didn't think she had scuttled, though.

'Do they know how the sabre-tooth got out?' Elise said, steering the topic away from herself.

'No, but they are assessing the matter. I have full confidence that it was a mere technical error. We will learn from the experience and move on,' Harriet said, the waver in her tone not aligning with her words.

For once, Harriet was so lost in her own thoughts that she had nothing to add. Elise did not push, grateful for some quiet.

When they arrived at the canteen, Harriet briefly informed Elise that all of her meals would be provided by the museum. Elise added up the additional tickets she could save and mentally set these aside.

The service machine had two options for sandwiches: cheese and pickle on brown bread, or ham and mustard on brown bread. Elise paused before making her selection, unaccustomed to choosing meals. At school she had written essays about choice leading to waste. As well as a cheese sandwich, she selected a small packet of cookies that she stuffed into her pocket before Harriet could see. Elise was so hungry she didn't care whether she was allowed two items.

'I'll show you through to where you will be sleeping. You will have your own room in the east block, which is for Sapiens,' Harriet said, coming out of her daze. 'Not many employees sleep at the museum overnight, only the Companions, a few Rangers, canteen staff and some security personnel. Oh, and Samuel Adair, the Collections Assistant and your Overseer; he barely ever leaves the place. Unhealthy attachment, if you ask me. The Medius rooms and suites set aside for visiting Potiors are in the west block near to where the dinosaur skeletons are displayed.'

As they walked through the deserted corridors, Elise made a conscious effort to remember the route, knowing that she had to find her way back to the canteen in the morning.

'You will not be expected to start working with Twenty-One until tomorrow. Luca, who is the other Companion, will come and collect you in the morning around eight. He will train you over the next few days and once you have completed the initial stages, you will be passed to Samuel for general supervision.'

As they moved through a glass walkway, Elise realised that she had lost all track of the time. When she glanced upwards, all she could see was her own reflection in the glass; there was no light from outside.

'And this brings us to the end of the tour,' Harriet said, stopping outside a door similar to the one Elise had seen earlier, just without the steel sliding bars.

Elise's name was printed next to the identification disc, which gave her a small sense of belonging. Holding her hand against the disc, she waited for her identity to be confirmed. Elise pushed open the door and Harriet followed. The recycled rubber matting contrasted sharply with the concrete flooring in the hallway. Elise prodded the wall; it was springy to touch but also slightly damp, as if the walls were sweating. There were no windows and the air was stale. She didn't close the door.

'This is a standard-issue Sapien room with its own bathroom, entirely made from recycled materials, of course, to comply with Decree Number 19. All Sapien reparation guidelines are strictly adhered to in the museum, so don't think that there will be a slackening of the rules now that you are here.'

Harriet paused to see if Elise would raise any objections.

Elise knew all about Decree Number 19; it was the reason her parents' home was a patchwork quilt of recycled materials covered in turf. Her eyes darted to the sleeping platform in the corner and she could think of nothing else. She stared blankly at Harriet as she received the finale to her lecture.

'Reparations are key to the Museum of Evolution,' Harriet said, pacing. 'The very reason the Potiors built the museum is to begin to unravel the damage Homo sapiens have progressively inflicted on the world over the past eighty thousand years. A large part of that was their systematic assault on other species. The Potiors are trying to bring back as many of the extinct species as possible, including the other species of human that disappeared many thousands of years ago.'

Elise had heard a similar speech every day when she was at school. There was no end to reparations. No future date on which the past would finally be set aside and she would be judged by her own actions.

'Your work with Twenty-One is vital to Fintorian's vision for Thymine Base. Your commitment to this project is, therefore, expected in full. Luca will collect you in the morning and will be reporting on your progress at every step.'

Elise felt alert again; no one had spoken to her of her duties until now.

'As you are aware, Twenty-One is the twenty-first Homo neanderthalensis the Potiors have managed to copy and reintroduce to this world. Due to unfortunate circumstances, he is one of only fourteen that are still alive to date. It is your job to make sure he stays that way . . . or you're out.'

Without saying goodbye, Harriet closed the door firmly behind her. Elise tried not to think about what she had said. Instead, she dragged her rucksack, which had been placed by the door, closer to the sleeping platform. The effort made her realise how tired she was. Earlier in the day, she had been able to run with it; now, she could barely lift it.

She changed into the leggings and long-sleeved top she normally slept in, the familiar clothes easing her into the alien room. After using the bathroom, she pulled back the sheets to inspect the mattress. It was made of hay and wool but appeared to have been recently restuffed so that it was softer than the one she had at home. Curling into a ball, she hugged her knees to her chest for warmth and comfort.

The newest Companion to the twenty-first Neanderthal to be brought back from extinction quickly fell asleep.

CHAPTER 4

Startled, Elise sat up. After listening intently, she thought she must have imagined the noise. It wasn't until she started to lower herself back onto the mattress that she heard it again, an insistent rapping. Disorientated, as there were no windows in the room, she had no idea what time it was or how long she had been asleep.

Throwing back the covers, she couldn't remember how to turn the lights on. Tracing her arm along the wall, she navigated through the darkness until her fingers touched the ridge of the door. Unsure whom to expect, she only pulled it wide enough to poke her head around.

'Morning, beautiful,' a voice sang out. 'Nice hair. I like that it sticks to your face on one side and stands straight out on the other. It's as if you have your own cyclone in there.'

Elise stared at the young man leaning against the wall, enjoying himself at her expense. 'Luca?'

'Indeedy. You're late, so scram, I'll meet you in the canteen in ten minutes.'

Elise closed the door and managed to get ready in eight. There was nothing she could do about her hair so she dunked her head under the tap and smoothed it straight back. Glancing at her screen, she groaned. It was 5.40 a.m.; she hoped that this wouldn't be her standard start time.

Jogging to the canteen, she slowed before walking in; she didn't want to seem completely ruffled. Except for Luca, who was sitting at a table in the far corner, it was deserted. She headed straight to him, wondering why he was cracking nuts open. There were two neat piles positioned to either side of his hands, one made up of the shells and one smaller pile of the hazelnuts found within. Smiling, Elise took a seat and hoped that he wasn't unhappy with her being late.

Luca glanced up at her. 'The slicked-back hair is good.' He leant in. 'But I'm hoping the cyclone look makes a return.'

'I'm sorry I'm late; I didn't know we'd be starting this early. I thought Harriet said you'd collect me at eight,' Elise said, unsure how to handle Luca's comments.

'Not a problem, Thanton. Harriet must've missed the start time for the first day. Anyway. This gives us a chance to have a chat about the role before we head in. Nut?' he asked, offering her one.

Elise took it and, using the other nutcracker, enjoyed the satisfaction of the hard shell buckling under the pressure. She found it therapeutic to have something to do with her hands and, without asking, continued to help Luca. Now that she was more awake, she took the opportunity to view him with fresher eyes.

No one would call him handsome. All of his features were a little oversized. Alone, they would be admirable, but together it was as if they were fighting for control of his face. He did have unusually ash-blond curly hair, though, which Elise imagined was springy to touch.

Whenever she met someone new, she always picked her favourite feature and concentrated on that. She found that, after a while, and particularly if she liked them, they became embodied by that one feature and, consequently, attractive. Samuel had capable hands, which were both strong and dexterous, and Georgina was epitomised by her neat little nose, which turned up slightly at the end. Elise decided that his short, coiled hair would embody Luca. Harriet could stay ugly.

'So what do you know about the Companion role, Thanton?'

'Not much, really. They didn't tell me anything in the interview and the Neanderthals have never been on display. No one knows anything about them outside the museum. Except that they exist.' Elise paused, waiting for Luca to explain. When he remained silent, she continued, 'They chose me because I know sign language and I was told he can't speak the same language as us. I'll have to spend a lot of time with him and try to get to know him and—'

'You're basically on suicide watch,' Luca said without looking up.

'Oh, that narrows it down. So Twenty-One's not very happy then?'

'It's not just Twenty-One; none of them are. But we don't say that to anyone out there. After Two drowned herself in Guanine Base's Museum of Evolution twenty-three years ago, they made the quick decision to take all the Neanderthals off display. And they haven't been back on since. They told the public it was an accident and the Neanderthals would be safer in a more contained environment.'

Luca glanced up at Elise and sighed. 'Try to imagine living in what is effectively a cage all day with no one else around you. The Supes won't let them live together as clans yet. They're worried that if a little internal war breaks out, they could lose half their stock in a few minutes. That's the eventual aim, though. Clan families, I mean, not Neanderthal civil war.'

'Supes?' Elise said.

Luca laughed. 'The Potiors. Everyone calls them Supes round here. Where did they ship you in from? The Outer Circle?' When Elise didn't respond, he grinned. 'You really are a green one growing up all the way out there.'

'We can't all grow up in the Inner or Mid Circles; there's got to be someone on the outside,' Elise said, smiling to hide her annoyance.

'Can't argue with that logic. So, anyway, that's where we come in,' he continued, still shelling the nuts. 'It wasn't until they lost the first seven in a row through self-harm, extreme depressive disorders and stress-related illnesses that the museums realised the cause. Neanderthals are not meant to be lone wolves. They're like us. Clan animals. And with no group to live with, they tend to go a bit mad. So that's when the Companion role was created.'

'How much do they know about their situation?' Elise asked.

'Well, that's the million-ticket question, Elise,' Luca said, glancing up at her. 'You're a smart one; I'm going to have to keep my eye on you.' He continued to stare at Elise thoughtfully. He chewed one of the nuts. 'They know they'll be looked after, but have no real freedom to decide anything themselves. They know they're related to the Supes, Midders and us, but there are still differences between us all. They know that the Supes have brought them back from the dead. They're taught that, after not being around for forty thousand years, it falls to them to start the next generation of Neanderthals. There's a lot they have to accept is for the greater good of the survival of their species.' Luca pulled a piece of shell from his jumper. 'There's a lot they just have to accept.'

'It sounds like they have to be pretty strong to survive with those pressures,' Elise said, her voice rising with concern. 'So what can I do? How can I help him?'

'Well, you can lower it down a pitch for a start,' Luca said, flinching. 'No use trying to help them with the bigger picture. If they think about that too much, they definitely will go mad. Just take it down to the day-to-day. Keep him occupied; they want to feel that they have some sort of purpose. We all do. Help Twenty-One with that. And, above all, try to keep his mood up. If you lose him, you lose your job. They don't give second chances here.'

Elise wondered how she was going to do any of that without coming across as unhinged. She imagined herself grinning inanely at Twenty-One, suggesting hobbies in a singsong voice. No, she'd have to give this thought.

'So grab something to eat and we'll get in there,' Luca said, gesturing at one of the service machines with his elbow.

'We're going in this morning?' Elise said.

'No, you're mistaken. *We* are not going in there. *You* are going in there alone. I'll just be watching from the platform.' Luca paused and stared up at Elise. 'Is that a problem?'

'No, no problem at all,' Elise said as she jumped up and headed to the vending machine.

Her heart started to hammer. If there was a covert camera in the canteen it would be interested in her.

When she returned to the table with her sandwich, Luca was carefully tipping the shelled nuts into a paper bag.

'Are you Seventeen's Companion?' Elise asked between bites.

Luca nodded.

'Is she the pregnant one?'

'For the moment.'

It was clear to Elise he didn't want to discuss it further. Finishing her sandwich, she didn't ask any more questions.

When she was done, Luca rose and stared down at her. 'Don't look so worried, Thanton. You'll be fine.' He half smiled. 'Or you won't be. But in that case, you'll want to leave the museum straight away and the Supes will be pleased to see you go. Therefore, it really is a no-lose situation.'

Elise was careful not to react. She had to find a way to show him they were right to choose her.

'Now, I trust we can get from here to Twenty-One's pod without you running off after any Midders or Supes?' Luca said.

'You heard about that?'

'Everyone's heard about that. You're famous. Well, infamous. But it's close enough.'

Elise tried to console herself that at least in the pod she would be away from the museum staff. In only one day she had managed to get herself a reputation as a Midder-chaser.

When they arrived outside Twenty-One's pod, Luca turned to Elise. 'Look, it's really not that hard. Just get inside and start a conversation with him and see where you go from there. It's early, so I'll be the only one watching. They'll record you, of course, but I doubt anyone will watch it, except Samuel. All eyes are on Seventeen at the moment. Try to stay in there as long as you can. And take these as a gift.' He pressed the bag of shelled hazelnuts into Elise's hand. 'They're quite formal, so they always appreciate a "token of introduction", as Samuel puts it.'

Taking them silently, Elise turned to the door and held her hand against the panel.

Luca drew back the thick metal bars. 'I'll leave these open for the rest of the day for you. Just touch out when you're done.'

The door closed behind her. Taking her first step into the habitat, Elise appreciated how much thought had gone into the creation of this enclosed world. Although the pod was not as large as some of the ones in the main museum, it was still able to comfortably hold three pine trees in a distant corner. Lush green ferns were scattered about, so dense in some areas that she couldn't see what lay beyond. She heard trickling water mixed with the soft chirping of birds from the trees; there were other animals in there besides Elise and Twenty-One. She thought she could hear something small rustling in a bush near to her feet. When she stepped towards it, the rustling stopped. Whatever it was, it still feared predators in this man-made paradise.

She breathed in the crisp air. It smelled fresh and clean, preferable to her own dark, stuffy room. She zipped up her jacket to her chin; it was cooler than she had expected. Not knowing where else to go, she followed the trodden path that led deeper into the pod.

After she had crossed the small meadow, the foliage became denser and bramble branches caught on her clothes. Pulling her sleeve over her hand, she pushed them aside. It was getting darker, as the rays from the skylight struggled to penetrate deep into the pod. She wiped moisture from her face left by the damp leaves and tried not to think about what was hiding in the undergrowth.

Stopping, she realised she wasn't ready to meet Twenty-One. She had no idea what he would look like or how to approach him. Her mind went blank. Reasoning that her hesitation wasn't going to win any points with Luca, she forced herself to start moving again.

A few steps farther and she emerged into a small clearing. A crystal-clear stream tumbled through the pod and its sound unnerved Elise. Her fear of unknown water sources had been instilled in her since childhood. She wouldn't even let it splash her clothes. Her eyes ran up and down the small stream searching for a crossing; it was then that she saw Twenty-One.

He was sitting cross-legged by the river, engrossed in some task. Elise didn't think that he had seen her. Pleased that she would have a few more moments to prepare, she watched him from across the water. He was repeatedly scraping some material that lay across his knee and didn't look up. Although he was seated, Elise thought he wasn't much taller than her. Whatever he lacked in height, though, he made up in muscular strength. Despite her guess that he was only a couple of years older than her, he was still one of the most powerfully built men she had seen. He had a wide, barrel chest, over which he wore a loose tunic and trousers. The muscles came in thick strips from his neck to his shoulders. Although his legs were twice the width of Elise's, they were also slightly shorter than hers; he carried more of his height through his torso.

Elise hadn't expected him to have light brown hair with auburn tinges. She had been prepared for short, dark hair that covered most of his body. Instead, he had loosely tied his long hair at the nape of his neck with a thin piece of leather cord. His skin was smooth and there were only light patches of fuzz over his forearms. Elise knew many Sapien men who were hairier.

His head was bent low so she couldn't see the features of his face. The back of his head was shaped differently to hers; his skull protruded slightly, which she hadn't seen in any other species of human. Despite this, he could still have been mistaken for a stocky male Sapien.

Taking in his powerful build, Elise reassured herself that if Twenty-One were dangerous then she wouldn't be allowed in the pod by herself. She was not dispensable; Samuel had said they couldn't afford to lose a Companion. *It must be safe; it must be.* She repeated the mantra to herself.

Still unsure how she was going to cross the small brook, she was relieved when her gaze fell on some raised stepping stones downstream. Elise thought that someone must have positioned them in the water; they were too perfectly staged to be coincidental. Shaking her head, she had to remind herself that someone had positioned everything; she kept on forgetting it was not a natural landscape.

Elise neatly hopped across the stones, careful not to touch the water. She landed noisily on the other side of the bank. Twenty-One remained still.

She walked over, smiling widely, preparing herself for when he looked up. His head remained firmly down. Elise set her features so that she wouldn't react when he did look at her. She had never seen a living Neanderthal's face before and didn't know what to expect. She was now only a few feet from him and he had still not moved.

As she continued forwards, she willed him to raise his head. When her feet were in his line of sight, she reached the uncomfortable conclusion that he was ignoring her. Flummoxed as to what to do, she recalled that Luca had advised that they appreciated formalities.

Deciding not to delay, Elise crossed her legs and sat directly in front of Twenty-One. Without saying anything, she held the bag of nuts out to him, cradling it in both of her hands. She was careful not to stare at him and instead lowered her eyes, the same as she would when meeting a Medius or Potior for the first time. After a moment, she felt a warm hand gently remove the bag. She then raised her head to look directly at him.

She was first drawn to his heavy, protruding brow ridge. It dominated his face and cast a slight shadow over his eyes, giving them a sunken appearance, even though they were large. His nose was broad and prominent, but not unusually shaped. His chin was almost non-existent and disappeared below his wide mouth. What held Elise's gaze, though, were the similarities, not the differences. She admired his strong features and large, intelligent eyes. He was not so very different; she might have glanced at him twice, but no more. There was nothing so unusual that it would cause her to stare.

Twenty-One stared at Elise. She couldn't read anything from his expression. No thoughts or indication of his mood made the slightest appearance. He was still. After a few more seconds, Elise grew uncomfortable under his uncompromising gaze. She decided to take the lead.

Smiling broadly, she signed as clearly as she could. 'Hello, my name is Elise.'

There was no response or flicker of recognition. He continued to stare. His gaze was not aggressive or challenging, just impartial.

She decided to press on. 'I am the new Companion and yesterday was my first day. I am looking forward to working with you.'

Elise paused to give him a chance to respond. She was start-ing to get desperate; Luca would be watching. If Twenty-One wouldn't engage with her then she knew she wouldn't pass the training. Unsure whether he could even understand her, she thought that she might be signing too fast or that her language was too complex.

Out of desperation, she asked a question that she already knew the answer to, like she would with a small child. 'What is your name?'

'My name is Kit, not Twenty-One,' he signed, his face almost expressionless.

He did not use his facial expressions or movement to the same extent as Elise and her family would to add tone and con-text to his meaning. It left his words flat and difficult to fully understand without the layers and nuances she would normally rely on.

Relieved that he had spoken to her, Elise's smile was genuine. 'I'll use that in the future, Kit.'

Kit nodded and lowered his head. He continued to scrape the leather that was resting on his knee.

Unsure what to do, Elise pulled at some of the long, thick grasses next to her. Laying them out, she began to weave them together as her mum had shown her when she was younger. They would use the mats to collect vegetables from the garden, the prettier ones to serve food. She wished she had more hazel-nuts to shell, but this would have to do for the moment.

Elise's fingers moved automatically as they fell into the familiar rhythm. It gave her a chance to let her thoughts wander as she considered what she should do next. She hadn't been prepared for Kit being uninterested in her presence. She had thought he would be desperate for company after being alone. For the first time, Elise wondered what had happened to his previous Companions; no one had mentioned them. She decided that the only thing she could do was ask more questions, to work out what interested him. Bolstering herself, she decided to ask Kit's age. Finishing one corner of the mat, she turned it in a diagonal direction so that she could create a geometric design with the weave.

Glancing up, she stopped. She had caught Kit watching, but he was now looking away.

'Would you like me to show you?' Elise signed.

Kit nodded and Elise plucked stems for him. She chose the widest ones, knowing he would find it difficult to weave the finer blades with his large hands. After she had shown him the basic method, he started on his own mat. Continuing with hers, Elise occasionally glanced up to check his progress. Kit would hold his mat up to her when he wanted to change direction and she would help him lace the next section.

The hours passed and Elise marvelled at Kit's concentration. He was absorbed by what he was creating, barely changing his position. Her back began to ache, but she didn't want to move and disturb this moment. Ignoring the nagging pain, she resolved to build up her own strength in her spare time.

Elise jumped when she heard the clank of the steel door opening and quickly shutting. Kit stood and stretched his arms above his head. It was only then that Elise fully comprehended how powerfully built he was, completely solid with a chest as thick and round as a tree trunk. As Kit disappeared into the undergrowth towards the door, Elise realised that she wouldn't stand a chance if he decided to attack her. The odds were about the same as when she had been in the pod with the sabre-tooth tiger. The only thing she might be able to do would be to out-run him. If he got hold of her, he could crush her with just his bare arms. His strength was a weapon in itself.

Elise had a decision to make. She would either have to be forever on edge, ready to flee at a moment's notice, or she would have to trust that he wouldn't want to hurt her. For the moment, she was edging towards fleeing.

Elise heard Kit returning before she saw him. He was moving quickly through the bushes; he had circled around her. Her heartbeat increased and it reminded her of how many times it had in just two days; this job was already taking its toll. Subtly shifting her position, Elise pulled her legs around so she could spring up if needed. Kit was moving swiftly and with purpose, but she was unsure exactly where he was. Dropping her mat to free her arms, Elise tensed.

Without warning, Kit emerged from the bushes behind her. Elise jumped up. She turned anxiously and backed away a step, unable to read his intent.

Kit stared at her.

'I have our food,' he signed.

He was carrying two small containers, one of which he placed at Elise's feet before he sat. He pulled at the metal latches of the box and scooped out a chicken leg. Delicately picking the meat off the bone with his teeth, he placed his mat next to Elise's, his eyes flicking between the two.

Sitting opposite Kit, Elise opened up the container that he had brought for her. As she ate, she watched him comparing the mats, turning them one way and the other. She made her decision; firmly tucking her legs underneath herself, she lowered her head and continued her work.

CHAPTER 5

Over the next few days, Elise and Kit fell into a quiet routine. Arriving early in the morning, Elise would sit with him as he worked. He would alternate treating leather with weaving grass mats. The work was continuous and he didn't show any desire for relaxation. The once small pile of grass mats was growing and Elise knew he would get tired of them soon; he had almost mastered the technique and had even started to weave patterns she had not previously imagined.

Kit had not spoken to her since delivering her food. He didn't ask questions and ignored the few that she asked. He was never rude or aggressive; it was instead as if she had not entered his pod. The grass mats were the only evidence that she had made any impact on his world.

Frustrated with her lack of progress, Elise thought about new ways to make a breakthrough. She always came back to the need for further projects, but there was nothing in the pod for them to do. She had systematically explored every corner. Running her hands along the ivy-covered walls, she had felt the steel panels behind the foliage. Although the pod looked like the ones outside, there were no chances being taken; Kit was enclosed on every side.

During her investigations, she had discovered Kit's sleeping area at the back near the pine trees. There was only a small sleeping mat and furs. Closed to the sky, there was no rain or wind; the pod was a shelter in itself. Someone had carved shelving into a tree stump nearby and Kit had placed a few personal items onto its ledges. Elise did not pry, acutely aware that even though it had no clear boundaries, this section was private. Besides the sleeping area, there was nothing else that confirmed Kit's presence; he had not made attempts to alter his environment.

They would take turns collecting their meals from the only door into the pod. After breakfast, Kit exercised, his routine never altering. After running around the edge for an hour, he would then pull his substantial weight up onto a low tree branch. Elise, grateful for some exertion, copied what he did. She could easily keep up with the running, but her upper body strength was poor. She could barely pull her chin above the branch before she had to let go. Kit would silently watch and then proceed to pull himself up effortlessly twenty times in a row. Elise wouldn't have been surprised if he could do it with one arm.

With nothing else to explore, Elise began to mull over what she could teach Kit to help him expand his insular world. The options were limitless.

Ignoring her requests for advice, Luca would only say that she was doing better than he had expected. He no longer watched her all day and she was not sure if the pod was being monitored at all.

By the time she left in the late evening, the viewing platform was deserted. No one waited for her after work and the canteen was always empty. She would collect cookies from the vending machine and head straight to her room before falling asleep. The cycle would then be repeated.

In three days, the only conversation Elise had was with Georgina. Even the few people she met in the morning on the way to Kit's pod looked away when she passed; the rumours about her first day had spread.

Being invisible was preferable to what happened with the two Sapien girls she had to pass on the way to Georgina's clinic. They were leaning against a wall part-way down the corridor. One was tall with a single plait running from the top of her head down her back. She could have been mistaken for a Medius, but Elise knew she must be Sapien as she worked in the canteen. The other was short and dumpy. She clung to every word and gesture the taller girl made with a faint air of worship. As Elise walked by, they gave each other pointed looks.

'That's the one I was telling you about. Thinks she's a Midder. Keeps on running after Samuel and don't remember where she came from,' the shorter girl said, not bothering to whisper.

The taller one waited until Elise passed before saying in a dismissive drawl, 'Luca said she's nothing special. Outer Circle production plugger. Mightn't even pass her induction.'

Elise's heart sank. It was like being back at school, except there was no Holly to step in. Her parents had always drilled her to walk away, to do anything to avoid conflict that might escalate and draw unwanted attention, but this inability to stand up for herself had led to her unintentionally isolating herself from her classmates.

Elise's pleasure at seeing Georgina must have been evident, as she dispensed with formalities and gave Elise a quick hug after she entered the treatment room.

'How's the arm?' Georgina asked once Elise had hopped onto the bed.

'Oh, that; it's great. Back to normal, I think,' Elise said, testing her voice, which hadn't been used properly for days.

It sounded rusty and she had to clear her throat a few times. Elise smiled at Georgina apologetically.

'And how's it going with Kit?' Georgina continued, unwrapping the bandages from Elise's arm.

Elise hadn't heard anyone else call him by that name; it was always Twenty-One. The familiarity encouraged her to confide.

'He ignores me. I'm not even sure he understands what I'm saying most of the time.'

'Oh, he understands you just fine,' Georgina said without looking up from Elise's arm. 'Don't ever underestimate his ability to comprehend what is happening around him.'

'Do you know a lot about him?'

'As much as any nurse knows about her patients. Kit's a little different to the other Neanderthals I've seen. Most sink into depressive states. They just sleep and either eat all day or lose their appetite entirely. But he's resilient. He tries to keep himself busy, which I'm sure helps.'

'But he won't even speak to me.'

'It's not you,' Georgina explained. 'He's just slow to trust. Always try to imagine what you'd be thinking, feeling, in his position.'

'I can't seem to get him to notice I'm even there. Do you think he has other ways of communicating, besides sign language?'

Georgina stopped what she was doing and looked up at Elise. 'Well, it's only a theory of mine, but that big old lump at the back of his head has to be used for something. We don't have them. The scans show there is a small section of brain tissue there.' Georgina sat up. 'So the question I keep on asking myself is: What does it do?'

The possibilities flicked through Elise's mind, each more outlandish.

'What do you think?' she asked.

'I have theories, but no proof. The Supes think it's to do with spatial awareness, but I'm not so sure. You're the one sitting with him all day; perhaps you can work it out.'

'But how can I when he won't even speak with me?' Elise said, her mind flicking back to the possibility she wasn't going to pass her induction. The girl in the corridor's words still lingered.

Georgina snapped off her latex gloves. 'If he won't speak to you, it's your job to convince him that you're worth speaking to.'

Elise stared down at her hands; she knew Georgina was right. She couldn't expect Kit to treat her like a friend; she had done nothing to earn his trust. It was up to her to make the effort. She was able to leave the pod every day, but he couldn't escape her company.

Georgina smiled at the evident concern on Elise's face. 'Well, there's no infection and it's healing nicely. But I want to be sure you're as good as new. Another splash of Dermadew and you'll be back to normal by next week.'

'I wasn't worrying about my arm,' Elise said. 'I'm sure it's better. I was just thinking about Kit and what I should do. But I've got a plan now. Things have to change.'

'Well, you make sure you go through the proper channels before making any of those changes. You'll be out of here quicker than you can say, "I was only trying to help," if Fintorian catches you messing around with his plans.'

Elise was pulling back the covers to climb into bed when she heard a gentle knock. She never had visitors. Intrigued, she pulled open the door and was surprised that Samuel was standing outside. She hadn't seen him since her first day. He filled the narrow corridor and Elise realised for the first time how tall he was. What other genes had his parents tweaked?

Samuel avoided looking at Elise and took a step back until he was standing by the opposite wall. 'I'm sorry to call on you this late, but I realise that I haven't checked on how you are progressing. Seventeen and the barrier failure seem to be taking up all my time at the moment.'

'Do you want to come in?' Elise asked politely, holding the door open.

'No. No, thank you. Perhaps it would be better if we went to the canteen. I'll give you a minute to get dressed.'

Elise, embarrassed by her naivety, quickly closed the door. A Medius and a Sapien alone in sleeping quarters late at night would never be tolerated. Shedding her leggings and T-shirt, she hastily pulled on the trousers and grey hooded top she'd been wearing earlier. Not for the first time, she wished that she had something new to wear. She tried to flatten her spiky hair and gave up when it refused to be tamed.

She pulled open the door. 'I'm sorry, sir. I wasn't thinking properly. I haven't been sleeping much.'

Brushing aside the awkward moment, Samuel started to walk down the corridor. 'Yes, I have noted that you've been clocking up the hours with Twenty-One. It's not giving you much time for rest.'

'Kit . . . I mean Twenty-One, doesn't sleep much.'

'No, he does not,' Samuel said, pushing back his hair. 'And he's been sleeping even less in the past few months. I'm concerned that this might be the start of some sort of decline.'

Elise took a deep breath. 'I was wondering, sir, if I could speak to you about something?'

'Yes, of course. And please don't call me "sir". It makes me feel old.'

Elise smiled; she still didn't know if Samuel was two years older than her or fifty.

'Thank you,' she said before pushing on. 'I wanted to ask why Twenty-One is only allowed to build and make things. He must be so bored. Couldn't I teach him something else? Music or art, or even see if he could learn to read and write?'

Samuel didn't respond. Instead, he led her over to the far corner of the canteen, to the same table she had shared with Luca. Before sitting, Samuel scanned the room. Without warning, he abruptly pushed a chair and the sound echoed around the empty canteen. Elise jumped at the noise, heart beating faster as her body prepared to run if she needed it to.

A few seconds later, she felt the slightest draft pass her ear; a camera had come to investigate.

'Sorry about that. I have a tendency to be a little clumsy at times. Would you please take a seat, Elise?'

Saying nothing in response, Elise sat opposite him. She had lost sight of the camera but knew it wouldn't have finished with them yet.

Samuel stared down at his screen. 'I can see that you have been spending, on average, seventeen hours a day with Twenty-One. How are you finding the work?'

He looked up at Elise for a second before returning to his screen.

'I enjoy it much more than I thought possible,' Elise responded. 'We've been weaving some grass mats together and he's already better at it than me. It's made me think about what else he could do, if he were given the chance.'

'Well, that is certainly a question we at the museum have been asking ourselves,' Samuel said, still peering at his screen. 'How is your arm?'

'Much better,' Elise said, her senses reaching out to detect whether the camera was still around them.

'I'm glad it's healing and you can rest assured that you won't be expected to pay for the treatment out of your own Medi-stamps.' Samuel was still looking at his screen. 'Twenty-One's stats all seem to be around average, apart from the decreased sleeping time. He also doesn't seem to spend time relaxing throughout the day. But, then, neither do you. He seems to treat everything as a full-time job. Perhaps this is something you could explore with him over the coming weeks?'

Samuel's shoulders relaxed a little and Elise guessed that the camera had captured what it needed and moved on. She didn't fully trust Samuel, though; besides being a Medius, he had also lied to Fintorian. If he could lie to a Potior, he could lie to anyone. Was Samuel just pretending that the camera had gone?

Perhaps he now wanted to record her speaking more freely. She was starting to think like her parents.

'As to your previous question, it would never be agreed to by the Potiors. They are puritans when it comes to the museum.' Samuel picked up his screen and started to fold it up so it would fit in his pocket. His eyes darted over to the doorway. 'There is no evidence that Neanderthals discovered music before they died out and limited evidence for art. Even the Sapiens living at the same time only had cave paintings and possibly a few simple percussion instruments; they didn't start writing until six thousand years ago. Whatever you do with Twenty-One, it can be nothing more than he would have done forty thousand years ago. I suggest you find some other type of pursuit to practise with him.'

Samuel started to push back his chair, gently this time so it didn't make any noise.

Frustrated, Elise leant forwards. She didn't know when she would get to speak to him next. 'They must've done something besides craft kitchenware.' She caught herself. 'I'm sorry; I just think there's so much more I could do. So much more he could do.'

Samuel looked at her with surprise and met her gaze for the first time. He then leant back in his chair. 'I'm sure you've heard the rumours, courtesy of Luca, that we have a similar problem in every base. I agree; I think we are underestimating their capabilities and needs. But I shouldn't even be speaking to you about this.'

'Tell me what they were like before, then,' Elise said.

Sighing, Samuel took off his glasses and rubbed his eyes. 'Life for them was predominantly about survival, as it was for our ancestors. They did what was necessary to stay alive and continue their line. They had a large range of tools and cooked with fire. They made utensils and bowls: kitchenware, if you will.' Samuel raised an eyebrow. 'They made and wore clothing, hunted and foraged. But they also had a complex language, which we haven't even begun to decipher yet, and they probably used this to keep their histories alive through stories and legends. They buried and mourned their dead. They may've even had gods. But no music, no writing. They just didn't live long enough to develop it.'

Elise pondered this new information. There was little she could do with gods and she could hardly help discover the depth of his language if he wouldn't even speak with her.

'Hunted and cooked with fire?' Elise said, holding on to this.

'Yes. They regularly hunted. They would supplement this with produce that they could pick or dig from the ground. They would cook all of this using fire, either communally or in smaller units.'

Elise's eyes widened as she latched onto a plan. 'What if I learnt to hunt and cook with Twenty-One, same way he would have done forty thousand years ago?'

'No. No, you couldn't,' Samuel said, the frustration clear. 'Firstly, Sapiens didn't necessarily hunt in the same way as Neanderthals. Sapiens often threw spears from a distance. Neanderthals were more likely to get close to their prey and thrust their spears at the animals, although there is some evidence of them throwing spears. Secondly, you are talking about arming a Neanderthal and giving him fire while you're in an enclosed metal cage with him. He could turn on you in a second and there would be nothing you, or anyone, could do about it. The Potiors would never allow it.'

'He could've snuffed me out in a second already,' Elise said. 'I could never fight him off; he's too strong.'

Samuel stared at her. 'I know that Kit would never intentionally hurt you, but the Potiors don't. You could still be accidentally hurt, though. A fire could get out of control or a spear be thrown the wrong way.'

'We'd be careful. I'd learn how to hunt like a Sapien. He'd learn to hunt like a Neanderthal. We wouldn't fight each other.' She paused to think. 'We could agree that the fire-making equipment would only be used when I'm there and never left in the pod. And maybe an extinguisher outside, by the door, just in case.'

Samuel pushed his hair away from his eyes and stared at the ceiling. 'Are you really serious about this? You would risk your own safety, just so that Kit can have a broader range of pastimes?'

'I want to help and I can't if we're just weaving grass mats every day. Please, just ask Fintorian for me. If he doesn't agree then I won't mention it again.'

'I'll speak with Fintorian, but only because I think he'll say no.' Samuel moved around the table before looking down at her. 'When you go home this weekend, be sure to bring back some warmer clothes. We'll be dropping the temperature soon for the seasonal change.'

Elise didn't know how to respond. She didn't own many clothes, let alone warm ones.

Samuel stared down at her lowered head. 'Well, ah, I actually have a few items you can have.'

'I don't have any spare tickets,' Elise said, trying to cover her embarrassment.

'No payment of any kind expected. Just consider it an investment of mine to ensure that I don't catch any colds from you. I'm not very good at being ill. Very grumpy, awful to be around.'

Elise smiled up at him, but he had already stepped around her and was walking away.

'Thanks!' she shouted out after him.

'Get some sleep!' he called out without turning around. 'Both of you!'

CHAPTER 6

The following day was a Sunday and Elise was due to go home. She felt uncomfortable leaving Kit alone, all too aware that she was free to leave the pod while he was not. She didn't want to tell him she was visiting her family and so, giving no explanation, she just said that she would be back in the morning. Kit looked up at her with his sunken brown eyes, not a visible thought passing across his face. Elise wasn't sure if he had even understood her.

When she rounded the corner to her parents' home, her heart sank; Deeta Thinckle and her daughter, Shauna, were walking towards her. She thought about making another lap of the paths, but they had already noticed her. There was nothing she could do to avoid them without appearing rude. Smiling widely, she waved and continued to jog past them, hoping that the encounter was over.

'Elise!' Deeta called out. 'I've been waiting to hear all about your new job!'

Trying to hide her disappointment, Elise turned and walked back to them. She had learnt that it was best to overwhelm Deeta with information. That way, Deeta would think she had gleaned some gossip and Elise could quickly escape.

Deeta reached out and clasped Elise's forearm. 'I want to hear everything! It's not often we have someone on this pathway working in the Inner Circle!'

Elise stared down at Deeta's pawing hand and resisted the urge to shake it off.

Instead, she smiled. 'It's going well. The most interesting bit was the tour I had with a very short Midder from the Worker Profiling Department.'

Elise then started to recite Harriet's introductory speech word for word. Shauna yawned and didn't bother to cover her mouth.

'No, no. It's like being back at school,' Deeta said, looking confused. 'I don't want to hear that. I want to hear about the Ned you're looking after!'

Elise's smile faded as she realised she wasn't going to get away as quickly as she had hoped.

'What's he like? Is he dangerous? Have they broken him in yet? Do you get to brush his coat?' Deeta said, her eyes wide.

'He's very calm. And also nothing like a horse, so he doesn't need to be broken in or brushed down.'

'But he's a h'animal, isn't he?' asked Shauna in her low voice.

She was permanently bunged up and, consequently, breathed through her mouth, which she never closed.

'Yes. But so are we.'

'No, we're not. We're human. Along with Potiors and Midders. It's different.'

'Humans are still animals. The Neanderthals are human too.'

'Bet he don't have ideas and talk to you about them. Does he?' Shauna said, taking a step closer.

'But . . .' Elise said, slightly stumped.

She was pretty sure Kit did have ideas, but he certainly didn't talk to her about them. There was still the nagging doubt that she was projecting too much onto him, that he wasn't as capable as she hoped.

'And if he don't have ideas. And he don't talk to you about 'em. Then he's a h'animal. Never hear a horse tell you his plans for the future, do you? That's 'cause he's a h'animal,' Shauna concluded.

Deeta was nodding sagely at her daughter's words. Elise could see that this could easily escalate; she was familiar with Shauna's logic from their time at school. When Shauna felt that she had been wronged, something would happen to the person she nurtured a grievance against, no matter how long she had to wait. When Katy Thorble had called Shauna a 'mouth-breather' at school, two months later a camera had caught Katy cheating in her final exams. Elise had heard that Shauna had tipped off the teacher after befriending Katy and telling her how easy it would be to smuggle in a few notes. Katy wasn't even able to get a job on the production line, as she couldn't be trusted, so she had to work in the Recycling Centre. Elise reasoned to herself that there was no point antagonising Shauna until she knew more about what Kit was capable of.

'Mum told me you won the lottery,' Elise said, turning to Deeta.

Deeta tried to swell with pride, but it was a little half-hearted. 'Well, I've been entering every month for twenty years, so it's about my turn, I reckon.'

'So your next child will be Medius, then; they'll be moving up in the world.'

'Um, no, not this time . . . I thought to pass the winnings on to Shauna for when she has children. Having a Medius grandchild will be just as good as having a Medius child,' Deeta said with a firm nod.

'Mum thought she weren't likely to have more children and as I'm the oldest we thought it best passed to me instead,' Shauna said, smiling smugly.

Elise looked at them and wondered how many other lottery wins had caused friction in families.

'Well, you still won, Deeta. It's so rare; that's something to be proud of in itself.'

'Yes, it is, isn't it? Perhaps my luck will continue,' Deeta said, brightening. 'I've heard they're going to have an annual lottery to modify a child up to the level of a Potior.'

'Is that even possible?' Elise asked.

'Course it is, dear. If you had ten modifications, that would do it. Maybe I'll have another grandchild who's a Potior!' Deeta said, eyes misting.

'What traits will your child have, Shauna?' Elise asked, intrigued.

'Warrior gene. Height. Strength.'

'Shauna wants to build a right little defender, don't you?' Deeta said, smiling up at her daughter.

'I want them to be able to take care of themselves in any situation. Maybe get into the Protection Department for the Potiors. If they got to go to Adenine Base and help the leaders all day, then my child couldn't ask for a better job. It's the right thing to do, as well, serving the Potiors and ensuring they're safe. Owe them everything, we do.'

Elise was surprised that Shauna had such far-flung dreams for her child. Adenine Base was where all the decisions for Zone 3 were made: 'Guidance and Governance.'

Feeling she had spent long enough with Shauna, Elise smiled firmly. 'I must get back. Mum and Dad will want to hear my news.'

With a brief wave, she carried on down the lane and closed the front door firmly behind her in case Deeta had followed.

'Did you have a run-in with Deeta?' Sofi said when she saw her daughter's expression. 'I hope you were nice to her; she's not got much else but her family and neighbours.'

'I was very nice to her; it's Shauna I could do without. She's so black and white, you can't ever get any other points of view in there.'

'That might be true, but she'll still be here this evening and you won't. So I want to hear all of your news. We should really wait until your dad's back, though.' Sofi paused, gazing around the room. 'But I'm sure he won't mind if you tell me a bit about the people you're working with. He's got no interest in younger people, especially anyone new you've met,' she concluded with a smile.

Elise knew what Sofi meant, so she gave her what she wanted. She spoke only of Luca, though, as she wanted her to know there were other Sapiens in the museum, that she wasn't alone. She painted a happy working partnership and embellished the amount of time they spent together. She didn't mention the Sapien girls in the corridor, embarrassed that she didn't fit in.

When Elise had finished, Sofi appeared satisfied, so Elise nodded at the door. 'I'll go see Nathan now, if that's okay?'

As Elise passed her mum, she was scooped up into a big hug.

'I've missed you, Elise.'

'I've missed you too,' Elise responded, not expecting the feeling to be so intense.

It was lovely to be somewhere people wanted to speak with her and didn't look down at her for being an Outer Circle Sapien or call her a Midder-chaser. She couldn't win; she was either too Sapien or not Sapien enough.

Sofi stared at her appraisingly. 'Working life's suiting you; you look so pretty today. Are you wearing new clothes?'

Elise looked down at herself. She was wearing the pair of soft grey slacks and the loose cotton shirt she had found outside her pod door that morning. They had been wrapped up in sturdy brown paper along with two thick jumpers. There had been a note, but all it said was: 'To Elise, from Samuel.' Everything was too big, as he was a foot and a half taller than her, but she had dealt with this by rolling the trousers up and tying the shirt in a knot at her waist. He had also given her a knitted hooded top that had been promoted to her favourite item of clothing. They were all simply designed, but the materials were more expensive than anything else she had ever owned. They didn't crease either, which she still couldn't get used to.

'Yes, do you like them? I was given them by my Overseer; he had them spare.'

'Well, that was very kind of Luca,' Sofi said. 'He sounds like a very nice boy and is welcome to visit us whenever he wants.'

Elise smiled and didn't correct her.

Taking note of the sign Nathan had made asking everyone to 'PLEASE OPEN DOOR ONLY SLIGHTLY AND WAIT BEFORE ENTERING', Elise paused before opening his door only a few inches and closing it a few times so that Nathan would have a fair chance of seeing that she was coming. He was at an age when privacy had started to become important; it didn't stop him from bursting into Elise's room when he was excited, though. One of the good things about living at the museum was that she no longer needed to wedge a chair under the door handle every time she wanted to get changed.

Nathan was still in bed, blankets pulled over his head. Sitting next to him, Elise gently pulled them down so she could wake him up. She tried not to gasp when she saw his face.

'What happened?' she said as she gently turned the side of his cheek towards her. There was a large light-coloured bruise near his ear. It hadn't been there earlier in the week and had not yet fully ripened into the dark colours it promised.

Nathan looked up at Elise, his large brown eyes following the shape of the words as they left her lips.

'Oh, that. Nothing. I just tripped in the playground,' he signed, pulling only one of his hands free from the covers.

All of the family would use one-handed signs at times; it meant that they didn't have to drop everything they were hold-ing when they wanted to speak.

'Are you sure?' Elise signed.

Nathan squirmed and turned away.

'You don't have to be embarrassed; everyone makes mistakes they wish hadn't happened.'

Elise watched as Nathan blushed. 'Some kids at school said I have a fault because I can't hear. That I have faulty genes.' He paused and rubbed his eye. 'I tried to tell them that I couldn't hear after I got sick. I said I wasn't born like this, but they just laughed at me. They threw a rock. I dodged it, but I tripped and fell.'

Drawing Nathan to her, Elise held him while he tried not to cry. Pleased he couldn't see her face, she considered what she should do.

When Nathan was still, she gently pulled away from him. Smoothing down his hair, which stuck up like her own, she smiled at him. 'You're not faulty, Nathan. People can't be faulty. And you don't have to tell them about when you got ill; you don't have to explain anything to them. You're just you.' Elise paused to see if what she was saying was having any effect. 'What happened after you fell?'

Nathan grinned. 'A girl in the year above, Jada, ran over and accidentally on purpose kicked them in the knee. Maddy did as well. I really wanted to, but Mum and Dad always told me not to bring attention to myself.'

'A good accidental knee-kicking is probably what they needed. What's Jada like?'

'She's a year older, but she's still nice to me. Maddy's her sister and she's in the year below me. Maddy can't walk very fast, but she's really good at painting, better than even the eleven-year-olds.'

'Well, if you like them, ask them over after school. Dad could make one of his blackberry crumbles.'

'And even if they won't come round, I can have all the topping from the crumble as you won't be here,' Nathan signed.

Elise grinned at Nathan's opportunistic reasoning. 'I think I'm seeing Holly later. Do you mind if I speak to her about what happened? You know she always tries to keep an eye out for you.'

'Yeah, sure – if you want. I'm going to ask Jada and Maddy over tomorrow,' Nathan signed, pushing back the covers.

Halfway to the door, he turned round. 'What's it like working at the museum?'

'It's better than I imagined. Maybe when you're older you can come and be a Companion with me.'

'I'd like that. Maybe we could be Companions in another base's Museum of Evolution. I'd like to see Adenine.'

Elise just smiled in response and nodded; she felt he was still too young to know how limited their options were. When she heard the bathroom door close, she went to speak with Sofi.

'Can you ask Dad to make a blackberry crumble today? Nathan might be having two friends back from school tomorrow. He told me he's being pushed around for being deaf, but these girls kicked back for him.'

'We thought something was going on, but he wouldn't tell us. Kept on saying he'd just tripped,' Sofi said. 'But the Medius teachers won't do anything; I think they agree with the kids.'

Elise struggled to remain calm; she didn't want to ruin her only day at home. 'You've got to stop this "fade into the background" stuff with Nathan. You did that with me, but he's having a rougher time than I ever did. Instead of Dad teaching him how to run faster, get him to teach him how to stand up for himself.' Elise paused to see if her words were having any effect. 'If Dad teaches him how to do that, he can stop running. He's old enough.'

Sighing, Sofi sat at the table and rested her head in her hands. 'Oh, I know you're right. We were just so worried that he'd bring attention to himself, that he might even start fighting everyone. It's clearly not working, though. I'll speak with your dad and we'll come up with something. Maybe he could start teaching him to block, like he did with you. If they start some training, it'll take everyone's mind off you being away as well.'

Elise was torn. She didn't want her dad to turn all his attention on Nathan. She had trained with Aiden for hours every day growing up, learning simple blocking moves that had become more advanced as she got older. Never in public, though; any form of fighting was banned, but her dad still insisted on it. Defence was always his main concern.

'Just some simple moves. Don't let him take over like he did with me,' Elise said.

'He only did it for your safety.'

'There has to be balance, though, and it's up to you to make sure Dad realises that.'

She didn't wait for her mum to respond.

Aiden was late to return, which was often the case with his production centre. Elise could see how tired he was as soon as she walked into the kitchen. She had spent the afternoon with Nathan wandering the pathways, catching up on the events of the last week, and had only just got back to the house.

Elise busied herself getting a glass of water for Aiden before signing, 'Could you not use some of your leave days you've been storing? Maybe spend a few days just sleeping and gardening. It'd do you some good.'

Aiden took the glass and gulped it down before handing it back to Elise for her to refill. She checked the water tank by the kitchen sink out of habit before turning on the tap. They had nearly run out of treated water for the day. Everyone must have had their ninety-second shower. The showers were set on timers, one press per family member. If you became dirty again, the only option was to wait until midnight when the timers reset. She decided not to mention the low water levels and instead filled his glass. They would get their next delivery in the morning anyway.

Aiden finished the second glass before signing his response. 'Not at the moment. I want to save them for if there's an emergency. I'm fine. Nothing a few early nights won't cure.' He rubbed his face with both hands. 'So what's been happening at the museum then?'

Elise recounted a happy tale of weaving grass mats and never seeing anyone due to the long hours she was working.

'So you don't want to leave, then?' Sofi signed. 'I was hoping you'd miss us enough to want to come home again.'

'I'm sorry, Mum. Kit needs my help—'

'Who's Kit?' Aiden interjected before she could go any further.

'It's Twenty-One's name for himself,' Nathan signed, clearly pleased to know more than his parents about Elise's work.

'You named Twenty-One?' Aiden asked Elise.

'No, he named himself.'

'Well, I never . . . What else can he do?'

'I'm not really sure, Dad. He doesn't talk to me at the moment, but I think I can work on that. He's very gentle, though, and even collects my lunch for me when it's delivered.'

'Well, that's better than I expected. We never saw them when they were on display when I was a girl,' Sofi signed. 'The one in Thymine never left her shelter. I'd end up staring at an empty pod when I went on my annual tour at school. But there can be other Companions. It doesn't have to be you who helps him learn to sign.'

'But that's the thing. I think that he can already sign fluently. He just chooses not to. I think he also has other ways of communicating, but we haven't discovered them yet.'

'We?' Aiden signed. 'Who's we? You know perfectly well that you're not part of that picture and you shouldn't get your hopes up either.'

Elise caught herself. Her dad's words stung, but she knew they were true.

'Who've you been speaking to at the museum?' he continued.

'No one, Dad. I'm in there with Kit for so long that I don't really see anyone else. I barely ever see my Overseers either; they're focused on Seventeen, who's pregnant. It's more lonely than dangerous.'

'Well, lonely's good in my book.'

Elise decided not to mention her run-in with the Potior and the sabre-tooth. She had let her guard down that day. If her dad knew what Samuel had seen, he would lock her in her bedroom. She tugged her sleeve down to make sure it covered the bandage on her arm.

'I know it's not part of my job, and that no one would ever listen to me even if I did make a breakthrough. But I just think Kit can do a lot more than he's letting on,' Elise signed, realising she wasn't as sure as she sounded.

Sofi looked thoughtful. 'Your granddad had the same theories too, Elise, but they were just based on what he'd gleaned from Infactualities.'

'Did Granddad speak about it with you?'

'No, not really. He just read that old encyclopaedia from cover to cover and liked to discuss what he'd learnt.'

Elise tried not to think about her granddad; she missed the calm logic he had brought to their home. He'd had the most inquisitive mind she had ever known, even more so than Holly, and it had been left to languish on the production line. Before Elise had been born, he had risked everything to acquire an illegal Pre-Pandemic encyclopaedia, which he had treasured above everything. When he had died, Aiden had burnt the encyclopaedia, despite Elise's reassurances that she would keep it safely hidden. She had attended two cremations that day.

'Your granddad always said there was a lot more to the Neanderthals than just being a simple-minded species of human,' Sofi signed. 'But they must've become extinct for a reason. We either killed them all and they weren't advanced enough to defend themselves or they weren't able to work out how to adapt to the climate change.'

Elise mulled this over; there was no other explanation she could think of either.

Undeterred, she pressed on. 'That might be true, but they have a second chance and I want to be part of it. So I'll be going back. I'm sorry, but I have to.'

Aiden seemed likely to object, but stopped once he saw the look Sofi gave him.

'If that's your decision, we'll support you,' Sofi signed. 'But we want you to know that you can come home anytime and we'll work out what to tell the museum together.'

'Thanks, I won't forget it.'

Elise was relieved that they wouldn't have to discuss it further.

The evening passed and everyone made a point of not discussing Elise's decision. When it was nearly time for her to leave, Holly came to the house and they sat in Elise's bedroom. Elise told Holly about her job, leaving out nearly as much detail as she had with her parents. She knew Holly would not approve of her chasing after a Potior or pushing to teach Kit how to hunt; even Holly had her limits.

But Holly was distracted and barely listened anyway. Elise watched her circle the room, occasionally picking things up and glancing at them before putting them back.

'Is there something rumbling around your head that needs to come out?' Elise finally asked.

'Oh, I'm sorry. I've been listening; it's just a few things have happened since you've been away.'

'Good or bad?'

'Good, definitely good,' Holly said. 'I've started spending some time with Lewis Thetter and, well, you know . . .'

Elise was stumped, firstly that someone had made Holly shy and secondly that it was Lewis Thetter. She didn't approve; they had both known Lewis for years and he had always been loud and opinionated.

'I thought you didn't like Lewis; you called him a puffed-up ticket chaser to his face!' she said, laughing.

Glancing at Holly, Elise could see that this was not a joking matter. She had no experience of this type of conversation, though, having avoided any serious relationships with the Sapien boys while growing up. They had never held any interest for her beyond friendship and a few test runs to see what all the fuss was about.

'That was years ago. People change. He's got some amazing ideas about Sapiens and where we are now. He's a really interesting man.'

'What sort of ideas?'

'I shouldn't really talk about them here,' Holly said in a hushed tone, 'but he thinks Sapiens should petition the Potiors for their own lands. Live separately from Midders. He doesn't think we need the Midders, that we were doing just fine before they came along.'

Elise couldn't hide her shock. What Holly had said was one of the most serious of crimes: Denial. There could be no sincere Reparations if there was no acceptance of past events. Denial, along with violent crimes, meant expulsion from the base. Once or twice a year, interested spectators would gather at the edge of the Thymine Base and watch as someone was marched across the fern boundary line by a member of the Protection Department. With nothing but the clothes they were wearing, they would be forced into the woods. If they tried to rejoin their family and friends, or refused to move farther, one of the Protection Department would cross the boundary line and beat them until they left, never to return. Violence wasn't a criminal act outside of the safe lines of the base. After they stumbled away the second time, no one ever saw them again. Without treated water, they would die within days.

'You can't say anything, Elise, please! Promise me you won't say anything!' The urgency in Holly's tone was still there even though she was whispering.

'Of course I won't say anything, but you have to be careful. He can't just run around saying things like that. He'll get caught. If someone heard him or a camera followed him—'

'He's not stupid. Of course he doesn't say those things in public. They have meetings. I've been to one.'

Elise didn't know what to say. She knew why Holly was frustrated in her work, but she didn't think that all the Medius were the problem; Georgina had always been friendly to her.

'I've met a Midder at the museum and she's fine with me. She talks to me like I'm no different to her,' Elise said, knowing that what she was saying sounded weak. She didn't expect the force of Holly's reaction, though.

'What did I tell you! It's only half-baked charity. She doesn't actually care about you or what you think!'

Holly was no longer whispering.

'It doesn't feel like charity, well, not from Georgina anyway,' Elise said, looking away.

'Georgina!' Holly exploded. 'Now on first name terms, are you? Well, our first names say everything, El-ise. They're different for a reason.' Holly glared around the room. 'Lewis said this would happen if you went and worked with them.'

Elise was mortified that Holly and Lewis had talked about her in this way. She had always hoped that Holly never spoke about her when she wasn't with her, that their friendship was their own.

'I only get to see you a few hours a week and I don't want us to argue,' Elise said. 'I've only been away five days and it already feels like things are changing. Did you hear about what happened to Nathan?'

Holly often acted as an interpreter for Nathan in his lessons but Elise knew that Holly wasn't with him all of the time.

Holly softened. 'One of the other teaching assistants told me. Don't worry; I'll keep an eye on him. I'll push the Midders into doing something if it happens again. Or I'll deal with it myself.'

Holly paused, but didn't elaborate. 'You know he's like a little brother to me too.'

Elise touched Holly's arm. 'Thanks. That makes me feel better about leaving him.'

Holly squeezed her hand. 'I know you're not the one I'm cross with. I just get so frustrated with everything, and I think this might be the answer. I really do.'

'Just please be careful.'

'Of course I will. That goes for you as well, okay?'

Elise just nodded.

CHAPTER 7

. . . .

The following week, Elise peeled off her bandages in her airtight bedroom. She was pleased to see that her arm had healed. There was not even the trace of a silver line to show where the claw had torn her skin. She had been given a rare taste of how life was for a Medius or Potior.

Collecting some of the grass mats, Elise decided to drop by the nurses' station to give them to Georgina as a thank you. It wasn't much, but it was all she had.

When she entered, she was surprised to see Harriet leaving the treatment room. Not wanting to pry, Elise lowered her head and sat. The waft of a camera passed her left ear. Two tiny feet enclosed in sturdy shoes, with heels nearly as high as the sho were long, stopped in Elise's line of sight. Elise tried not to at the flesh poking over the leather seams.

'Ah, the new Companion. I hope you're not back f ther Dermadew; you've already had more than ne are very lucky that we didn't deduct your tickets

With a sinking feeling, Elise nodded and from the corner of her eye as she crossed th camera following. As soon as she was alone, Elise jumped up and rapped on Georgina's door.

'Come in,' Georgina called out. 'Elise, lovely to see you. How's the arm?'

Georgina gratefully accepted the grass mats and Elise studied her face. 'What happened? Harriet said something about deductions for the Dermadew.'

'I was hoping she wouldn't mention that.' Georgina glanced up at Elise from her wheeled stool. 'There was a camera in here, the first time I treated you. I didn't know it was here, didn't hear it come in above the noise of the machines. It must have settled in one of the corners, amongst my equipment.'

Elise's eyes widened as she tried to recall what they had talked about.

'Don't worry; they showed me most of the footage and there was nothing incriminating, for you, at least. They're not very happy with me, though . . . said I shouldn't use Dermadew on a Sapien scar unless it's a facial disfigurement. Apparently, you should just wear long-sleeved shirts for the rest of your life.'

'How many tickets?'

'Not so many that you need to worry about it.' Georgina smiled up at her.

'How many?'

Georgina sighed. 'A hundred.'

' hundred!' Elise exclaimed, reaching for the wall behind her.

it's not for you to worry about. I have everything I need.

paid a lot more than you. I can take the deduction.'

to
'ou back . . .' Elise said, as she tried to work out how
three
her parents she would have no salary for the next

Georgina stood and fixed Elise with a look that stopped her mid-sentence. 'You most certainly will not. That scar should have been repaired, and I'd do it again. Even if I have to pay for it myself.'

Elise opened her mouth to protest.

Georgina pointed the grass mats at her. 'I'd do it again, so no regrets or reparations about this, okay?'

Elise nodded. 'Thank you. If you can think of any way I can pay you back . . .'

Georgina shook her head and ushered Elise out of the door.

As she left Georgina's clinic, Elise ran her hand over her healed arm and decided to go to the canteen to get cookies from the vending machine. A habit was developing, one that couldn't be indulged in Kit's pod either. The rules were strict: she could only eat the same foods as Kit in his pod and he was restricted to eating only what would have been available forty thousand years ago. This did not include chocolate-peanut swirls. Elise wondered what he would think of them if he did try them. Smiling to herself, she punched in the code at the service machine.

'Hungry again, Thanton?' Luca said behind her.

'All part of the salary, Luca.'

'Well, you could probably do with something extra; you're already skinnier than when you arrived.'

'Is there something you want?'

'Yes, there is. Come, sit,' Luca said, pointing to a table.

The shorter girl from the corridor was sitting at a table nearby. She only greeted Luca when they passed. Elise was relieved when Luca led her to a table at the other end of the room.

'First thing, you've passed your introductory period,' Luca said, looking at his screen and ignoring Elise's wide grin. 'Just. You nearly failed as you haven't got much out of Twenty-One so far, but he seems happy enough. So, overall, you passed. There's still a lot of room for improvement, though, so don't pat yourself on the back too hard. But I hear that you've a few ideas on what to do.'

'Does that mean Samuel is my Overseer now?'

'Yes, it does. We'll switch to being co-Companions and you can stop being so polite if you want.'

Elise couldn't help but smile, realising that she wanted Luca's approval. At least he spoke to her, which was more than any of the other Sapiens did.

'Well, I'd need to know your surname first, so I can address you in a similar way.'

Luca paused before answering. 'It's Addison. I'm from Adenine Base. There's nothing more to tell. I came here young and I don't remember it, so there's no point in asking.'

'Not a problem, Addison. I might stick with Luca, though, as I don't want you to get all high and mighty about coming from Adenine Base.'

Luca snorted. 'There's no chance of that; I'm as Thymine as they get.' He paused before glancing up at her and smiling. 'There's something else as well. Fintorian has passed your completely insane plan to learn how to hunt with Twenty-One. Oh, and practise how to cook with him and probably burn the pod down. Great idea, that one.'

'You won't think it's so crazy when I become an awe-inspiring spear thrower,' Elise said, mimicking Luca, who always tipped his chair onto its back legs.

'You're never going to be an awe-inspiring spear thrower, Thanton,' Luca responded with a raised eyebrow. 'With those puny little arm muscles, you won't even be able to lift a spear, let alone launch it at anything. Perhaps you could help by dragging along Twenty-One's spear for him?'

Elise couldn't help but laugh.

Luca grinned back at her. 'You know, you're much more fun when you relax a bit, Thanton.'

'Prepare to be awe-inspired, Luca. I want to see open mouths and perhaps a poem on my skill and finesse. Me and my new spear are going places.'

As she headed out of the canteen to tell Kit the good news, she could hear Luca reciting:

> 'There was a young-ish girl called Thanton,
>   Her arms were as strong as a wonton,
>   She picked up a spear,
>   Tried to throw it at a deer,
>   Failed, and threw a tantrum.'

Elise turned around and made a gesture at Luca. Not a witty response, but it made him laugh. The short girl from the corridor snorted and, on a whim, Elise made the same gesture at her too.

Elise was surprised to find the metal bars on Kit's pod drawn back; he did not have many visitors. As she was holding her hand up to be scanned, the door opened from the inside and she jumped to avoid being hit. Samuel came out of the pod looking lost in his thoughts, but stopped when he saw Elise.

'Glad you're here. I was hoping to have a word with you before you went in.'

He rubbed his glasses on his sleeve. After he put them back on, he closed the door behind him and tried to lean casually against the wall. The effect was anything but casual; he kept on adjusting his position and moving his screen between his hands.

His awkwardness made Elise nervous and she thought she should fill the silence.

'I was just going to tell Kit the good news. About Fintorian agreeing to us learning to hunt and cook.'

'Yes, I've just been in to tell him myself.'

Elise felt a rising annoyance at Samuel; she had wanted to tell Kit. It was her idea and Samuel had probably told Kit it was his. She wouldn't be surprised after what had happened with the sedative pen on her first day.

'What did you want to speak to me about?'

'It's just about the investigation into the barriers. Fintorian wants me to speak with everyone who was around the pod. He wants me to ask if you saw anyone else who shouldn't have been there.'

'I thought it was a mechanical failure.'

'Nothing's been officially released, but a mechanical failure is unlikely. Impossible, actually. Someone overrode the system.'

Elise cast her mind back to her first day. 'I didn't see anyone, except you and Fintorian. How do the gates work anyway?'

'Each animal has a tag. The cages consist of magnetised force fields. If the animal goes too close to the fences, it gets repelled and thrown backwards a few feet.' Samuel repositioned himself against the wall. 'They soon learn where the boundaries are.'

'So that's why we can pass through the pods? Because we don't have the tags?'

'Exactly. The problem we have is that we can't de-tag the animals every time we want to move them, so instead we have an override code. It takes two people to deactivate the barriers at the same time, though, and they have to be at an Overseer's level. It ensures there are no mistakes, intentional or otherwise. We've been working on a chip which, when injected, temporarily blocks the signals from the original tag, but with little success as we can't get it to dissolve properly after use. We can't have lots of old chips rumbling around inside of them.'

'So you think two people overrode the codes? Why'd they do that?'

'That is not what we are saying at this stage . . . but, yes, that's what I think happened. I honestly don't know why they would do it, though; it's creating chaos.'

'It's happened since then, hasn't it?' Elise asked before thinking about whom she was speaking to.

Samuel rolled his eyes. 'Yes, it's happened again. And stop asking questions when I'm tired.' He paused, as though weighing up what to say next. 'We managed to contain it because it was only a possum family. Hardly the same impact as a sabretooth tiger. Also much easier to round up.' He straightened. 'Right, well, I had better get on. We won't start anything with the new project until tomorrow. So no fire and no spears today. Understood?'

Elise nodded, pleased that she wouldn't have to wait longer than a day to begin training. Pushing open the door to Kit's pod, she took the familiar path to the stream. She no longer worried about where Kit was any more and had begun to feel at ease in his environment. The temperature had dropped in the last couple of days to provide the seasonal change into winter. Still walking, she pulled on the knitted jacket Samuel had given her and a scarf she was carrying. She had always felt the cold and was grateful for the extra layers.

After hopping across the first few stepping stones, she stopped dead. Kit had raised his head and held his hand up to her. Not once in two weeks had he acknowledged her presence when she entered the pod. Elise smiled her widest smile and held her hand up to him in return.

Feeling lighter than she had in weeks, she walked over to where he was sitting and sat cross-legged in front of him. He put down the grass mat he was working on and gave her his usual blank stare. Spirits dampened, she wondered whether she had imagined the greeting.

'Good morning, Kit,' she signed slowly and deliberately. 'I've been told that we can start learning to hunt and cook together from tomorrow.'

Kit signed without a pause, 'Samuel told me. He said that it was your idea. Thank you.'

He then narrowed his eyes so that the corners creased and pulled the sides of his lips up. The look was not threatening. In fact, Elise thought it might be his version of a smile.

Not wanting to lose momentum, she quickly signed, 'I thought I'd spend the day checking to see if there are any vegetables or fruit growing in here that we can cook with. Do you want to come with me?'

Kit nodded and stood, waiting for Elise to join him. She was still in mild shock; he had finally spoken to her. She jumped up and followed Kit as he started walking to the far corner of the pod. Once he could touch the corners of both walls with each hand, he began systematically to inspect every plant and tree.

Elise followed, trying to give him the space to complete the task by himself. He gently teased the roots of a few plants to see if there were vegetables below the surface. If he wasn't sure about a plant, he would tear off a tiny corner of a leaf, chew it and spit it out. He worked his way down the side of the wall and then walked a few steps up and moved down the adjacent line. On a couple of occasions, Elise was able to point out a few plants she recognised from her parents' garden, but she let Kit inspect most of them.

They worked quietly, cataloguing the contents of the pod. By lunchtime, they had reached the halfway point of the stream. They had not found much that was edible; most of the plants were for decoration, or to section off different areas of the pod. Elise spread out the sweet potatoes, carrots, mint and rosemary that she had collected by the riverbank. They had been careful only to take a little of each, even when they grew in abundance, to ensure that the plants would continue to provide for them.

Elise thought if they were careful they would have enough to cook with, but she was concerned about the lack of variety. Making a quick decision, she signed to Kit that she was going to wait for their lunch to arrive. As she picked her way through the undergrowth, she stopped to inspect certain plants or bushes. While crouching, she took some seeds from her pocket and pushed them in the soil, followed by a drizzle of water. She continued doing this every few metres near bushes or trees that she would be able to locate again. In thirty minutes, she had hopefully doubled their supplies to include radishes, green onions, okra and courgettes. She silently thanked her mum for recommending these quick-growing vegetables.

When she returned with their lunches, Kit was sitting in their usual spot, high on the bank at the top of the stream. For once, he was not working, waiting patiently for her instead.

As she handed him the metal container, he signed, 'Thank you, Elle.'

'That's the first time anyone has ever shortened my name.'

Names were important in Thymine as each syllable signalled someone's position in society so no one ever used abbreviations.

Opening his food package he signed, 'Do you mind?'

Elise thought about it for a moment. 'No, not at all. In fact, I like it.'

Kit nodded and gave his eye-scrunching smile to signal his approval.

CHAPTER 8

Elise was pacing outside Kit's pod at 6 a.m. the next morning, eager to start work. Reasoning with herself that she wouldn't wake him up if she stayed away from his sleeping area, she gently pulled back the two metal bars as quietly as she could and slipped inside.

Unsure what time Samuel would arrive, she stayed close to the door and positioned the two straw-stuffed pillows she had brought at one side of the pod. Hands on hips, she stood at the other end and cocked her head as she inspected them from a distance. Roaming wildebeest they were not, but they would have to do for the moment.

Gingerly picking up a few sticks, Elise weighed them in her hand. Weapons of any description were prohibited, sporting equipment was obsolete and recreational games were discouraged; she had never taken aim at anything in her life. Pleased that she was alone, she stared at the bag on the right, narrowed her eyes and threw the short stick at it. She watched with pleasure as it spun through the air and made a soft thump when it hit the coarse straw target. Wanting to check whether it was a fluke, she launched a second stick at the same pillow. Again, she heard a satisfying thunk. Without pausing, she threw the last stick with her left hand this time; three strikes in a row.

Bouncing on the balls of her feet, she gathered up the same sticks. Knowing she couldn't make the targets move, she tried running sideways before launching the sticks at the bags. Two out of three were successful; she missed the third when her ankle tipped over in a dip just as she was launching her makeshift weapon. Trying again, she got all three while sprinting across the far end of the pod.

Bending to collect the sticks, she straightened when she heard the steel door opening. She watched as Samuel inched around the side of the door clasping three spears of differing heights. One of them got stuck in the door and he dropped another as he tried to release it. He swivelled awkwardly. Elise smiled in amusement and jogged over to help. When she crouched to pick the spear up, Samuel bent at the same time and they only narrowly avoided knocking foreheads.

Elise's smile froze when Samuel's lips brushed her ear. 'Miss a few. That's not normal.' He stood up. 'Thanks for the help.'

Straightening, she retreated behind her passive mask while her brain went into overdrive. She hadn't known; she'd thought everyone would hit what they were aiming for. If anything, she had been annoyed at herself for missing one.

Turning, she went to the far end of the pod and took aim. Missing the sack by a foot, she walked closer and took aim again. This time she skimmed the top of it; the third one hit the corner.

'That's really good; shows what a bit of practice can do.'

Elise smiled, trying to hide her panic. 'Have you been watching for long? I've missed quite a few.'

'Just from the viewing gallery,' Samuel said in an offhand manner. 'It's really quiet up there this morning but will fill up soon. It was a bit lonely really, so I thought we would start early.'

Elise tried to calm herself as Samuel walked over, dragging the three spears. Guessing that only he had seen her, she promised herself she wouldn't make any more mistakes. That still left Samuel, though, and he had clearly begun to make his own assumptions about her capabilities. Elise realised she was going to have to speak to him soon before he jumped to any unwanted conclusions.

She distracted herself from these unpleasant thoughts by inspecting the three spears Samuel was carrying. Even the shortest one was nearly the same height as Elise.

'This one is for you; it's the smallest Sapien spear I could find in the displays.' Samuel handed her the middle one. 'It's a replica so you don't have to worry about breaking it.'

Elise took the spear. At the tip, there was a stone point that had been wedged into the end and secured with leather bands.

'Kit's is quite different,' Samuel said, holding the shortest one out to Elise.

Holding it up against hers, she compared the two. Kit's was much shorter and sturdier. The construction was similar, but Kit's had a wider stone point and was heavier.

'Why are they different?'

'Both Sapiens and Neanderthals used either flint tips or spears made entirely from wood,' Samuel said, holding his spear up above his shoulder. 'However, Fintorian wants there to be a clear difference in the hunting styles, he doesn't want any crossover. So, we'll concentrate on the more classic methods of hunting for the two species.'

Without hesitation, Samuel turned and launched the spear at the sack farthest away from him. The spear flew through the air and lodged itself firmly in the centre. Elise was not surprised; after seeing him leap twenty feet off a metal walkway, she knew that he had many hidden talents.

Taking the shortest spear from Elise, Samuel held it with both hands and jabbed it forwards. 'Neanderthals, on the other hand, would usually get close to their prey and ambush animals, impaling them instead. They were so much stronger than Sapiens that they were able to muster the force to do this.' Samuel held out the throwing spear to Elise. 'You have a go.'

Taking it, Elise copied the way Samuel had held it with one arm above his shoulder. She had to adjust it several times to get the perfect balancing point as the stone tip made it top heavy. Throwing it, she watched the spear soar in the right direction, but fall well short of the sack. Annoyed, she ran over and retrieved it before returning to where Samuel was standing. Changing her positioning, she used all of her force as she threw the spear again. The effort slightly skewed her aim but didn't improve the distance it travelled by much. It landed well short of the sack again.

Elise was even more embarrassed when she realised that Kit had been watching her last few efforts. He had an innate ability to blend in with the scenery. It was only by chance that she spotted him standing perfectly still, leaning against one of the trees in a shaded area, his grey tunic standing out against the greenery. When she caught his eye, he held his hand up in greeting and she returned the gesture.

Kit then pushed off from the tree and jogged over to Samuel. Elise's shame was briefly forgotten as Samuel offered Kit the shortest spear. Kit held it in both hands as if it was the most precious thing in the world. Turning to Elise, he gave her a scrunched-eye smile before inspecting every detail of the spear. He tested the weight and tried different ways of holding it, finally settling on clasping it with two hands to the side of his body. Occasionally, he would glance at Samuel for reassurance or turn to Elise and give her his unique smile. Kit and Samuel then began to spar hesitantly, taking it in turns to jab and block, testing the spears and each other.

After Elise had watched Kit for half an hour, she returned to throwing her spear at the closest sack. No matter how she held it or adjusted her stance, she could only throw it a few metres. When she was up close, her throws were deadly accurate, even allowing for the occasional intentional miss. Her perfect aim did not help her with strength, though. However much she tried, she could not throw it far or with much force. Consequently, even close up, it regularly bounced off the sack rather than impaling it.

Stopping occasionally to rest her arm, she watched with envy as Samuel and Kit sparred. Samuel had wrapped cloth around the ends of both their spears and they were practising trying to land blows. Samuel was clearly enjoying himself; he was laughing while dodging Kit's ever more confident aim. He caught Elise watching him and smiled widely at her. His eyes crinkled at the corners, just like Kit's, which gave his face a warmth she hadn't seen before. Kit took advantage of Samuel's momentary distraction and jabbed him in the ribs. Clasping his side, Samuel turned and, with doubled gusto, jabbed back.

At exactly ten, the metal door opened. Elise was running to pick up her spear again and nearly tripped. Fintorian had entered the pod.

'I hope you don't mind the intrusion, but I just had to see how you are getting on,' Fintorian said to Samuel, beaming at Kit.

'Of course not, Fintorian. You're always welcome,' Samuel said, gesturing for him to come closer.

Elise scooped up her spear and stood to one side while Samuel and Kit continued sparring. Out of the corner of her eye, she could see Fintorian circling around them so he could watch from every angle. He was coming closer to her. She tried not to stare, but it was impossible. She realised that she only had two modes with Fintorian: staring in the opposite direction or peering at him in near open-mouthed wonder. She hated herself for it. She didn't want to be like Harriet, all wide-eyed and eyelashes aflutter; she just wanted to be able to act normally around him.

When he stopped next to her, she realised she only came up to his chest; he was a whole two feet taller than her. She glanced up. His hair was so smooth that it reflected the sunlight; he seemed to glow.

'Elise, isn't it?' he said, staring ahead at Kit and Samuel.

'Yes, sir,' Elise responded quickly.

'Please, call me Fintorian. I'm not one for formalities.'

Elise just nodded.

'Remarkable, isn't it?' Fintorian commented. 'How one little idea can boost the wellbeing of another. If this is successful, it could spread to the other museums.'

Elise could feel her skin warming up; she hoped she wasn't blushing.

She coughed. 'I hope it helps.'

'Please do everything in your power to ensure that it does. I must impress on you how important this is to the museum. To

Thymine Base. We cannot afford to lose another one. It would be a tragedy if we did.'

'I'll do everything I can.'

'Thank you, Elise. I look forward to seeing the results.'

Without another word, he crossed back over to Samuel and Kit. Squeezing Kit's shoulder as he passed, he nodded goodbye to Samuel and closed the pod door behind him.

Elise practised for the rest of the morning, but with no improvement. She was hot and tired, and her shoulder ached continuously. Frustrated, she stopped to take off the jacket Samuel had given her. Feeling that she had wasted her morning, she tied the arms of the jacket around her waist and wearily picked up the spear again. Before she could lift it up to her shoulder, Samuel's hand gently pushed it back down.

'Why don't you take a break?'

'Because I won't get any better if I don't practise,' Elise said, sighing. 'Sorry, I just hoped I'd be good at this.'

'Your problem isn't practice; it's strength. Or lack of it, to be accurate. That will take time, so there is no point in injuring yourself.' Samuel looked over at Kit. 'A morning won't change anything.'

Elise knew he was right; she dropped her spear to the ground and started massaging her shoulder to try to ease the aching.

'Perhaps you can begin learning how to start a fire. Then you can show Kit tomorrow when I'm not here,' Samuel suggested, pointing at his bag. 'All the equipment is in there and you will find an article on my screen with instructions.'

After studying the screen, Elise grabbed the items from Samuel's bag and headed to her normal seating area by the stream. She wanted to be alone this time.

Sitting cross-legged, she spread out the equipment in front of her: iron pyrite, flint, dry grass, tinder, some small sticks and some larger ones. Taking a piece of iron pyrite in one hand and a piece of flint in the other, she hit the iron pyrite with the flint as instructed. Nothing happened. She repeated the action rapidly, but still no promised sparks. Turning around, she could not see Samuel or Kit, so she pulled her jacket from around her waist and draped it over her head. Feeling foolish, she bent forwards and tried again. The darkness revealed the occasional minute spark that rapidly went out before hitting the dry grass, like tiny fireworks that hadn't made it back to the ground.

Taking comfort in the fact that she was at least creating a spark, no matter how feeble, Elise adjusted her position. Uncrossing her legs, she knelt over the grass and rapidly hit the two stones together, watching how her angle changed the direction the spark travelled. Once she had successfully controlled the movement, she removed the jacket from her head. Even though she couldn't see the sparks as well in the bright light, she could at least see the dried grass better.

Forty rapid strikes. Nothing. Then, the tiniest corner of the grass sizzled and turned black. It would mean nothing to most, but Elise was elated; she had started to move on to the next step.

After lunch, she went back to practising. She had to learn how to lean down quickly enough to blow some life into the sizzling grass. One of the positives about living in a carefully controlled pod was that there were no sudden gusts of wind to blow out her tentative attempts. By the end of the day, she had created two tiny little flames, so small that she could barely feel their heat when she ran her hand over them. She was happy that she had at least managed to learn one thing that day.

In the evening, Kit ambled over with their metal containers, rubbing his shoulders. All three sat beside the stream and ate. Samuel tapped a few controls on his screen and a soft twilight expanded through the pod. Usually, Elise and Kit had to sit in the fading light, until it was completely dark and they couldn't work any longer. However, tonight, there was the atmosphere of a small celebration; Samuel explained that he could take lighting liberties occasionally.

All three ate fast, tired from their day. They then stretched out around Elise's small campfire, which she had proudly exhibited. The fire wasn't strong enough to cook with, but the dancing flames held each of their gazes. Samuel would occasionally feed the small fire with twigs. Elise lay on her side, resting her head on her bent arm.

Disorientated, Elise felt herself being nudged awake. She sat up quickly; Kit was next to her, gently prodding her on the shoulder. Samuel was extinguishing the fire and gathering the equipment back into the small bag.

Stretching, Elise realised that she had fallen asleep in a locked metal cage with a Medius and a Neanderthal. She couldn't help but smile at the absurdity, and how angry her dad would be if he knew.

'Why are you smiling, Elle?' Kit signed.

It was the first time he had ever asked her a question and Elise took a moment to respond. 'I was thinking of how funny it was, us three sitting together. And how normal it felt as well.'

Kit scrunched his eyes up and Elise was glad that he understood.

'Thank you for today,' Kit signed to them both. 'I'm going to sleep now.'

He padded off to his sleeping area.

Elise watched him as he disappeared into the dense foliage, the spear still tucked underneath his arm. Standing, she picked up her belongings and began to make her way to the steel door.

'Elise, wait,' Samuel called after her.

She stopped.

'I wanted to say thank you,' he said when he finally caught up. 'I saw Kit call you "Elle" earlier today. He told me you didn't mind him calling you that. It is probably the first time a Sapien has intentionally shortened their name for two hundred years. That means a lot. To Kit, and me.'

Samuel peered at Elise's face in the half-light when she didn't respond. 'Have you been crying? Just give it some time and you will get better.'

'I haven't been crying. And if I did, it wouldn't be over that,' Elise signed, not wanting Kit to overhear her, no matter how far away he was.

'Then what?' Samuel signed back.

'It's because I get to leave, and he never will,' Elise signed rapidly before stopping herself.

'Not here,' he signed back.

Elise knew he was right. She walked towards the door again, too tired to worry any longer what Samuel thought of her. She had given him enough rope to hang her with if he wanted.

Samuel kept up with her and helped push open the steel door, which he then closed and locked behind them. He did this as quietly as he could and Elise appreciated the gesture.

On the way to her room, she turned to him. 'Thanks for telling Kit it was my idea. That meant a lot to me.'

'Of course I did,' Samuel said, looking perplexed. 'I wasn't going to tell him it was anyone else's.'

Elise didn't say anything in response and just stared at her feet.

'What?' Samuel said.

'It wouldn't be the first time you've . . .' Elise said, stopping herself when she realised how petty she sounded. She wished she could suck the words back in.

Samuel stopped and looked at her. 'Do you mean on your first day? When I said that I injected the sabre-tooth tiger rather than you?' He pushed his hand through his hair. 'I wasn't trying to pretend I'd saved the day, Elise. I was trying to protect you.'

Elise met Samuel's gaze, hoping her words would carry some weight. 'It was a mistake for me to think that I could help a Medius and a Potior. I've learnt that now. Other than that, there's nothing to protect, as I've nothing to hide.'

'You were at risk of drawing too much attention to yourself.'

'It was just a lucky move, that's all.'

Elise was not comforted by Samuel's silence.

CHAPTER 9

* *

Elise continued to practise every day for the next week, but didn't have the strength to launch the cumbersome spear farther than a few metres. Trying not to show her disappointment, she reminded herself that she had requested the training for Kit's benefit, not hers, and he was progressing rapidly. Every morning when Elise arrived in the pod, he was already awake and practising. He would have continued straight through until dark if she didn't remind him to eat.

After a frustrating morning, Elise spent her afternoons perfecting her fire-making. She could now produce a healthy flame in less than ten minutes. Using the campfire, she had started to cook some of the sweet potatoes that grew in the pod to supplement their meals. Stirring the potatoes, she would watch enviously as Kit practised. Even to her untrained eye, he was significantly better. Elise resigned herself to only being able to make the fire and she became quieter as the days passed.

Samuel would occasionally drop in and practise with Kit, the concentration on his face increasing every day as he worked harder to avoid Kit's blows. Wary of Samuel's cryptic messages,

Elise made sure that she was elsewhere in the pod when he visited. But after a week of her avoiding him, he came to find her.

Elise was crouching by one of the bushes where she had planted okra, checking to see if any of the seedlings had taken. Pleased to see a few green shoots, her smile faded as Samuel approached.

'Ah, there you are,' Samuel said, keeping his distance. 'I've been thinking about your difficulties with the spear and I've come up with a solution. I've got some work to do now, but I'll show you later.'

Despite her growing unease around Samuel, Elise didn't feel that she could refuse to meet him. Reluctantly, she agreed to wait in her room for him to collect her that evening. After finishing her shift, she said goodbye to Kit and gently closed the steel door, trying to lessen the sound of the metal bolts locking him in for the night.

Elise was pleased to see that Luca was leaning against the opposite wall, waiting for her. They had fallen into an easy routine and, without saying a word, they headed to the canteen. Luca was preoccupied with Seventeen's progressing pregnancy and Elise had learnt to just let him speak when he was ready.

Once they had settled at their usual table, Luca tipped his chair onto its two back legs. 'So when do you want to meet Seventeen?'

'Whenever you want,' Elise said, happy finally to be invited to meet the only other Neanderthal in the museum besides Kit.

'I think in the next couple of weeks would be good. Maybe you can help prepare her for the birth.'

'I don't think I'll be much help with that,' Elise said, concerned Luca had made the assumption that as a female she would have an extensive knowledge of birthing procedures.

'Samuel seems to think she's doing well and that everything should go smoothly. He said current research implies that Neanderthals have a higher chance of a successful birth without intervention than Sapiens. I stopped listening, though, when he went into details; I do not need to know about the width of birth canals.' He paused and looked up at Elise. 'I think once she has the baby, her depression will lift. It's got to, right?'

'I would have thought so. But none of my friends have babies and I was too young to remember much about when Mum had Nathan.'

'I know. I'm just not sure how to help. And you seem to have a way with Twenty-One.' Luca traced his finger along the table without looking up. 'I thought you might be able to take a look at Seventeen as well. She's one of the oldest still alive . . .'

'I'll do what I can, as long as it doesn't involve throwing a spear, because that's clearly going to be one of my long-term failures.'

'Still having problems with it?'

'As long as the antelope comes within touching distance, I'll be fine. Well, if they stand very still. Or maybe lie down.'

'You can't be great at everything, Thanton; at least Kit's enjoying himself. I was reviewing his stats and his serotonin levels have risen in the last few weeks. That's got to be because of you.'

Elise blushed and lowered her head, unsure what to say. 'Samuel thinks he may have come up with a way of getting around my severe lack of skill. No details, but he's going to show me tonight.'

Her smile faded as she watched Luca's face. A flash of irritation passed across his usually warm features. He quickly recovered, though.

'Samuel seems to want to spend a lot of time with you; people will start talking if you're not careful.'

Elise's head snapped up.

'Talking about what?' she said, annoyed. 'What are you saying? That I'm still running after him, like the others whisper about me? Or are you saying something else? Because if you are – no one even considers it.'

Luca leant forwards and touched Elise's hand. 'I know. I'm sorry. No one is saying anything. It's just me being clumsy.'

Elise softened but pulled her hand away, still unsure what Luca was suggesting.

'Friends?' she said.

Luca glanced up at her. 'I was—'

A tray slammed down next to them.

'Sorry, do you mind if I join?' Georgina said, already pulling out a seat.

'Well, er . . .' Luca said.

Elise interjected. 'Of course we don't. How're you doing? I haven't seen you for ages.'

'I am all good, thanks, despite what this place does to try and prevent that,' Georgina said, loading her fork.

She had a huge plate of food, which she ate with fervour.

Unsure how to respond to Georgina's open criticism of the museum, Elise turned back to her own food, grateful for the distraction. She was acutely aware that she was still heavily in Georgina's debt.

'I wanted to say thank you again, for the mats. I took them home yesterday and they look lovely scattered around,' Georgina said between mouthfuls.

'It was nothing,' Elise said, embarrassed at the gift.

'No, it was definitely something,' Georgina said, smiling. 'I haven't had a present for years.'

'What, not even from your family?' Elise asked.

She tried not to flinch as Luca kicked her under the table.

'I don't have a family any more.'

Elise blushed.

Luca looked at them, fork halfway to his mouth. 'So, Thanton here is going to make Companion of the year if I'm not careful.'

Elise smiled up at him, grateful he was there.

'That's good to hear. We could do with a decent Companion after the last one.'

'Who were they?' Elise asked. 'No one ever mentions them.'

'Kit's had a couple here. The dreaded Martha was the last one.' Georgina pushed her plate away and rested both hands on her still flat stomach. 'She was, without a doubt, the most useless Companion I have met in years.'

Luca snorted and balanced his chair on the two back legs again. 'Do you remember when Samuel caught her patting Twenty-One on the head?'

'Oh my stars, yes. I thought Samuel was going to have an aneurysm. I had to lead him away into my office for some breathing exercises.' Georgina smiled, running her tongue over her teeth.

'What happened to her?' Elise asked, caught up in their recollections.

'She was dismissed,' Luca said. 'Samuel petitioned Fintorian and Harriet did the deed. I honestly think Harriet had fun doing it, which is the only dampener on the story really.'

'That doesn't surprise me,' Elise said.

'You shouldn't be so hard on Harriet,' Georgina said, glancing between them. 'She has no family either. All she has is this place and it's tough for her here. All the other Medius look down on her because she's so . . . well, so . . .'

'Sapien-looking?' Luca responded.

'Well, yes. You know I don't go in for any of that. I avoid nearly all the Medius in this stars-forsaken place, but Harriet so desperately wants to belong. And she never will, whatever she does. So she'll always lose in life. That's got to be something to pity rather than enjoy.'

Luca leant farther back on his chair legs and raised an eyebrow. 'Maybe you're right. But until she starts being even vaguely pleasant to me, I'm not losing any sleep over her parents' rubbish job of tweaking her genes.' He turned to Elise. 'I wish you'd met Martha; you'd see how well you're doing in comparison. She thought Twenty-One was a pet. She had no idea.'

'What did Twenty-One do when she patted him on the head?' Elise asked.

'What he always does,' Georgina said. 'Stared passively at her and stored it for later.'

While Elise waited in her room for Samuel, she thought about what Georgina had said. She had definitely made progress with Kit, but she hadn't begun to tap into the breadth of his capabilities. Ultimately, she suspected that he still didn't fully trust her.

She was jolted back to the present when she heard the tapping at her door. Stepping into the hallway, she closed the door behind her without inviting Samuel in. She didn't want to repeat her previous mistake. He was dressed more casually in dark, loose trousers and a soft knitted hooded top, similar to the one Elise was wearing.

'You're not wearing glasses,' she said, surprised.

'Ah, contact lenses tonight. You'll see why in a minute.'

Elise zipped up her jacket and dug her hands into her pockets. She felt on edge around Samuel and wanted their late-night expedition to be over quickly so she could go back to avoiding him. Deciding to say as little as possible, she dropped behind him so they didn't speak as they passed through the deserted corridors. Watching his ungainly walk, she wondered again how he managed to look like he was gliding when he ran.

He was leading her to one of the antiquities rooms at the other end of the museum. Elise rarely had the time to go into the main museum any more, as she was so involved in working with Kit.

It was the first time she had passed through the main displays at night and she found it unsettling. Unnaturally still, the pods were only lit by moonlight stretching down through the glass roof. Most of the pods appeared empty, although Elise knew better. She strained to pick out familiar shapes. She dismissed two large formations to her right for rocks, until one of them raised its trunk and Elise realised it was a mammoth. A distant howl made her jump. She put her head down and caught up with Samuel.

The antiquities room held some of the displays that Elise hadn't seen since her last museum tour when she was a student.

Emptied of the usual visitors, the bright electric lights gave the room an unnaturally eerie glow, which made Elise feel even tenser. Rows and rows of spears of differing heights and sizes lined the walls. These were interspersed with clubs and axes; the Potiors favoured chronological categorisation rather than weapon type.

'So I was thinking about your, umm, strength issue,' Samuel said, heading to a cabinet on the other side of the room. 'And with a little research, I may have come up with a solution. Forty thousand years ago, Sapiens didn't just hunt with spears. They may have used these as well.' He tapped on the glass of one of the cabinets.

Elise came up behind him and peered at the display cabinet. She wasn't really sure what she was looking at. It was just a length of cord, twice as long as her arm, with a small pouch in the middle. She wondered if it was a lasso, which she had read about in her granddad's encyclopaedia.

'What is it?'

'A sling. There is a debate about whether it was used forty thousand years ago, but most agree it was possible. We haven't found any from that time, but that can easily be explained; they were made of cord or leather and, therefore, biodegradable – unlike flint spears.' Samuel tapped the cabinet again. 'This one is about four thousand years old and we were lucky to find it in such good condition.'

He dug into his pocket and pulled out another sling and held it out to Elise. 'I, ah, made this one for you. It should work just as well, even better maybe.'

Elise took it gratefully and smiled up at him. She carefully inspected the sling, pulling it through her hands as Samuel continued to talk.

'It's made from braided flax with a leather pouch in the middle. The pouch is where you put the stone, which you throw.' He pointed at one end where there was a small leather loop. 'You hold a finger in here.' He then pointed at the other end where there was a tab of leather. 'This is the release tab.'

'So it'll help me throw stones?' Elise said, trying to keep the disappointment from her voice.

Samuel grinned. 'Well, essentially, yes. But don't underestimate its power. A well-aimed stone can kill a larger animal such as a wolf, even a sabre-tooth tiger if the shot is perfect.'

'When can I start? We could go now, I don't need much sleep.'

'We can use one of the empty pods if you like,' Samuel said.

Before he'd even finished speaking, Elise was already jogging to the door.

Samuel pulled back the metal bars to the pod across the corridor from Kit's. A few taps on his screen and there was bright daylight. While he was occupied, Elise searched the ground for some small, smooth stones – the kind she would carefully skim over the stream when she was a child.

She gave half to Samuel and watched as he loaded one into the diamond-shaped leather pouch. He held both ends of the sling in one hand and, with a fluid motion, swung it in a circle around his head. He quickly released one end of the sling; there was a deafening crack. The stone flew so quickly that Elise struggled to follow its path.

'Wow,' was all she could say.

'My aim is pretty awful as I've only had time to practise the loading and throwing motion, which isn't easy. It took a few days.'

'You practised this for me?'

'Well, yes. I couldn't just hand you the sling and tell you to get on with it,' Samuel said, half smiling and pushing his hair back.

'Thank you so much,' Elise said, touching his arm.

Samuel whipped his arm away and stepped backwards. Elise was shocked by his reaction and unsure what to say. They were both silent for a moment.

'Ah, sorry, hard habit to break,' Samuel said, staring at his feet.

Flustered, Elise loaded the stone into the sling and circled it around her head. After a few attempts, she was able to balance it so that it didn't fall out of the leather pouch halfway round. She released the end of the sling and Samuel ducked as, with a snapping noise, the stone flew dangerously close to his head.

'Now you see why the specs were left behind today,' he said, straightening.

It was agreed that Samuel would stand behind Elise. With his back to her, he also practised circling and throwing the stones.

With careful adjustments, Elise grew more confident and could soon smoothly load and spin the sling. The difficult bit was when to release the end, as this was what affected the aim. She loved the noise it made when the stone fired through the air. It made her feel strong.

Lost in learning her new weapon, she did not speak until Samuel told her it was time to go; the sprinkler systems were about to be switched on. Elise checked his screen. It was 2 a.m.; they had been practising solidly for three hours. Still elated, she practically skipped out of the pod and, for once, it was Samuel who had to rush to keep up.

'Thanks again.'

'You don't have to thank me. I just wanted you to have something of your own.'

Elise was touched, but made sure she kept her distance from him. 'How did you learn to use it?'

'I found some drawings of one being used before the Pandemic.'

'They used slings before the Pandemic?'

Samuel laughed. 'No, not really. A few people did because they were interested in how early humans lived, or they wanted to keep ancient hunting methods alive that didn't involve guns.'

Elise halted in the deserted corridor. She carefully scanned the area and reached out with her senses to try and locate any surveillance cameras. Samuel cleared his throat and she opened her eyes.

'It's okay; we're alone,' he said.

'So the diagrams you found were Infactualities?' Elise asked in disbelief. 'What if they find out you had them? You could be dismissed . . . or worse.'

'Technically, it's labelled an Infactuality, but that doesn't mean it isn't true.'

Casting her mind back to her granddad's encyclopaedia, she couldn't argue with that. 'Why are you telling me all this? Why would you risk everything just to help a Sapien?'

Bracing herself for his response, she looked at him directly.

Samuel rubbed his forehead and was silent for a moment. 'Because I think you have potential, and I want to see where it takes you.'

CHAPTER 10

A month later, Elise reluctantly took the familiar route home. All she wanted was to practise with the sling; everything else was an interruption. Her time at home was noticeably more awkward; her parents sensed the growing distance. The only thing that kept Elise going back for her weekly visits was Nathan. She missed his company and wished she could take him back to the museum with her and away from her dad's overbearing presence. Nathan had found his own escape route, though, and had started spending his spare time with his new friends, Jada and Maddy.

Sitting at the kitchen table, Elise tried to hide her disappointment when she heard that Nathan was staying at Jada's house for the weekend. Running her eyes over the cluttered kitchen surfaces, she weighed up how long she would have to stay before she could make her excuses and return to the museum.

Sofi glanced at Elise across the kitchen table. 'I saw a recording of the Potior at the museum talking about a Neanderthal birth that's going to happen soon. Is that the one Luca works with?'

'Yes, that's Seventeen; I haven't met her yet. What did Fintorian say?'

'That it's the first time in forty thousand years and will be an amazing achievement for Thymine Base. They are going to screen the birth too. He was very impressive. Have you met him?'

'Yes, and he's even more so in person. It's hard not to stare. He's so passionate about the Neanderthal project that he sweeps everyone up with him.'

Sofi frowned and looked down at the family screen.

'For the first time in years, we've some tickets about to expire,' she said as she tapped away. 'It's all down to you; the tickets you bring in have left us with extra this month. I think you should have them.'

Elise walked around the table and peered over Sofi's shoulder. There were no physical tickets handed out or exchanged. Instead, every ticket was logged as a number on a personal or family account. All purchases were made through this account and the oldest tickets were used first. Tickets given to Sapiens had to be spent within a month or they would expire. Decree Number 7 said that Sapiens were not allowed to hoard tickets; history had shown that they could not be trusted with the accumulation of currency. The Potiors had decided that an equal measure of staple goods combined with some freedom of choice was the fairest method of distribution and the Medius agreed. The Sapiens were not consulted.

Elise's first thought was to buy something for Kit, but she soon realised she wouldn't be allowed to take anything from the outside world to him. The 40,000-year rule was growing increasingly annoying. Instead, she decided on an alternative and collected Holly, who was always open to some frivolous spending.

As they made their way to the enormous warehouse in the Outer Circle, they took their time strolling the pathways. Elise had always felt safe here, and it was where they were encouraged to spend most of their time. She held her face up to the sun and enjoyed the feeling of the light breeze against her skin. She hadn't realised how much she had missed the outside elements compared to the cold, implausibly still compartments of the museum. Holly was making a noticeable effort to be nice to Elise, and she happily accepted the attention. They chatted about Holly's work and Elise checked how Nathan was doing at his school.

When they entered the Emporium, Elise unfolded her family screen and presented it to confirm that she had tickets to spend. They then hopped onto one of the electric buggies and, as always, Holly drove.

As they careered down aisle after aisle of non-perishable goods, Elise ogled everything available, if only you had the tickets: light leather jackets, intricately glazed clay pots and mirrors of every size whizzed by. Most of the year, Thymine Base was a hub of manufacturing; but once every sixth month, everything would grind to a halt as they prepared to transport the goods to the other bases. On these two days, all the production centre workers would load crates onto the automated steel pulley systems that zigzagged their way down to the coast five miles away. The pulleys were only raised on these two days; the rest of the time, they were lowered to the ground, no longer a blemish on the landscape. At the port, the crates were unloaded by the Protection Department, who transferred them onto ships with enormous, blustering sails. For the next few days, these transport ships would snake their way round the coast, nudging their way down rivers to deliver the fruits of Thymine's labour to the other three bases.

Only glancing at the aisle ahead, Holly turned to Elise. 'I'm thinking of leaving my job at the school.'

'What!' Elise exclaimed, pulling her gaze from the displays. 'But I thought you liked working with the children.'

'It's not the job itself; I enjoy that.' Holly glanced at Elise, who was staring at her open-mouthed. 'It's being around Midders all day. I'd rather work somewhere it's just Sapiens.'

'If that's what you want to do . . .' Elise trailed off, unsure how to continue when she didn't believe in what her friend was saying.

'It'll be better this way.' Holly looked back at the aisle, just in time to take a particularly sharp corner. 'I'll have more time to think in one of the production centres.'

'But you've always hated the idea of working at a production centre. It's why you took the job at the school,' Elise said, clinging on to her seat as Holly threw the buggy around the corner.

'I know, but I've been going to these meetings and they're more important to me than the school. I can put my time to good use instead of running around after Midders all day, trying to make their jobs easier. I want to start studying with Lewis, so I have to start making some changes.'

'What'll you be studying?' Elise asked, unsure if she wanted to know.

With just one hand on the wheel, Holly turned to Elise and put her mouth up against her ear. 'Infactualities.'

'Can I see them?' Elise said without pausing.

*

Two hours later, Elise was sitting on Lewis Thetter's couch, accepting a cup of tea from his mum. The upholstered seat was zipped up in plastic covers, and she could feel her bare legs sticking to it. She was under strict instructions not to mention their real reason for visiting; Lewis's mum had no idea about her son's wider interests. They had already been there for thirty minutes and the pauses between conversations were growing longer.

'I'm sure he'll be back in a tick,' Lewis's mum reassured them, circling the room for the third time, plumping the overstuffed cushions.

Elise braced herself when the front door opened. Taller than most men and as heavily built as Elise's dad, he was a rare Sapien anomaly who could easily be mistaken for a Medius. Consequently, he'd never been short of Sapien girls hanging on his every word.

He didn't look surprised to see Elise perched on the end of his couch. He crossed the room in a few steps and rested his hand on Holly's shoulder.

'Good to see you, Elise,' he said, smiling at her. He turned to his mum. 'We're just going to my room for a bit. Elise wanted to see those statues I've been carving.'

'Course, dear,' his mum responded. 'You're in for a treat, Louise; he has a rare gift for whittling.'

Elise didn't bother to correct her name and instead concentrated on trying to peel herself off the plastic couch covers without making too much noise.

After Lewis shut the door, he cleared a space on his bed for Holly and Elise to sit on. The room was larger than Elise's, but he had its entire contents spread out across the floor and all the other surfaces.

Elise hadn't seen Lewis much in the last couple of years since they left school, but she could already tell he had changed. He was quieter, more serious, and it was Holly who filled the silence with chitchat. Holly followed every movement he made, never taking her eyes from him, even when Elise addressed her directly. When Lewis cleared a space for himself, he moved with intensity, as if he had channelled his previous gregarious nature into whatever task occupied him.

Once settled, he leant on his hands and stared appraisingly at Elise. Feeling uncomfortable under his gaze, she shifted on the bed, pulling her skirt farther down her thighs.

Holly was still talking about nothing much when he interrupted. 'I hear you're working down at the Museum of Evolution.'

Holly stopped mid-sentence and folded her hands on her lap.

Elise met his gaze. 'Been there a couple of months now.'

'Elise wanted to see some of the carvings you'd been showing me,' Holly interjected. 'She's very interested in them and, as my friend, I promise that she'll be careful with them.'

'Are you sure?' Lewis said to Holly, his eyes not leaving Elise. 'I trust her.'

'You know how much trouble Holly would get into if anything was lost, or found its way into the wrong hands, right?'

Elise nodded. 'I'd never do that.'

Lewis stood. 'I don't have much on me, but I do have this.' Moving towards his wardrobe, he knelt and felt underneath its solid ledge, then pulled out a handmade book taped underneath. Holding the book with both hands, he walked back to Elise. 'All that's left is what was printed. Most information was in electronic format before the Pandemic, but that was wiped years ago.' He held out the book to Elise. 'These are Pre-Pandemic newspaper articles, from when there were just Sapiens.'

Elise opened the leather book, careful not to bend the binding too much as it was hand-stitched. Before now, she had only seen the posters that were put up around Thymine when important announcements were being made, never a printed newspaper article. Browning, delicate sheets had been stuck onto the thick, rough pages. Some were slightly distorted from moisture; others were curling at the corners. Most were missing a hastily chopped out sentence or two, but as she flicked through their theme was clear. Page after page of reports: a man running into a burning house to save his neighbour's son; donations of blood, kidneys and other organs; doctors travelling around the world to help victims of natural disasters; animal sanctuaries staffed entirely by volunteers.

As Elise read, she wondered if they were real. If they weren't, then this was an elaborate hoax; the pages were made of different materials and the fonts varied. She looked up at Holly for reassurance.

Holly leant over and squeezed her hand. 'I felt the same when I first saw them.'

'But, they can't be true,' Elise said. 'Everyone knows Sapiens were consumed by destruction and greed.'

Lewis was still standing over her. 'They were just the same as us; there were some who were good and some who weren't. But we are only told about the negatives.'

Elise swallowed, unsure what to say. Her mind ticked over this new information and the assumptions she leapt to were terrifying.

'So we didn't just kill and maim and destroy everything in our path?'

'No, course not. Have you ever wanted to kill someone for fun or intentionally starve someone?' Holly said, raising her voice.

'No.'

'Then why couldn't there have been people like you before the Pandemic?' Lewis interjected.

'Because of the Medius and Potior,' Elise said. 'They keep our motives in check . . .'

'Listen to yourself,' Holly said, rolling her eyes.

Lewis glared at Holly and crouched in front of Elise. 'So you can see now; Sapiens weren't just on some power-crazy, destructive rampage across the world. There were selfless acts as well. But the Midders want us to believe that we're unable to govern ourselves. Can't be trusted with currency, education, even planning our own homes.'

Elise stared at Lewis, her mind whirring. 'So what do you suggest we do?'

Lewis straightened and started pacing as he ticked a list off on his fingers. 'We need to secure our own lands, govern ourselves, live separately from the Midders, open up our own universities. We don't need them as much as they need us to work in their production centres.'

'Lewis has so many ideas,' Holly said, reaching for him with both hands.

Lewis loosely held Holly's hands between his large palms, all his focus directed towards Elise. 'Just take some time to think about it. We could use someone with your access to the museum.'

It was a relief to get back into Kit's pod. More and more Elise found herself craving the solace and simplicity of being in this controlled environment. She found comfort in practising with

her sling, the repetitive action clearing her mind. She had per-
fected the art of loading and swinging; the timing for the release
was going to need a lot more work, though, even to hit a stationary object. A second's difference would result in the stone
flying in a different direction by several feet. It was this that she
practised throughout the day.

At lunchtime, she wandered to the stream to eat. Their food
was still delivered, which left more time for her to work on her
aim. Elise called Kit from his practice and they sat, neither speaking. Although always friendly, Kit didn't ever want to talk much.
Elise knew she couldn't ask him how he was feeling and he
refused to engage in small talk.

Instead, she let her mind meander as she thought about what
Lewis had said. It went against everything they had been taught
at school. The endless wars, mindless killings, lootings, burning
of homes, and destruction of entire populations and environments were all they had been shown. There had been no mention of the individual acts of kindness, generosity, altruism and
self-sacrifice. Her mind kept flicking back to who taught them,
who decided the content.

Kit tapping her on the knee interrupted her solitary musings.

'Elle. I saw you practising. You are getting much better,' he
signed.

Elise was surprised; she hadn't been aware of him watching
her. 'Thanks, Kit. I want to get as good as you.'

'We will soon be able to hunt together.'

'I hope so.'

'Come, I want to show you something.'

Elise followed him through the pod into his sleeping area,
where the foliage was denser and the light was only able to

trickle through the branches. His step was light for such a heavily built man; he managed to make no noise as he passed through the pod.

Elise usually avoided this section, aware of Kit's limited privacy. Now that she had been invited, she looked around his living area with interest. She breathed in the scent of the pine needles and admired the woven mats scattered across the ground. Leaning against the tree stump was a small broom made of soft rushes. Her gaze ranged over the shelves cut into the stump and was held by the tiny carvings lined up along the edge. Picking one up, Kit held it out to her. His hand was twice the size of hers and felt warmer. Studying the carving, she admired the detailed wooden model of a man. Kit had managed to shape the face and features even though the figurine was no bigger than the palm of her hand. Turning it over, she ran her thumb over the smoothness of the grain, which had been carefully sanded. She peered at its face; there were tiny circles around the eyes.

'Is it Samuel?'

'Yes, I made it years ago. I came with him from the other place they call Guanine.'

'You came from Guanine Base with Samuel?' Elise said, forgetting to sign.

'Yes. He is the person I have the longest memories of,' Kit signed, his face still as always. 'He is like family to me. We chose my name together.' Elise was about to ask more when Kit continued. 'Elle, can I ask you a question?'

'Of course you can, anything.'

'Have you met Seventeen?'

Elise paused, unsure how much she should say. She felt as if they were straying into the 'bigger picture', as Luca put it.

She decided to tell him the truth. 'No, not yet. But Luca wants me to meet her soon.'

Kit nodded. 'Will you tell me about her when you do?'

'Yes, if you want.'

Kit glanced over at his shelves.

'All of these,' he signed, nodding towards the shelf that held the carefully spaced carvings, 'are people I have known well. Some have died, but I still keep them here with me.' He selected one from the shelf. 'This is the newest one.'

Elise inspected the carving, which she thought was of a boy, as he had short hair. The face was smooth with no eyes or mouth, just a nose. Hanging down from the clenched hand was a rope.

Elise was too embarrassed to ask in case she was wrong.

'It is you,' Kit signed.

'It's beautiful, thank you,' Elise signed. 'I am honoured to be included.' Turning the statue around, she studied the face again. 'But when did you have the time to carve it?'

'I made it in the afternoons when you go home to your family.'

Elise avoided Kit's gaze and turned the figure around in her hand. 'Why are there no eyes or mouth?'

'Because your eyes and mouth are usually controlled. They say nothing unless you want them to, so they don't exist. Only your nose tells your secrets,' Kit signed, scrunching his eyes.

Elise laughed. 'How does my nose tell my secrets?'

'When you want to control your face and hide your thoughts, your nose widens. When you don't like something, you pull it up. When you are happy, it gets really wide,' Kit signed back, still scrunching his eyes.

'That's amazing. Can you do this with everyone?' Elise signed, making a conscious effort to keep her nose still.

'Yes,' was Kit's simple answer. 'I can also understand your words if you speak them, as I can hear them. It is saying them that is not so easy. When I speak, I have difficulty linking the single sounds that make a word. It takes me too long if there are many syllables, that is why I sign. But I prefer it if you sign to me rather than speak as it helps me read more of your meaning.'

'Can you read my hands like my nose?' Elise signed, intrigued.

'Yes, everything helps.'

Kit stretched upwards. Elise stayed still, acutely aware of any potential underlying signals she might be sending.

Stopping part-way though the stretch, Kit looked at Elise and dropped his hands to sign. 'Don't worry; you don't normally send bad thoughts. Only when you are annoyed at me for not talking to you.'

Elise groaned and Kit's eyes scrunched up even further.

At the end of her shift, Elise was pleased to see Luca waiting for her outside the pod.

'I've been watching you from the viewing gallery with your new toy, Thanton. You've got some power there, but your aim is a bit twonked.'

'Give me a few more weeks and I'll knock one of those baby curls right off your head.'

'Ouch. What's wrong with you?' Luca said, clutching his hair to his head.

'Oh, it's nothing, just something Kit said.'

'Did he say your aim was rubbish too?'

Elise couldn't help but smile; Luca always softened her moods by making her laugh at herself.

As they walked to the canteen, Elise decided to broach the subject. 'Can, er, Seventeen read extra meaning in what you're saying?'

'I'm not really sure what you mean, Thanton. I'd be happy if she bothered to lift her head to read what I'm signing at the moment,' Luca said, his tone losing its lightness.

Elise realised this was a risky subject and decided to change it. 'I didn't know that Kit came with Samuel from Guanine Base.'

'Yeah, it was before my time. About three years ago, I think.' Luca pulled out a seat at their favourite table. 'Thymine Base needed a new male Neanderthal and Samuel came with him as a Collections Assistant. I think Samuel practically raised Kit and didn't want to leave him.'

'I wonder what Guanine Base is like,' Elise said, pulling a chair out for herself.

'It's where all the Midders go to university: "Education and Enlightenment". I heard it's perched on top of a mountain and to get there you have to climb three thousand narrow steps that were carved into the rock face. It's part of a test for the Midders to prove they want to be there.'

'And you don't remember Adenine at all?'

'No, but it's the grandest of the bases. Samuel was born there as well. He told me it's on an island in the middle of a lake, completely protected by water. Cytosine is on the edge of a cliff face and it's the most isolated from the other three, but still closest to Thymine.'

'You seem to know a lot about the other bases.'

'I'd give anything to visit them,' Luca responded, before saying in a quieter tone, 'Maybe I will one day.'

'We'd never be allowed; Sapiens aren't important enough to cross. You know that.'

'Perhaps,' Luca answered, before lowering his voice. 'But not everything has to be their way.'

'How, though?' Elise asked, leaning in. 'Even if you did it without permission, the crossings are nearly impossible. A day's worth of water isn't enough to get you to Cytosine Base, let alone the other ones.'

Luca moved farther across the table and rested his chin in his hands, covering both sides of his mouth as he spoke. 'There must be a way of getting some. Samuel crossed, didn't he? They give the water to the Midders; it's just us who aren't allowed it.'

Elise thought about what Luca had said. It was true that some Medius and Potiors made the crossings, but Luca was the only Sapien she knew who had and he was too young to remember. From what she understood, they were all immune to the original virus, but if it mutated, they would not be so naturally resilient the second time. Treated water was an essential and they were only provided with enough to get through a single day.

'Even if you could get the water, I heard that there are other viruses that are airborne,' Elise whispered, scanning the empty canteen for cameras.

She was learning to always look out for them now; she'd had several conversations in the last few weeks that would have been punished with more than a fine.

'What other viruses?' Luca mouthed. 'That's just a rumour spread to stop anyone from taking the chance of leaving. It's just another method, like the supplies of food and water. No one has the skills to defend themselves, hunt or forage any more either. Even with the water, no one could take care of themselves out there.' Luca stared at Elise. 'Except you.'

CHAPTER 11

Elise was not surprised to see Luca leaning against the wall outside her bedroom. For the past couple of weeks since their conversation in the canteen, he had made a habit of accompanying her through the corridors before she cocooned herself in Kit's pod for the day. He then went to visit Seventeen. Luca would frequently steer the conversation to her progression with the sling, and even raised the possibility of learning to use the throwing spear himself.

'I thought I'd introduce you to Seventeen this morning, Thanton,' he said, straightening. 'You can take a look at the shelter I've just made for her. All natural, of course, and adhering to the strict forty-K rule.'

Keen to meet Seventeen, Elise set aside the doubts she had about Luca's newfound interest in carpentry.

As they pushed their way through the dense foliage inside Seventeen's pod, Luca started whistling loudly. The unfamiliar tune echoed around the pod, silencing the few birds that normally filled the mornings with their song.

'That's beautiful, Luca. Did it take long to learn?'

'It's for practical reasons, not a musical thing,' Luca said, holding back some brambles for Elise. 'I like to let Seventeen know that I'm coming and where I am in the pod. Prevents any awkward privacy issues.'

Elise smiled up at Luca, appreciating this small, thoughtful act.

Hopping over the stepping stones, she turned to him. 'It's identical to Kit's, isn't it?'

'Well spotted, Thanton,' Luca responded, following her across the stream. 'The Supes designed the perfect environment to house the Neanderthals and cater to all their needs. They weren't going to change the layout of each pod as well.' With an added grandness, he continued, 'That would be both unnecessary and inefficient.'

Elise laughed at the perfect imitation of a Medius or Potior and, once they were safely over the shallow stream, playfully pushed Luca in response. Smiling, he grabbed her hand and didn't let go, not even when she stopped her brief struggle to free her arm.

His hand enclosed hers and she was surprised at how natural this brief transition felt. She ran her thumb down the inside of his palm and his grip tightened. Elise smiled without looking at him, somehow aware that he was doing the same. As they left the steep bank of the stream, Luca started his reverberating whistle again. The sound reminded Elise of the reason they were there and she gently pulled her hand from his. Knowing they would soon be in the sleeping area, her thoughts turned to meeting Seventeen.

When they emerged into the clearing, Elise stopped to admire the new shelter Luca had built. He had lashed branches together in a triangular shape that ran back several metres. Over the top, he had hung brown animal skins and at the tip of the triangle, three proud feathers stood pointing to the sky.

'They'd normally live and sleep in caves like Sapiens did at the time, but I managed to persuade Fintorian that I could build a temporary structure – like the ones they might use on hunting expeditions,' Luca explained, running his hand over the back of his neck. 'I didn't really have much to work from, so I just sort of made it up as I went along.'

Without saying anything, Elise walked over to the frame and pushed it slightly. It didn't budge. She then knelt to inspect the bottom of the branches that Luca had dug into the earth.

Brushing the dirt from her hands, she stared up at him. 'It looks sturdy. And I'm guessing it's weather-proof as well.'

'It's always good to have something to keep us busy,' he said, shrugging.

Bending at the opening, he pulled back the two animal skins there and tied them in place. Following him inside, Elise sat near the entrance where there was the most light. Once her eyes had adjusted, she could see someone was curled on their side farther inside the shelter.

Luca coughed and the figure raised their head.

'I've brought Elise to meet you. The one I told you about,' he signed.

Sitting, the figure stretched and pushed back the rugs covering her legs. Taking her time to push herself up, she walked slowly towards them. Unlike Elise, she did not have to bend her head as she moved through the shelter; it was the perfect height for her.

As she approached, Elise busied herself making room for all three of them to sit in a circle. She was aware of Seventeen's laboured movements and didn't want to stare at her slow approach. Once Seventeen had lowered herself to the ground, Elise smiled and turned to look at her for the first time. Her smile froze and it took her a moment to recover.

'Hello, I'm Seventeen,' the girl signed to Elise.

Every movement seemed to take a great effort and as soon as she finished she let her hands drop into her lap.

Elise swallowed, struggling to regain her composure. Seventeen appeared the same age as her, maybe even younger. She had thought Seventeen would be in her twenties. A barrage of questions flooded Elise's mind and she tried to remind herself that she couldn't help with the bigger picture; she just had to concentrate on the day-to-day. The thought didn't make her feel better.

She broadened her smile. 'It's lovely to meet you finally. Luca talks about you all the time.'

She was unnerved by how familiar Seventeen's face was, even more so than Kit's. Seventeen's features were bolder than some Sapien women's, but they certainly weren't masculine. Seventeen still had the same strong eyebrow ridge as Kit, the same large, sunken eyes, but these were softened by her long, strawberry-blonde hair.

'You have beautiful hair,' Elise signed, unsure what to say; she didn't want to mention the pregnancy, as she didn't know how Seventeen felt about it.

Seventeen looked a little coy and ran a lock through her fingers, inspecting the ends. Elise realised that she could read Seventeen's facial expressions; they were not hidden like Kit's.

'Thank you. I like your hair too. It's like a boy's.'

Luca laughed.

Elise blushed and touched her hair. 'I keep it short as it's easier to look after.'

'You should let it grow. It would be like mine then, but darker,' Seventeen responded, giving her the same scrunchy-eyed smile as Kit, with her lips slightly pulled up.

Unlike Kit, Seventeen used her full range of facial expressions and body language, adding further meaning to her sign language, the same as Elise and Luca.

'You should do that, Thanton. Much prettier,' Luca signed.

Seventeen stared at Luca, then at Elise. She gave an even tighter scrunchy-eyed smile but then winced. Both Luca and Elise leant closer to her as she touched her stomach.

'What is it?' Luca signed, his hands a flurry of movement. 'Are you okay?'

Seventeen breathed out slowly before wearily lifting just one hand. 'I'm fine. The baby just kicked. See?'

She pulled both of their hands to her stomach. Even through the soft material of the tunic, Elise could clearly feel a little nudge. She glanced up at Luca and their eyes met. They both turned to Seventeen.

Seventeen released their hands, yawned and stretched upwards again.

'I'm sorry, but I'm very tired. Please come again, though,' she signed, scrunching her eyes at Elise.

'I'd like that,' was all Elise could manage as she watched Seventeen awkwardly push herself to her feet and pad back to her sleeping mat.

Without saying anything, Elise and Luca stood at the same time. With their heads bent, Luca held back to let Elise leave first. She blinked at the bright light and, without waiting for Luca, started to walk in a trance towards the stream.

When she heard him calling, she shoved her hands into her pockets and waited for him to catch up. As soon as he was next to her, she continued walking, her head still lowered. She only half listened to Luca as he chattered.

'That went well,' he said, putting his arm around her shoulder. She did not lean into him. 'It's the most I've got out of her in days; she just sleeps all the time now. I even have to wake her up to eat. Fintorian thinks it's normal, though; he has a theory that they hibernate in the last trimester.' Luca laughed. 'Stars, I must be the only nineteen-year-old male Sapien who has an intimate knowledge of trimesters. I should not know this stuff!'

They passed some tall grasses, and Elise absent-mindedly ran one of the blades through her finger and thumb. The edge was so sharp it threatened to slice through her skin, but she didn't pull away, running it through to the end.

'How old is she?' she asked.

'She's sixteen, will be seventeen next month,' Luca replied, dropping his arm and moving in front of Elise so that he was facing her and walking backwards. 'Perhaps we should do something for her birthday. Seventeen will be seventeen. I'm sensing a potential theme, right?'

Elise stopped walking as she processed what he had said. She was just over a year older than Seventeen. Her mind made the next leap without any warning; it could have been her. In a different world, it could have been Elise, confined, pregnant and alone, all through no choice of her own.

Luca stopped as well, a look of confusion on his face. Glancing up at him, Elise continued walking. He moved out of the way and fell back to her side.

She avoided catching his eye. 'How was it done?'

Luca took a moment to realise what Elise meant. 'Oh no, nothing like that. I would never let them . . .' He trailed off. 'It was artificial insemination. Just like transferring a seedling to a garden bed, they said. She agreed to them doing it as well.' He was gabbling in an effort to reassure her. 'Although, after several meetings with Fintorian, I think *I* would've agreed to have a baby for him. He can be pretty persuasive.'

Elise felt sick. Her mind overloaded as she imagined what had happened, and the smart arguments and angles used to persuade Seventeen that it was the right thing to do.

Sensing Elise's distress, Luca slowed. 'I think she wanted to do it, wanted something of her own to look after, to love.'

Elise didn't ask any more questions. Once she got to the door, she mumbled an excuse about feeling unwell and made her way back to her room. Picking at the rubber matting on the walls, she could only stand the room's suffocating atmosphere for a few minutes before she had to leave. Without thinking about where she was going, she circled the corridors of the museum until she found herself outside Samuel's office. But before she could lift her hand to knock on the oak door, he pulled it open and ushered her inside.

After studying her face, he guided her over to a chair. He then leant against his desk and waited for her to speak. He did not say anything as she glanced around his office. She would normally have been intrigued by the piles of papers stacked in teetering columns around the room, but she barely registered them.

Elise raised her head. 'Was it your idea to do that to Seventeen?'

She watched every twitch, every minute movement as he processed her question.

'No, it wasn't. The order came direct from Adenine Base.' Taking off his glasses, he rubbed his eyes with one hand. 'I was against it from the start, but I don't have the authority to refuse their wishes. No one does.'

He looked directly at Elise without flinching or lowering his gaze.

She believed him. 'What can I do to help?'

Samuel rubbed his eyes again before putting his glasses back on. His usually flawless skin was dull and blotchy; he was a faded version of himself. He could have brightened his complexion in minutes with Dermadew, but he didn't seem to pay any attention to his appearance, unlike most Medius.

'I honestly don't know what to do. Any medical assistance has been banned unless she or the baby is dying. Even if I defied Fintorian's orders, he would just recall all the doctors in a second.' Samuel gripped the edge of the desk. 'When it happens, she will be on her own, no medical assistance, just some drone cameras to capture every moment.'

Elise dropped her head into both of her hands and pushed her mind into examining the options, discounting all of them.

'Did they use medicine? Did Neanderthals use medicine?' she asked without raising her head.

'We think so,' Samuel said, pointing to one of the piles of papers. 'We've studied many of their remains. Some had horrific injuries, probably from hunting accidents. Yet tests showed they lived for years after these injuries. There's little sign of infection, so someone must have healed them and helped care for them while they recovered. The evidence is pretty conclusive that they had knowledge of painkillers as well, maybe even some natural antibiotics.'

'If they used medicine then they would have known how to help during labour; it's one of the most common medical conditions,' Elise said, her mind jumping ahead to the possibilities. 'We could use the forty-thousand rule,' she continued, lifting her head from her hands. 'Argue that it's historically inaccurate for her to be by herself. That she would've had help from other people in her clan. Maybe even a woman who specialised in births, a midwife. Georgina maybe?'

Samuel stood. 'Stars, I've been so stupid. I've been so fixated on what modern medicine and surgery could do to help her that I haven't thought about what they could have done at the time.'

'If you can show there was a midwife, then you can argue that Georgina should be in there with her, not me or Luca. We'd be useless. It has to be someone with some medical knowledge,' Elise said, her confidence rising.

Samuel nodded. 'We have some work to do.'

Over the next few weeks, Elise split her time between Kit, Seventeen and helping Samuel with his research. In the mornings, she would practise using her sling with Kit and then she and Luca would swap pods. Luca was happy with the change; it gave him some respite from worrying about Seventeen and the chance to start practising with the throwing spear. But it meant that Luca and Elise barely saw each other; all of her spare time she spent with Samuel gathering evidence to present to Fintorian.

To everyone's surprise, Fintorian agreed to Georgina acting as midwife. Georgina took the role as seriously as they had hoped; she would regularly be found wandering the corridors, reciting methodology under her breath.

In the afternoons, Elise sat with Seventeen, who slept most of the time. Even when Elise managed to get her to eat something, she would struggle to keep her eyes open longer than a few minutes and would glance longingly at her sleeping mat. Propping her up, Elise would encourage Seventeen to circle the shelter with her a few times before allowing her to go back to sleep. Not knowing whether she was doing the right thing, Elise could only trust her instinct that Seventeen's desire to sleep was not normal and that she should be moving around more.

One afternoon, after walking around the pod with Elise, Seventeen didn't ask to go back to her sleeping mat straight away. Instead, she settled herself next to Elise. Seventeen lifted her hands to sign, but then dropped them into her lap several times.

Finally, she raised them again and hurriedly signed, 'Will you tell me about Twenty-One?'

Elise stretched out her arms, giving herself a moment to think. They were probably being recorded, but she didn't want to deny Seventeen one of her few requests.

'Of course. What do you want to know?'

'There is so much I do not know about him. Except that he is younger than me.'

'He looks older than you,' Elise signed.

'Describe him in five words.'

Elise smiled at Seventeen. 'Kind, strong, loyal, brave and handsome.'

Seventeen actually blushed. 'That is enough for today. It will give me something else to think about.'

Seventeen absent-mindedly ran her hands over her swollen belly. Glancing up at her, Elise smiled, recognising the familiar movement that pregnant Sapien women made as well.

'Do you think it will be a boy or a girl?' Seventeen signed.

'I don't know. What do you want?' Elise replied, for a moment stopping the adjustments she was making to her sling so she could sign.

'I hope it's a girl, so they don't separate us. I think they won't separate us if it's a girl.'

Before Elise could answer, Seventeen leant over and brushed the hair out of Elise's eyes. Seventeen's skin was just as soft as Elise's and her touch was gentle. Elise thought back to when she had first gone into Kit's pod, how frightened she had been of him because she had believed the rumours that he was no more than another wild animal.

Elise leant over and briefly squeezed Seventeen's hand. 'I think that, either way, boy or girl, we'll try to keep you together.'

'Who knows in this place? It's with the stars now,' Seventeen signed, staring up at the sky through the glass ceiling. Turning back to Elise, she straightened. 'You look much prettier now you are letting your hair grow; you should keep going. I don't understand why you would want to look like a boy.'

Elise smiled. She had become used to Seventeen's honest observations; she even enjoyed it when they were directed at Luca or Samuel. Seventeen glanced over at the shelter and Elise hopped up. Seventeen had gotten so big she needed one of them to help her stand most of the time. When Seventeen had told Luca that his left eyebrow was his best feature, he had threatened to leave her on the ground for the rest of the day if she didn't at least include both eyebrows.

Crouching, Elise offered Seventeen her arm and together they strained to stand. Seventeen was shorter than Elise but weighed more. She was solidly built with a round, barrel chest, which had grown even bigger with her advancing pregnancy. Her arms and legs were slimmer than Kit's, but like his, they were muscular.

Finally up, they staggered a few steps before regaining their balance. Elise let go of Seventeen and they walked to the shelter together.

Before Seventeen pulled back the opening, she turned to Elise. 'You do mean it, don't you? You will help us stay together?'

'I promise, I will do everything I can,' Elise signed without hesitation.

Smiling at each other, they touched hands before Seventeen disappeared inside.

'Are they going to separate them?' Elise said to Samuel as soon as she closed his office door.

'Who? Seventeen and her baby?' Samuel said, glancing up from his papers.

Elise nodded and waited for his answer.

Samuel leant back in his chair and motioned for Elise to sit on the one opposite his desk. 'It's possible, but I am pushing for them to remain together. I have made a proposal to conduct a study on the nurturing process of Neanderthals and I'm expecting a response soon.' He half smiled at Elise. 'And I can't do that without a mother and baby to study, can I?'

Elise relaxed a little. Samuel was on board.

'And if they don't agree to it, what'll happen?'

'The main reason for them not to agree would be wanting the baby in another base. And I'm sorry, but that is out of my control.'

'You followed Kit,' Elise said, leaning forwards. 'Maybe one of us could go with the baby, make sure they're alright. That might help Seventeen a little if she knows they're not alone.'

Samuel stared at Elise. 'I'm sorry, but that's not how it works. I had to pull in every favour I could to be transferred with Kit.' He stood and came around the desk. He towered over Elise and it made her feel like a little girl, out of her depth. He sat on the edge of the desk in front of her. 'I can't leave Kit. And I don't think they would let you or Luca leave. They won't think it's, ah, necessary.'

Understanding his meaning, Elise tried not to crumple; she wasn't important enough to move bases. Standing, she pushed her chair back. She didn't like being towered over. She joined him on the edge of the desk and leant back on her hands.

'We'll just have to do everything we can to keep them together then,' she said, looking straight ahead.

'Indeed we will,' he replied; Elise thought she could hear from his voice that he was smiling. 'I spoke with Georgina today and she said that Seventeen is doing well. She's done so much preparation; I really don't think Seventeen could be in better hands.'

Elise grinned, pleased things were starting to go their way.

'So Seventeen and the baby have got a good chance now?' she asked, allowing her legs to swing a little off the edge of the desk.

'She's got more than a good chance. With Georgina present, there's no reason why she shouldn't have a smooth labour. You see, the birth canal—'

'No, no, stop. We need to find another term because I never want to hear those words again. It's just the word "canal". It makes me feel like I'm part estuary.' Elise grimaced and glanced across at him; Samuel looked confused. 'I like learning about all of this; I never got the chance at school. So please keep on teaching.'

'You know, it's funny; Luca said exactly the same thing to me about my choice of terminology. Perhaps you are right.'

Elise hesitated before deciding to ask about something she had wanted to know for a long time. 'Everyone says Kit is different to the other Neanderthals. How come?'

Samuel sat farther back on the desk and allowed his legs to dangle over the side as well. 'Kit certainly has a unique stoicism, but the main influencing factor is that he was raised differently. So many of them are just left to grow up by themselves by indifferent Companions. The Potiors have the power to bring back the Neanderthals, but not the sensitivity to know why it is failing.' Samuel paused and looked over at Elise. 'I've been around Kit for nearly half his life and I made sure that he was taught as much as I was allowed. I thought it would help him cope with the isolation of the pods.'

Elise didn't interrupt; Samuel had never spoken so openly before.

Pushing his hair back, Samuel swung his legs again. 'When I met Kit, he'd already had the best start I could have hoped for. He'd had the same Companion most of his life and she really cared about his development. Together, we taught him coping strategies and went from there.'

'What happened to Kit's Companion?'

'We had to leave her behind in Guanine Base; they wouldn't let her come with us. Kit misses her, but he is resilient. Have you seen his carvings? It's his way of keeping her with him.'

Samuel went quiet and Elise decided to ask another question. 'How old is Kit?'

'Fourteen.'

Elise's face must have shown her surprise.

'His clan would have considered him a man at twelve.'

'We become adults here at fourteen, but most of the boys don't actually look like men,' Elise said.

'That's because Neanderthals are more muscular than Sapiens, which makes them look older.'

Elise stared at her feet, daring herself to ask the next question. 'How old are you?'

Samuel laughed. 'Are you wondering if I'm fifty-two, Elise?' He smiled at her. 'Well, I'm sorry to disappoint, but I'm a very unexciting twenty-four. I started working with Kit when I first started university in Guanine Base at eighteen; he was the "practical" element of my course. Most of the Neanderthals are in Guanine so they can be studied by the students there.'

Elise leant back on her hands as she considered this information. 'How did you make the crossings between bases?'

Samuel turned to look at Elise. 'Why are you asking?'

'I'm just curious. The Medius seem to cross sometimes, but the Sapiens never do.'

'The first time, when I left Adenine to go to Guanine, I walked. It is the only way to get into Guanine. You have to prove you are worthy of the knowledge they will impart. I was given three days' worth of water and it took six days to get there. It took nearly half a day to climb the steps.'

Elise stared at him, transfixed.

'The second time, from Guanine to here, I had permission to travel with one of the empty ships that was sailing to Thymine Base to collect the biannual delivery of goods. I had Kit with me, so we had to travel in the prescribed way.'

Elise laughed. 'Stars, I couldn't imagine Kit on a boat. He's seen more of this world than I have!'

Samuel glanced at her. 'He didn't see anything. They sedated him in Guanine and didn't wake him up until he had been brought into the pod where he lives now. That is how they move the Neanderthals between bases. They can't have them learning too much about this world. That would only lead to unwanted questions.'

CHAPTER 12

* *

'I wonder what it will be like?' Seventeen signed for the third time.

'How about we come back later and tell you every detail?' Luca signed in response.

'Promise?'

'Hand on heart,' Luca signed, exaggerating a swoon.

The Worker Profiling Department had asked that all the museum's employees meet in the canteen at six o'clock. Luca had heard from the canteen staff that there was going to be a celebration for Fintorian's one-year anniversary as Head of Thymine Base's Museum of Evolution. From 4 p.m., the bathrooms had been heaving with people changing into their evening outfits. Elise had borrowed a navy blue silk dress from Georgina that clung tightly and emphasised the curves she had forgotten were there. The dress ended halfway down her thighs but Elise drew the line at heels and instead wore matching flat sandals that gently shimmered in the fading light. Elise had promised Seventeen that she would show her what she was wearing and had even been made to do a twirl.

'You look beautiful. You've even done your hair nicely!' Seventeen signed, standing in the opening to her shelter.

Elise bobbed a little curtsy. Luca grinned and put his arm around her shoulder. He was wearing a soft grey jumper with a white shirt underneath and Elise leant into him, enjoying the moment.

Seventeen looked appraisingly at Luca.

'You look better,' she signed, before making them promise that they would wake her up later if they found her asleep.

As they walked towards the foliage that circled the sleeping area, Elise glanced back at Seventeen. She was still watching them. Elise silently wished she could take Seventeen with her, even swap places for the day. She waved at her again and Seventeen responded by signing, 'Enjoy yourselves.' Smiling, Elise let Luca take her hand as he pushed aside the leaves for her.

When they emerged onto the bank of the stream, Elise stopped to watch the last of the light dancing on the water. The pod was completely still and she breathed in the clean air.

'She's right about one thing; you are beautiful,' Luca said, pulling Elise round so that she was facing him.

He then slowly leant in and kissed her for the first time. Pulling away from each other, neither of them spoke for a moment. Elise matched Luca's smile and they held hands, this time with their fingers entwined, not even letting go as they crossed the stepping stones together.

No one noticed Harriet enter the canteen except for Elise, who was sitting closest to the door. Luca was chatting to the tall girl Elise had first seen in the corridor a few months ago. He had introduced them and Elise had learnt that her name was Rosa, but after that, Rosa had directed all of her conversation to Luca. Elise looked around. She could see Georgina in the far corner. She couldn't go over, though, as the announcement was about to begin.

Harriet cleared her throat a few times, but still everyone kept chatting. Eventually, she pulled out a chair and, leaning against a pillar for support, clambered onto it so that she was taller than most in the room. She tapped a spoon against the glass she was holding and the room began to fall silent. All of the faces turned to her and she paused for a few seconds, to ensure she held everyone's attention.

'It is with great pleasure that I am able to announce that today marks the first anniversary of Fintorian's arrival at Thymine Base's Museum of Evolution. I think you will all agree when I say that he has brought life to this museum. And for that we are grateful.'

The room erupted into cheers and people stamped their feet in celebration.

Harriet surveyed the room and allowed herself a brief smile. 'And now, please stand to show your appreciation for our very own museum director – Fintorian!'

Harriet, feet planted firmly on the seat of the chair, turned only the top half of her body and extended her clapping hands towards where Fintorian was standing. A clear path emerged as everyone pushed back to allow Fintorian to move effortlessly over to Harriet. He stopped next to her and smiled across at her; Harriet stayed standing on her chair.

Fintorian's gaze swept across the room and nothing else was required for everyone to stop applauding abruptly. The silence was sharp but full of anticipation, as if he were the conductor in front of his orchestra.

'Only a few words from me, as I know we all want to start the celebrations.' He paused to allow the brief burst of cheers and whoops to die down again. 'Firstly, I would like to thank Harriet for organising this very welcome surprise. It is a momentous day for me and I am grateful to Thymine Base. Soon, we will have achieved something no one dreamed of . . . even thirty years ago when the Neanderthal project began. The natural delivery of a Neanderthal takes us another step closer to returning order to this world.' Another round of cheers burst out and hammered around the canteen. 'And it is thanks to every single one of you that we have reached this moment. From the delightful canteen staff, who keep us fuelled every day . . .' Cheering and whistles exploded around Elise's table as Rosa and some of her friends took a bow. 'Right through to the museum Hosts who ensure that no one leaves with an unanswered question.' A more reserved smattering of applause followed these words, as the Hosts nodded their appreciation. 'All of you have contributed in some way to this project. And because of this, we shall be celebrating this evening with a party thrown by the museum in honour of all its employees.'

The cheers reached a crescendo as the staff reacted to what they had been hoping for. Rosa turned and hugged Luca, who looked surprised, but hugged her back.

Fintorian raised his glass. 'So everyone fill up your glasses and I propose a toast.' He beamed at everyone in the canteen and they all raised their glasses in unison. 'To the museum staff!'

'To the museum staff!' everyone echoed in harmony.

Two loud explosions bounced around the room as confetti cannons were set off. They were met with delighted screams as glittering green ticker tape fell over the crowd. Elise picked one from her hair and inspected it. Printed on one side was 'Thymine Base' and on the other 'Thank you'. She let it drop to the floor.

The steady bass sprang from the canteen speakers and people cleared a small space in the middle of the floor. The ones who had been drinking the longest moved into the centre and swayed, slightly out of time, to the music. The others filled up their glasses and raised their voices as they continued with their conversations. Mostly, they did not mix, and the room was divided between Medius and Sapiens, all determined to enjoy this rare opportunity to celebrate.

Luca tried to pull Elise into the middle of the near-empty dance floor, but she smiled and shook her hand free. 'Later,' when there's a bit more cover.'

Shrugging, he joined a small cluster of canteen workers determined to show the Medius how to have fun. Elise leant against the wall and smiled as she watched Luca keep perfect time to the beat, not a movement out of place. A couple of male Medius glanced over enviously as they tried to copy him, unsure what to do with their arms. She had to give it to Luca; he knew how to dance.

'He's good,' Samuel said, making her jump.

'Stars, Samuel. You scared me,' Elise said, laughing at herself.

'Sorry.'

The amusement was clear in his voice. Elise glanced over at him; he was dressed as he always was in a casual shirt with the sleeves rolled up to his elbows. He leant against the wall with his arms folded against his broad chest.

'Did it take you long to choose your outfit?' she asked.

She was careful not to touch him, even though the room was crowded.

'What? Of course not,' Samuel said, before realising that she was teasing him. He smiled ruefully. 'I don't like parties I'm ordered to attend.'

'There's no fun quite like mandatory fun,' Elise agreed.

Looking around, she knew that she and Samuel were in the minority. A few drinks down and people were getting braver as the dance floor swelled. Even Harriet was swaying gently at the sidelines.

'I wanted to tell you that Fintorian approved my request. The baby can stay with Seventeen,' Samuel said, leaning in closer so that Elise could hear him over the swelling noise.

One of the Sapien Keepers had turned the speakers up and it was growing impossible to have a conversation.

'What! That's amazing news. Now there's a reason to celebrate!' Elise switched to sign language. 'We have to tell Luca; are you coming?'

'No,' Samuel signed, frowning. 'You go. He would rather hear it from you anyway.'

Three hours later, after much dancing and a few too many celebratory drinks, Elise and Luca left the party. All of the food had been cleared and most of the canteen was now a dance floor. They decided to visit Seventeen to tell her the news and rejoin the party afterwards. They were sober compared to everyone else and Luca insisted that they would have some catching up to do.

Pulling aside the covering to Seventeen's shelter, they abruptly stopped their happy chatter. Loud moans were coming from the other end. It was dark and Elise stumbled through the entrance holding her hands low to the ground, trying to find where Seventeen was lying. Luca tried to follow, but she told him to hold back so he could keep the covering open to let in the feeble moonlight.

'We're here; don't worry,' Elise said as she swept her arms around her.

Another loud moan made Elise stop and swing to her left, where her hands finally touched Seventeen's tight tunic. As she ran her hand over Seventeen's side, she felt something wet.

'Luca, it's started. We have to get her out of here; it's too dark!'

Elise could hear Luca advancing and she used her voice to guide him. It was pitch-black and they couldn't even see the other's outline.

'Come on, Seventeen. I know you don't want to but we have to move you outside so that we can see,' Luca said when he was next to Elise.

Seventeen let out an ear-splitting scream that made Elise tremble. Trying to soothe her, Elise rubbed her back as they waited for the contraction to end.

Once it had subsided, Elise turned to Luca. 'Now. We have to move her now, before the next one.'

Both heaving from either side, they managed to get Seventeen to her feet as she groaned in protest. Stumbling through the shelter, Seventeen tried to help them, but Elise was buckling. Pulling open the shelter's entrance with one hand, she guided Seventeen outside, with Luca taking most of her weight.

'Hold her for a moment.' Elise pulled away to go back into the shelter and collect a sleeping mat for Seventeen to lie on.

'Why didn't the cameras pick up on this and alert us?' Luca said, supporting Seventeen with both arms.

'The cameras must have recorded her. There's no chance they wouldn't have been drawn to her heightened pulse,' Elise called out from the inside of the shelter. 'It's just that no one was watching. I bet whoever was supposed to be monitoring the footage tonight snuck off to the party and left the screens unattended.'

Even from inside the shelter, Elise could hear Luca swearing.

She emerged with a mat and a few furs. Placing the mat on the ground, she helped Luca lower Seventeen. Elise winced as Seventeen's body was racked by another heavy contraction.

'Go and get Georgina,' she shouted up at Luca, who had frozen, staring down at Seventeen's contorted face. 'Go!'

Luca spun and sprinted out of the sleeping area and Elise turned her attention back to Seventeen.

Outside the shelter, Elise could now see Seventeen's face in the moonlight. Everything was bleached of colour, leaving only differing shades of grey. Seventeen scrunched her eyes back up at Elise as the contraction ended.

'I'm so glad you came,' Seventeen signed. 'Is everything okay with the baby?'

'Yes, you're doing really well,' Elise signed, after stroking her forehead.

Elise felt the waft of the slightly larger camera pass her arm. Resisting the urge to swat it away, she gently draped a soft hide over Seventeen's stomach and legs. Another contraction hit the girl and Elise could only watch as she rode it out. She felt useless and didn't know whether to leave her and try to get help or stay. What if Luca couldn't find Georgina? She didn't know how to deliver a baby. She might do more damage than good. But she couldn't leave Seventeen by herself; she had already been alone for long enough. Seventeen's back arched and Elise signed words of encouragement as she prayed to the stars for Georgina to come soon.

'We just found out that the baby can stay with you. So only a bit longer and then you can be together. You're doing so well.'

Seventeen let out another scream and clutched the sleeping mat as her body shuddered. Once the contraction was over she turned her head to Elise and scrunched her eyes.

'Thank you,' she signed.

Peering into the darkness, Elise thought she could hear voices.

'I'm here, I'm here,' Georgina called out as she raced bare-foot into the clearing, her floor-length gown flying out behind her.

She was by them in a second and quickly examined Seventeen. 'Elise, you stay where you are. Luca, go and get my bag from my clinic. It's got everything I need. And find Samuel. I need the medical team on standby. And get him to turn the lights on!'

Without a word, Luca sprinted away again. Elise squeezed Georgina's hand in thanks as she passed her.

Moving up to speak with Seventeen, Georgina took her hand. 'You're doing everything right, sweetie, but we're nearly there and you'll have to push when the next contraction comes.' Georgina turned to Elise. 'Keep doing what you're doing. We need to keep her calm.'

Elise stared down at Seventeen and brushed her hair from her soaking forehead. Seventeen furrowed her eyebrows as the next wave hit.

'Come on, another push; we're nearly there,' Georgina said. 'I can see it! Nearly there. Short breaths now, like we practised.'

Seventeen tried to roll onto her side, racked with pain, and Elise gently pulled her back, never looking away from her face. Seventeen's eyes were tightly closed. She breathed out through her mouth.

'That's it. Soon be over. Last one,' Georgina said as the next contraction hit.

Seventeen let out another, even more piercing scream and Elise held her hand tightly, wincing under her grip. Seventeen shuddered one last time and Elise looked around at Georgina, who was leaning over a tiny baby. Its miniature fists were clawing at the air. It was clearly distressed at the traumatising experience of leaving the safety of its mother.

Georgina picked the baby up gently, taking care to support the head, and brought it to Seventeen's chest. Seventeen scrunched her eyes and placed one of her hands lightly over the baby, pulling her closer. Elise helped her support the baby, blinking back the tears that had formed.

'It's a girl,' Georgina said, smiling broadly.

'She's perfect,' Seventeen shakily signed with one hand, while drawing the other arm around her daughter.

Elise turned around as Luca skidded to a halt carrying Georgina's medical kit.

He dropped it by Georgina's feet, careful only to look over at the shelter.

'I'm going to stand over here,' he said, walking to the edge of the clearing and turning his back to give Seventeen some privacy.

'Right, I just have to cut the cord.' Georgina pulled equipment out of her bag. 'It's a girl, Luca!'

Luca whooped in response. 'I knew it!'

Elise bent to peer at the baby, wanting to take her first proper look. Seventeen was loosely holding her and she instinctively snuggled into her mother's chest. Elise smiled up at Seventeen and froze. Her eyes were closing. Elise stared at her, waiting for them to open. Maybe she was tired; she must be exhausted. Seventeen's eyes stayed closed.

'Is that blood or fluid?' Georgina said quietly to herself, and then, more loudly, 'Luca, go and tell them to turn the damned lights on!'

Elise had never heard Georgina so angry. She glanced back at Seventeen, whose breathing had become shallow.

'Georgina, you need to come up here,' she said as calmly as she could, while carefully lifting the baby from Seventeen.

Elise stood and cradled the little girl in her arms. She had begun to wail, just like a Sapien. Elise could only watch as Georgina scrabbled up to Seventeen's head and felt her neck for a pulse. '*Get the doctors in here!*' Georgina screamed at the viewing platform.

'No, no, no,' Elise muttered as she held the baby closer. 'Shhh . . . it's okay.'

She tried to comfort the little girl, but her eyes were transfixed by what was happening to Seventeen.

The lights snapped on and it was bright daylight. Georgina was breathing into Seventeen's mouth and then alternating it with pumping her chest, counting under her breath. There was blood all down the front of Georgina's violet dress and dark stains on the sleeping mat. Her brow was knitted in concentration. Elise strained to hear the now-familiar noise of people crashing through the undergrowth, but there was nothing. The only sounds were Georgina counting under her breath, the baby crying and Elise bargaining with the stars. It was a full five minutes before anyone came.

Fintorian was first. He ran straight to Elise.

'Is it alright?' he said, laying a fresh mat on the ground. 'Down here; place it down here.'

Elise complied and laid the baby as gently as she could on the mat.

'She's fine, I think,' she said as Fintorian examined the baby. 'Seventeen, though . . .'

She glanced up. Samüel had run into the clearing carrying what looked like a metal suitcase. He opened it up next to Seventeen in a second.

'Sudden cardiac arrest. No response,' Georgina said.

A doctor skidded to their side and knelt over Seventeen, blocking Elise's view.

'There's no pulse,' the doctor said. 'The defibrillator won't work now. I'm setting up automatic chest compressions.'

'She seems well,' Fintorian said, checking the baby.

He smiled up at Elise. For once, she wasn't dazzled by him.

'Come on, come on,' Georgina repeated over and over as she crouched next to Seventeen holding a mask over her mouth.

'A girl as well. A fine addition to the museum,' Fintorian continued. He glanced at Elise's stricken face. 'I'm sure Seventeen will stay with us. And if not, the other bases will understand. Won't they?'

Elise looked at him open-mouthed.

'Of course they will. Things like this happen all the time. We have a healthy baby girl, naturally delivered. That's what matters.'

The doctor craned his neck round to face Fintorian. Elise stared at him, willing him to say that he had found a pulse. That Seventeen would be fine. She had to be fine; she was young and strong and had everything to live for.

'I'm sorry. There's nothing. Permission to stop?'

The only sound now was Georgina sobbing. Elise opened her mouth to protest, to tell the doctor to do his job and keep trying, but Samuel shook his head and silenced her.

'Yes. It's time to stop. Come and check on Thirty-Two,' Fintorian said, pushing himself to his feet.

In a trance, Elise stood and stumbled to the closest bushes, where she retched until her stomach was empty.

Everyone had left with Thirty-Two except for Luca, Samuel and Elise. They were sitting cross-legged either end of a bundle of fur rugs and mats that had been covered in a blanket that someone had brought in. Luca looked as if he had been crying; his eyes were red and he kept wiping them and dropping his head. Samuel appeared shell-shocked, as if he couldn't take it in. Elise barely noticed them, though; all her attention was drawn to the blanket lying between them.

It could have been an inappropriate joke, some pillows covered in a sheet. She had done something similar when she wanted to leave her parents' house late at night. It wasn't, though. Some of Seventeen's strawberry-blonde hair spread out from underneath the covering. Elise leant over and took her time pushing it under the blanket, careful that every strand was hidden. It was as soft as she remembered. If it hadn't been for the hair, Elise would have struggled to believe it was Seventeen under there; she had been reduced to just a shape under a blanket. Elise sat back between Luca and Samuel; no one spoke.

They stayed there for hours, each locked in their own thoughts. Elise stood at one point and walked to the edge of the clearing to pick flowers. When she had an armful, she laid the little blue forget-me-nots at Seventeen's side. She knew Seventeen would have preferred big, bold blooms of peonies or roses, but the little blue flowers were all that the pod had to offer. She silently promised Seventeen that she would do better when she left the compound.

It was Luca who eventually broke the silence. 'I forgot about Kit. I ran in the last time to tell him the baby was on its way. He doesn't know.'

'I have to tell him,' Samuel said, standing.

'I'll come with you,' Elise said.

They turned expectantly to Luca, who slowly raised his head. 'I want to wait with her, just until she's collected.'

'Are you sure?' Elise said.

'They won't be long and I don't want her to be alone.' All emotion was gone from Luca's voice.

'I'll be back soon,' Samuel said.

When they walked down the corridor to Kit's pod, Elise could see two people kissing in the shadows. The distant thud of music told her that the party was still going strong. She jumped when someone ran laughing down the adjoining corridor and let off a party popper over the couple. Elise glared at them.

'What are you going to say?' she said.

'The truth, I suppose,' Samuel said, pulling back the steel bars.

When the door opened, Elise could see Kit standing on the other side, waiting.

He looked at their faces. 'Who was it? The baby or Seventeen?' He paused when they didn't respond. 'Or both?'

Samuel moved forwards. 'The baby is fine, a little girl. But Seventeen died. Georgina and Elise were with her until the end. I'm so sorry, Kit.'

Without responding, Kit turned and walked away.

Elise couldn't sleep that night. She had stayed with Kit until he told her he was going to his sleeping area. He had spent his time carving a new statue and Elise had sat with him and watched. When he had finished, he had given the carving to Elise and asked that she place it with Seventeen. She had held it tightly in her hand and only looked at it once she was safely in her bedroom; it was a tiny carving of a baby, wrapped in a shawl. Silent tears trickled down Elise's face and she hastily wiped them with her sleeve.

She had lain awake for so long that the back of her head ached. She continuously flipped from her side to her back in an effort to find a position that would soothe her to sleep. Her position was not the problem, though; it was the whirling, tripping thoughts that paddled their way through her mind. Round and round, oblivious that Elise no longer wanted to listen.

At half past five, she gave up. Pushing back the covers, she got dressed and paced her small room for a few minutes. The recycled rubber flooring had an unnatural spring she disliked. Pulling on her boots, she walked to the canteen.

Empty of the revellers, it was a sad little room. Dirty green ticker tape lay in drifts by the walls, waiting to be recycled;

balloons bumped against the ceilings, their journeys already over; and empty bottles stood on every table, filling the room with a sour smell.

She picked her way through the debris and made her way to the table in the far corner. Luca pushed a chair out for her with his foot. She smiled at him and slid into it. Georgina leant over, her eyes puffy and red. She filled a glass and nudged it towards Elise.

Samuel raised his glass. 'To Seventeen, whom we shall never forget.'

'To Seventeen,' the three of them echoed.

CHAPTER 13

....

A week later, sitting at the far end of the canteen, Elise looked everywhere but at the giant screen. Thankfully, the producers had decided that soft, orchestral music was a better accompaniment than the real-life sound effects of a girl giving birth, a nurse desperately trying to save her life and Elise bargaining with all the stars in the sky, offering them anything if they would only make the bleeding stop.

Samuel had tried to negotiate Elise and Luca's absence. But Fintorian had been resolute. They had to attend; this was a time for celebration, not grief.

Over the top of the floating music came the whimpering cry of a newborn growing stronger as it tested the first sounds it would make.

The presenter's deep voice chuckled at the baby's cries and then he continued with his commentary in a sombre tone. 'It is a sacrifice every mother would make for their offspring, and one that indebts us to all our mothers, no matter our species.' His voice then lightened. 'But the next generation has arrived, so we must look to the future and celebrate progress. Thymine Base has achieved what no other base believed possible . . .'

Elise wished she could squeeze her ears shut too; she started to hum under her breath, the vibration in her head a welcome distraction.

The screening ran for another ten minutes; shots of Thirty-Two, the museum, Kit as a child and Thymine Base seamlessly rolled by. Samuel had told Elise that the doctor who was supposed to be on call that evening had passed out drunk and that was why there was the delay while they found another. He had reassured her that the version used for the public screening would barely include Seventeen, as Fintorian had labelled it 'too realistic' for a mass audience. Elise took strange comfort from that.

When the lights went up, Elise left without turning and went straight to Kit's pod, where she remained until late into the night. Sometimes, she even slept there; she would wake at dawn and find that Kit had draped a fur over her.

Like Kit, Elise kept herself busy. Her desire for occupation had become as great as his and they followed their daily routine relentlessly, every hour taken care of. Kit had become subdued and barely spoke except to ask Elise disjointed questions about Seventeen. Besides exercising, foraging and cooking, they practised with their weapons. Elise could now hit a stationary object at thirty metres, ten times in a row. She still made sure she missed some, but for the first time in her life, she was angry that she had to conceal her abilities.

It was a new emotion for Elise, who had always been proud of her self-control and never questioned the need to hide what she was capable of. She was silently livid at the smallest things; it caught in her throat, burnt in her chest and she didn't know where to direct it. When she briefly saw her colleagues in the corridors, she would overhear their happy chatter about

Thymine Base's success. It made her feel as if she inhabited a different museum to them and had lost the ability to connect. So she stayed with Kit, away from everyone else, including Luca, Samuel and Georgina.

Not that they were knocking at her door. Samuel spent his time in his office and Georgina was always with Thirty-Two. She had slipped seamlessly from midwife to mother. Elise had only visited Thirty-Two briefly a couple of days after she was born. Not wanting to become attached, she had only stayed for a few minutes and hadn't been back since.

Elise still went home every Sunday, knowing her parents would storm the museum if she didn't turn up for one of her weekly visits. She relied on her permanently fixed mask to get her through these afternoons. She had become an expert at small talk and barely listened to the words that came out of her own mouth. To be able to remain working with Kit and still see Nathan, she had to convince her parents that nothing had changed.

The last time Elise had seen Luca, she had been slipping through the corridors late at night back to her room. Turning a corner, she had quickly stepped back and pressed herself up against the wall, holding her breath. Luca had stumbled out of one of the bedroom doors at the far end of the corridor. He hadn't seen her as he walked past; he'd been too busy buttoning his shirt. She had changed her route back so she could check the identification tag of the room he had come from. She should have guessed; it was Rosa's. She told herself nothing much had happened between herself and Luca; he didn't owe her any- thing. But her counsel was hollow; she was silently seething at Luca as well.

A few weeks passed. Elise would have stopped leaving Kit's pod altogether if it weren't for Samuel turning up one evening and marching her out of it.

When she protested, telling him she couldn't possibly leave Kit alone, she was silenced by Samuel's reply. 'It was Kit who told me what a state you've got yourself into.'

There was nothing she could say to that.

Looking down at her, Samuel beckoned with his hand. 'Come with me. There is a new display I want to show you.'

Elise peered into the glass cabinet, but she couldn't see much more than a few large branches standing out amidst the other foliage. She wondered whether Samuel wanted to show her some stick insects; she always had a hard time picking those out.

'Look over there, in the corner,' Samuel said, careful not to tap the glass.

Elise looked again and gave a small gasp as an eye rotated between two leaves.

'Is it a chameleon?' she said, turning to Samuel for confirmation.

'The first to live for nearly two hundred years. One of the teams of scientists from Cytosine Base found a preserved sample in Zone 4 last year. They have just completed the reproduction process and sent us one of the successful specimens as a gift.'

He pressed his nose against the glass and left a small smudge.

'You remembered from my interview,' Elise said, smiling at him. It had been the only question Samuel had asked.

'Of course. It was, without a doubt, the most ridiculous answer for a favourite animal I've ever heard,' Samuel said, pushing his glasses farther up his nose.

Elise laughed. 'It's better than a pony.'

'That it is. When did you even learn about them?'

'Here in the museum, amongst the displays of animals that hadn't been brought back yet.'

Elise didn't want to mention that she had also read about chameleons in her granddad's encyclopaedia and had been captivated with them since she was a little girl. She had always wanted to be able to slowly fade into the background whenever it suited her.

Samuel sat on the large wooden bench positioned across from the display cabinet. Elise stayed by the glass, willing the chameleon to change colour. She watched it stretching its leg, tentatively and at a slow pace.

'But that's not the main reason I brought you here,' Samuel said.

Elise's attention was still fixed on what she thought might be the stillest animal in the world. Just then, a snap of pink tongue flew out to another twig. The chameleon had secured its dinner; it was definitely her favourite animal.

'What do you mean?' she asked, pulling her eyes away.

Samuel had become silent. She glanced back at him.

A small rock was hurtling towards the cabinet – towards her chameleon. Before she could stop herself, she had stretched out her arm and caught it. She was left in a half-lunge, arm straight out, rock clasped in hand.

'Are you insane?' was all she could think to say.

'I knew it,' he said, a smile crossing his face. 'I knew it from your first day.'

'Knew what?' she said, as she tried to casually correct her stance without toppling.

'That your reflexes are unbelievably fast,' he said, grinning. 'I just needed to test it in a way that you couldn't think about too much. I didn't want you to feel you had to get mauled again. And the rock wouldn't have broken the glass; the display cabinets are virtually indestructible.'

'That's very considerate of you. And for the record—'

'Atch! No more!' Samuel said, glaring at her. 'I know what you can do now. Perfect aim and incredibly fast reactions. Is there anything else?'

Elise lowered her hand, still holding the rock, and considered throwing it at his head. Instead, she said nothing and turned to leave the room.

Samuel hopped up and grabbed her sleeve. 'If I was going to report you, I would have done it months ago.'

'*I don't know you, Samuel,*' Elise said, angry. 'How could I ever trust someone I don't know?'

'You've trusted me for months, and I you. That's what people do; they take a chance and they trust each other. Either that or they live out their lives as little hermits in self-imposed isolation.' He raised an eyebrow. 'Stars, I can't believe *I'm* having to explain interpersonal relationships to *you.*'

When Elise started to walk away, Samuel called out, 'But I can understand your hesitation. You'd have to be a fool to let anything slip in this place. So I am going to make it easier for you.'

Elise slowed.

'I, Samuel Adair, have some of the most highly graded engineering around. Well, for a Medius anyway.' Elise stopped walking, but didn't turn. 'I have a strengthened skeleton, which is practically impossible to break.' Samuel paused for effect and

Elise turned around. Smiling at her, he leant forwards. 'I have an IQ of 145. But don't tell anyone with an IQ of 140 or over – they are very competitive.'

'That's not exactly a secret, Samuel. Anyone who wants to talk about "birth canals" all the time must have lost some social skills to IQ.'

Samuel twitched his nose and pushed his hair back from his face.

Ignoring her, he continued with a flourish, 'I also have strengthened muscles, which, of course, includes my heart. That means I can run for miles without tiring and am stronger than most.'

Elise sat at the other end of the bench, away from him.

'What about when you knew there was something wrong before anyone else on my first day when the tiger got loose? Nobody else knew that the cleaner was going to enter the room except you,' she said, feigning a casual tone.

'Ah, well, you see. That's the crunch. My mother also had an interesting piece of high-grade engineering I inherited from her.' Samuel pulled at his earlobe. 'The ability to hear very soft sounds from far away, and very high sounds as well. I can also pinpoint where noises come from better than most.'

'Is there anything else?'

'Nothing remarkable from my father. In fact, I think he may have dulled a few of the gifts my mother might have passed on. He certainly gave me his poor eyesight.'

Elise looked at him. 'Sapiens will never catch up, will they? Even if we win the lottery, there are already children being born that are generations of engineering ahead. And only getting stronger . . .'

Samuel leant forwards and rested his arms on his knees. 'Now that's a conversation for another time. For the future, if all goes well.' He paused. 'So, tell me about you.'

Elise glanced around; it went against everything she had been taught growing up.

'There are no cameras; there's only me and I could have got you into trouble months ago.'

Elise began hesitantly. 'My parents knew my reflexes were fast when I was little . . . my aunt and uncle were the same. I don't know exactly what causes it, something to do with the nervous system. But my dad trained me from a young age, in case I ever had to defend myself.'

'And the perfect aim?' Samuel said.

'I've no idea where that came from.'

Samuel leant back and was silent while he considered. 'It might be a by-product of the proprioceptive training your father provided to you from a young age.' His eyes brightened. 'It really is fascinating.'

'The what training?'

'Proprioceptive training,' Samuel said, glancing up at Elise. 'Proprioception is your body's ability to know what it is doing even when you cannot see it. It stems from the Latin, *proprius*, which means "one's own", and "perception". We all have it, of course, or we'd be falling over constantly, but if this sense is trained from a young age, it can have remarkable results.'

Elise was sure her dad had never heard of proprioceptive training, but before she could say anything, Samuel continued, 'He wouldn't have to know he was specifically targeting it. Just training your reflexes, balance and blocking would help. The key is repetition.'

'There was certainly repetition.'

Samuel stood and put his hands in his pockets. 'You have learnt how to increase your body's awareness of itself, and extensions of it. Consequently, you can rely on those almost instinctively.' Elise thought he sounded excited. 'I think if you practised enough with the sling, you would be able to fire it accurately without consciously having to aim.'

'That's definitely something worth trying for,' Elise said, resisting the urge to make a weak joke. 'But what's annoying is I'm always having to miss them.'

'Just miss a few; it's important that you don't stand out. Stars knows what they would have planned for you if they found out,' Samuel said, a look of concern crossing his face. 'Probably some sort of security work in the Protection Department if they thought you were compliant enough, and if you weren't . . . well . . .'

His words had more impact than he could have imagined; this was what her dad had warned her about for years. It was strange to hear what she always thought of as her dad's paranoia and her mum's overreaction confirmed by Samuel.

'Anything else I should be careful about?'

'Yes. Don't isolate yourself from everyone,' Samuel said, looking down at her. 'Kit has it forced on him; don't belittle that sanction by voluntarily embracing it. The time might soon come when you both need as many friends as possible.' Samuel pushed his hair back. 'And it . . . ah, goes without saying that I would be counted among them.'

He awkwardly patted Elise's arm and she accepted this token of friendship.

*

'If I brought you more grass mats, would you throw them at me?' Elise said, popping her head round the nurses' station door.

That evening, she had decided to act on Samuel's advice. Build bridges and de-hermit herself.

'No, but I might have forgotten your name when I come to politely thank you for them,' Georgina responded, bouncing Thirty-Two in her arms.

'How about grass mats . . .' Elise said, waggling her right hand, which was holding them, '. . . and a mystery present?'

She moved around the door, leaving her left hand hidden.

'Ooh! I do like a mystery present,' Georgina said, joining in. 'Is it my very own baby woolly mammoth? No, no, too quiet. How about a serviced home in Adenine Base? No, think smart, Georgina; her arm is clearly not long enough for that.'

'Hmmm . . . you might have to lower those expectations a little,' Elise said. 'But it's definitely better than a grass mat.'

With that, she handed the small package to Georgina, who laid Thirty-Two back in her crib.

While Georgina enthusiastically unwrapped her present, Elise stood by the crib, peering at Thirty-Two. The baby was contentedly trying to pull her foot into her mouth; her alert eyes locked onto Elise. The legs and arms were sturdy, but in perfect proportion. She had very little chin but a large nose and eyes, which were overshadowed by her prominent brow ridge. Her neck was thick and Elise could see the shape of her skull clearly, as she only had a little hair. It was a different shape to a Sapien baby's. Instead of her forehead going straight up and back, it started sloping backwards much sooner, just a bit above her eyebrows. Elise could see the occipital bun at the back of her head and it made her think again about what it was for.

Georgina had tied the tufts of auburn hair at the top of Thirty-Two's head with some blue ribbon; Elise thought it made her look like a pineapple. She waved at Thirty-Two and received a scrunchy-eyed look for her efforts.

Elise's attention was drawn away by some excited squeals from Georgina. She smiled at the sight of her friend, whose feet had disappeared under torn tissue paper.

'Is it really for me?'

'Yes, I bought it ages ago, but I never found the right time to give it to you. It's to say thank you properly for my arm.'

Georgina was holding up the scarlet silk shirt and inspecting it from every angle. The colour perfectly matched her hair and lipstick.

'Well, it's very much appreciated. Thank you. But I don't think I deserve it. Are you sure? You would look lovely in it too.'

'I can't really imagine myself in a silk shirt, can you?'

'Well, no, but it really is too much. Thank you, though.'

Georgina looked overwhelmed. Elise thought it might have something to do with not often receiving presents.

'So how's it been going with Thirty-Two?' she asked, aware that she had missed the first month of her life.

'It's been hard, but really rewarding at the same time. She's developing so fast.' Georgina laid out the scarlet shirt over the back of a chair in the corner of the room, far from the baby to keep it safe. 'We've been thinking about names as well. Samuel thinks we should give her a proper name like he did with Kit. He thinks it helps with the isolation to have a clearer identity.'

'What names have you come up with?' Elise asked, leaning over the crib again and waving.

'Bay is the first choice; it was Samuel's suggestion, but I love the name too.'

'It's beautiful.' Elise peered over the side of the crib. 'Hello, Bay.' Another scrunchy-eyed smile had Elise melting. 'Seventeen would've loved her.'

'As she grows, I can see how similar they are. See, she has her nose and her hair, of course.' Georgina leant over the cot next to Elise. 'Maybe . . . I could have done more, should have prepped more.'

'No, no, Georgina. Don't say that. You did everything you could. Don't take the blame for something that wasn't your fault.'

Georgina just nodded.

'Luca comes to visit most days,' Georgina said, glancing at Elise. 'We're hoping he can be her Companion when the time comes.'

Elise stiffened. 'If you think that's best . . .'

Her anger at him and at the museum resurfaced and she struggled to push it down. But not away; it was a new emotion and it fuelled her.

Georgina sighed. 'I don't know what's happened between you, but Luca said you're avoiding him.' Elise opened her mouth to protest, but was cut off. 'He has probably done something idiotic, but unless you are truly heartbroken, don't lose a friendship over bruised pride. It's not like you've got friends to spare, is it? None of us do.'

Elise turned back to Bay and tried not to let the truth sting.

CHAPTER 14

The following Sunday, Elise tentatively knocked on her parents' front door. She winced when her knuckles, cracked from the cold, hit the solid wood. Her breath hung in the air and she thought how pretty it looked against the pale winter sun. Waiting, she stamped her feet to beat the cold out of them. She felt guilty about doubting her parents for so many years. She didn't know much about the Protection Department, but she knew she didn't want to work for them. To eject people from Thymine and intimidate them until they didn't return was unconscionable; she would rather spend the next sixty years in a production centre.

It was Aiden who answered. 'That's great, Nathan. Like that again . . . Elise!' He held the door open for her. 'It's good to see you.'

As soon as Elise closed the door, Sofi closely inspected her daughter's strained features. 'What happened? Are you hurt?'

'No, no, nothing like that. I'm fine. There's no danger; just, a lot's happened and I think I should tell you about it,' Elise signed, deciding that if she was honest with them, they might be open with her.

She had to make her parents tell her the truth about what had happened in the Rising.

She was ushered to the freshly scrubbed table. Her mum brought down the coffee tin and her dad filled a bowl with blackberry crumble, still warm from the oven, which she consumed in seconds. As the bustle of domestic life enveloped her, Nathan showed her his new blocking stances and Elise applauded in all the right places.

When everyone was sitting at the table and she was on her second bowl of crumble, she explained. She told them about the spear and sling, learning to make fire and her perfect aim. Before he could even protest, she reassured Aiden that she always missed around half of her shots and no one thought of her twice. She moved on to meeting Seventeen, how they had worked together to introduce medical care, had thought the pregnancy was going to be a success, only for Seventeen to die in front of her. She described having to watch the screening and then locking herself away with Kit. The only parts she left out were catching Luca slipping out of Rosa's bedroom and the evening with Samuel when she had told him about her inherited abilities.

When she had finished, Sofi was dabbing at her eye with a tissue and Nathan's mouth was hanging open.

They were all silent until Aiden stood and came around the table towards Elise. 'Can you show me the sling?'

Elise just laughed and pulled it out of her pocket; she carried it everywhere.

Up in the woods at the back of their house, the four of them stood in a loose semi-circle. They were wearing two layers of clothing and Nathan's stripy bobble hat had slipped to a jaunty angle. Aiden had already doubled back a couple of times to check they had not been followed.

Elise tested the weight of the few stones she had found amongst the fallen leaves. Her hands were almost numb from the cold, but she couldn't wear her mittens or she would lose dexterity. Bringing her hands to her mouth, she tried to breathe some life back into them. She eyed the three tins that Aiden had propped on top of a fallen log thirty metres away. They were spaced evenly apart and weighted with the earth he had packed inside them.

'They're very far away, Aiden. Perhaps we should move a bit closer,' Sofi signed, walking farther in.

Aiden looked over at Elise and she shook her head.

'Come back and stand behind me, or you might be mistaken for a tin,' Aiden responded, waving her over.

Nathan was clearly holding his breath; he was the only one who didn't have little puffs of air encircling him, so Elise thought she should get on with it before he passed out. The shattering crack boomed around them, twice as loud in the woods as it was in the pod, making Aiden and Sofi jump slightly. It was followed by the dull thud of the tin falling to the ground. Nathan jumped while waving his hands and was held back by his hood when he tried to run over to the tin to inspect it.

Elise loaded the sling again. Another shattering crack sounded, followed by the softer noise of a tin being shot off the log. Within a few slower circles of the sling, she had reloaded and knocked over the third can.

Out of the corner of her eye, she caught a flash; it was a grey rabbit, startled by the noise. Elise had never tried for a live animal before; the ones in the pod were too small to be worth eating and she didn't like the idea of killing for practice. She knew her parents would welcome the rabbit meat though, so she smoothly reloaded. Without hesitation, she released the tab at the rabbit scurrying for cover. Aiden ran over and Elise thought she must have missed, but she consoled herself that it was her first time aiming at something alive.

Aiden then bent over and when he stood, he was holding the rabbit by its back legs.

'Clean on the temple!' he shouted, while signing with one hand. 'I've never seen anything like it!'

Pride crossed his face, which Elise had never seen before.

Back in the house, Aiden busily skinned and prepared the rabbit.

'It's been years since I've done this,' he signed. 'Not since, well . . . not since the Rising.'

He was humming as he worked; for the first time in years, he looked full of life.

'Tell me about the Rising. You've never explained what happened,' Elise signed.

A look passed between her parents, but before Sofi could say anything, Nathan signed, 'I'm not going to bed; it's only four o'clock.'

He sat heavily on his chair and folded his arms.

'We both need to know,' Elise signed. 'We can't protect ourselves if we don't know the facts, where the danger lies and what the consequences are.'

She was surprised when Aiden turned to Sofi and signed, 'She's right. Ignorance won't help them.'

Sofi took a moment and nodded. 'Don't ever repeat a word outside of this house, Nathan, okay? Not even to Jada and Maddy.'

Nathan nodded with a solemnity that was fitting for the occasion. 'I promise.'

'It was nineteen years ago and your dad and I had just found out I was pregnant with you, Elise,' Sofi signed. 'Things were as bad as they could get that year. A new strain of meningitis was spreading through the production centres in Thymine Base and no one had enough Medi-stamps to buy the antibiotics to treat it.' She glanced at Nathan. 'People were dying. Even the healthy, strong ones. The Sapiens who recovered were immune, but they still had to watch people they loved die terrible, terrible deaths. Agonising for everyone.'

'Course, the Medius were okay,' Aiden signed, turning around from the kitchen counter. 'A few of them caught it too, but they got paid more, had the better jobs. So they just converted their spare stamps to Medi-stamps.'

Aiden glanced over at Sofi and started scrubbing his hands in the kitchen sink.

'You see, the Medi-stamps only had a month's expiry so no one could build up stocks of them,' Sofi signed. 'The Sapiens were getting desperate; a few had no one left to lose and the rest thought it might be them next. We'd heard rumours of riots in the other bases in the past. But there was no way for us to check the truth of it. Maybe they were made-up tales, but it helped to remember we weren't alone.

'It was a muggy summer's evening the night it began. They'd posted more guards around public buildings, but nothing had happened before then. Looking back, I don't think they could have predicted it, even now.'

Sofi stood and walked over to Aiden, who was still scrubbing his hands; she gently turned off the tap and held out a cloth, which he accepted. 'There was a widow who'd lost her husband years ago in an accident. Etta was her name. She'd been left to bring up four children by herself, on just her wages and whatever her neighbours could spare. We all knew Etta, of course; all our parents would help her out when they could. She was a nice lady, but she looked much older than she was. It was the pressure, you see, of being solely responsible for those children, never having any time to look after herself. It aged her terribly. She had completely grey hair, thick lines across her forehead and she was only forty-five.'

Sofi stayed standing by Aiden. They were both leaning against the kitchen counter, side by side.

'But she'd done it,' Sofi signed. 'She'd raised those children, and they'd all grown up healthy and strong. The oldest, Michael I think was his name, was about to leave school and start working at one of the production centres. It would have turned a corner in their lives, having another wage come in.

'But, of course, that never happened. She had nursed the three youngest, done everything she could, but they all died. One after the other. Only Michael was left and when he got sick, she couldn't bear it.'

Sofi glanced over at Nathan, who was still, trying to not get sent out of the room. 'She went to the Courthouse. Started begging and pleading with the guards to let her speak to a Potior. I suppose she thought that if she could only get to speak to one of them, she could tell them what had happened. Plead her case and ask for the antibiotics for Michael. The Medius guards were young—'

'*It was no excuse*,' Aiden signed. 'They should've shown some compassion.'

Elise glanced up at Aiden, willing him to direct his frustration away from her mum.

'Yes, you're right. But they were young, and that can often be dangerous when combined with a bit of newfound power,' Sofi signed. 'They got fed up with this old, tired-looking woman begging with them. I suppose it made them embarrassed as well, that she wouldn't be quiet, wouldn't go away. They saw it as a challenge to their fledgling authority. When she started tugging at their sleeves, one of them lost his temper. He hit her hard across the face with the back of his hand – he later called it self-defence – she lost her balance and toppled backwards down the stone stairs, cracked her head on the way. She died within minutes. They didn't even try to get her to hospital, just left her there.'

Elise sucked in her breath, imagining the blood trickling down the Courthouse steps.

'A few Sapiens saw what'd happened and word spread,' Aiden signed. 'We were scared and exhausted, but that didn't matter any more. That night, in the early hours of the morning, we all left our homes and streamed down into the central district. There were thousands of us, moving silently as one. I'd never seen anything like it and I probably never will again. I remember some Sapiens saying they'd never been down to the Inner Circle before. Can you imagine it? Twenty years old and never even left the Outer Circle . . .

'The riots went on for three days straight. The Potiors and Medius were overwhelmed. Some of the lower-grade Medius had even joined the Sapiens. They were fed up of being spoken down to, patronised, like the rest of us. We managed to take over most of the offices before they could get word out to the other bases.' Elise's dad rubbed his forehead. 'We knew they would come soon, though; they'd know that something was wrong when messages went unanswered. They couldn't lose the manufacturing base.

'We were at a stalemate. The Potiors and Medius had retreated out of most of the main buildings, but they still had the water treatment centre under their control. Looking back, we should've gone for that on the first day.' Aiden dried his hands with the cloth again before putting it down. 'We were low on water and people were panicking, terrified of having to drink the untreated water from the streams.'

'After a couple of days, one of the loudest, brashest Sapiens somehow managed to appoint himself leader,' Sofi signed, looking at Elise. 'You went to school with his son; Lewis Thetter, I think his name is.'

'That explains . . .' Elise mumbled under her breath, thinking of Holly's boyfriend.

'Adam Thetter and a small group of his closest friends went in there to negotiate. And a few hours later, they came out, proud as punch of securing a truce,' Sofi continued. 'Told us all what a good job they'd done, securing a change in the Medi-stamp system. They now wouldn't expire for five years.'

'All that for five-year Medi-stamps. *A thousand people* lost their lives in those riots,' Aiden signed. 'It *destroyed* whole communities. And Adam Thetter had the nerve to walk around as if he'd saved everyone. *It makes me want to—*'

Sofi touched his arm, but it was a while before it had the calming effect intended.

'Sorry,' Aiden signed after a moment. 'I just don't think they'd have done the same again, if they'd have known what they ended up fighting for.'

Sofi nodded in agreement. 'Of course, Adam persuaded most of the Sapiens that it was good deal. Said a tragedy like the one we'd been through would never happen again, as everyone could stockpile Medi-stamps. He was very charming, you see, very charismatic. Afterwards, they made us pay in other ways, tightening the surveillance. Said it was for our own good. And some people went missing, no questions asked. The Potiors kept their promise, though; they didn't try and change the Medi-stamps back.'

'I know Lewis Thetter,' Elise signed, pushing back her chair. 'Holly has started spending lots of time with him. He's got ideas of his own. Wants us to live separately from the Medius.'

'Oh stars, that idea has been around for years,' Sofi signed. 'Probably selling it as his own if he's anything like his dad.' She squeezed Aiden's hand. 'It's not one I personally agree with, but there are some pretty strong arguments on both sides.'

'What happened to Michael?' Nathan signed.

Sofi smiled at her son.

'He survived the sickness,' she signed, walking over to Nathan. 'After what happened to his mum, everyone dug deep and gave a spare ticket or two to him, until he had enough to convert to Medi-stamps for the antibiotics.

'In the days after the negotiation, there was chaos. The Potiors didn't know who'd lived and who'd died. He slipped away and left Thymine Base, and no one has heard from him since. We told the Potiors he'd died in the riots, crushed in a collapsing building, that the body was unrecognisable.'

Sofi glanced at Nathan. 'I'm sorry to say it, but he wouldn't have survived after leaving Thymine Base. He didn't have enough water to get to one of the other bases. It was his life, though, his choice to make. Perhaps he couldn't stay when he'd lost so much. It's so very sad; he would only have been fourteen.'

Elise thought about pushing for more information – they still hadn't told her what had happened to her aunt and uncle, and it had to be connected somehow, but she could see the strain on her parents' faces. These recollections had already taken their toll. She reluctantly decided to ask another time.

Before she left to return to the museum, she slipped into Nathan's room. She was pleased that his face was brighter than usual and, most importantly, it was clear of any unexplained bruises or marks.

'How're you doing, Nathan?' Elise signed.

'Good, thanks. I saw Maddy and Jada twice after school this week and we're going to build a rope swing from one of the trees today so that we have a base of operations. I'm teaching them to sign as well.'

'A base of operations, who came up with that idea?' Elise signed, leaning back on his bed.

'It was Jada. She's the oldest, so we made her the leader,' Nathan signed. 'I actually said that I'd meet them now. Do you think Mum will let me go?'

'I don't see why not. Just one thing, though; have the others at school started to leave you alone now that you have Jada and Maddy?'

'No one has done anything to me. And I haven't had to use my new blocking skills once, which is annoying,' Nathan signed, frowning.

Elise silently thanked the stars for Jada and Maddy and their knee-kicking abilities.

'I'm sorry I can't be back on Wednesday for your birthday, but I've got you this.' She pulled a neatly wrapped parcel out of her backpack.

'Can I open it now?' Nathan signed.

'That might be best. I don't know how Mum and Dad will feel about it.'

Elise watched as Nathan tore open the paper. She got the reaction she wanted when he pulled out the sling, grinning. She had asked Samuel to make it slightly shorter than her own, so it would be easier for Nathan to load and swing. She hugged him.

'Remember,' she signed, 'the key is lots of practice, but don't let anyone catch you doing it. You've the same reflexes as me, so you might have perfect aim too – and that needs to stay hidden. Even from Jada and Maddy. And if anyone catches you with it, tell them it's a skipping rope. Never let them find out it's a weapon.'

Winding her way along the near-empty pathways, Elise had already run halfway back to the museum when her thoughts were disturbed by the realisation that she was being followed. She could hear another set of feet a hundred metres behind her. Before she could decide whether to run faster or duck into one of the houses, she heard yet another join the chase; they were coming at her from both sides. Reasoning that she shouldn't jump to the worst conclusion, she decided to meet her followers head on.

Turning, she watched the lamplights flick on and off as the two figures drew closer. The lights were motion-sensitive and would only stay on for a few seconds as people passed underneath them. Closer and closer, the lamps flicked on and then abruptly switched off.

Peering into the darkness, she waited until she could see that the figures had their hoods pulled over their faces as they ran. Her right hand flitted over her jacket pocket, reassuring herself that the sling and some stones were easily accessible. When they skidded to a halt and lifted their faces to her, Elise frowned; it was Lewis Thetter and Holly. Instead of relief, she felt uneasy that they hadn't called out her name; they had wanted to scare her.

'Well, you sure can run,' Lewis said once he was breathing normally. 'We were beginning to worry. Hadn't seen you for a *long* time.'

'I've been busy.'

'If you say so,' Lewis said, looking her up and down. 'You haven't told anyone at the museum about our little chat?'

'No, of course not. I wouldn't do that to Holly,' Elise said, glancing at her. 'How've you been?'

'See, I told you . . .' Holly said, but she fell silent when Lewis twitched the fingers on his left hand and gestured towards Elise. Holly blinked and then turned to Elise. 'I've been good, been studying hard, and Lewis has been so patient with me. He's spent so much time making sure I understand the texts.'

'Have you thought any more about what we discussed?' Lewis asked, placing his arm over Holly's shoulder and pulling her towards him.

Holly smiled up at him and nuzzled her head into his chest.

Elise looked at them both before taking a deep breath. 'Yes, and I can't get involved. I don't know what you want me to do, but I think it's best it stays that way. I won't tell anyone what you showed me.'

'That's a pity,' Lewis said, his brow creasing. 'Perhaps we can do something to change your mind. Is it tickets you want? Turn them into Medi-stamps for your brother.'

'We don't need tickets at the moment, and my brother is fine as he is.'

'That's not what Holly told me.' Lewis absent-mindedly ran Holly's hair through his fingers.

Elise bristled and glared at him. 'I don't want your tickets and I don't want to hear about this again.'

'*Don't speak to him like that.*' Holly raised her head and shifted so she was standing in front of Lewis. 'He's only trying to help you, while helping us at the same time.'

Elise stared at Holly. There had been a time, even a couple of months ago, that she would have felt cowed by Holly's words, done anything to avoid arguing with her best friend.

'I don't believe that for a second,' she said. 'He only looks out for himself. Anyone can see that.'

The tendons in Holly's neck became pronounced. 'You're just a *Midder-lover* now that you've moved up to the museum.'

Lewis glanced between them.

'And you've completely lost yourself ever since you started worshipping him.' Elise nodded towards Lewis.

Holly raised her hand to slap Elise. Before it even got close to her face, Elise caught her arm and forced it back down. Holly looked at her hand in shock.

Elise stared at Holly. 'What's happened to you?'

'I think that's enough excitement for one evening,' Lewis interjected, watching the lamps flicker on the adjacent pathway.

'We might attract an audience.' He waved pleasantly at the people farther down the pathway who were drawing closer. 'Holly, come on now. We don't want to antagonise Elise if she's made up her mind.' He smiled at Elise. 'You know where to find us if you change it.'

Holly opened her mouth to respond, but then closed it and linked her arm with Lewis's.

Elise didn't turn her back on them until they were out of sight.

CHAPTER 15

Elise couldn't ignore them any longer; Luca had clearly beckoned her twice. Standing in the middle of the canteen, she fixed on her widest smile and pushed her way through the queues to sit at the only available table. She knew there was a good reason she never ate during normal serving hours.

'Nice of you to join us, Thanton,' he said. 'How's Kit? Georgina said you've had to spend more time with him.'

Elise had to lean in to hear him over the rumble of chatter from other tables. She couldn't help but stare; he had shaved all his baby curls off. She tried to concentrate on what he was saying, but other conversations kept leaking in, pulling her attention in different directions.

'He's not great. I think Seventeen's . . .' She trailed off, unsure how much she could say in the middle of the canteen. 'When do you hear about the Companion role for Thirty-Two?'

Elise tried to stop her eyes flicking over to Rosa, who was leaning back in her seat. Her long legs were draped over Luca's lap and she was wearing a very short skirt. Luca was idly running his thumb over her smooth calf. Rosa pulled herself up in her seat and Elise caught a flash of lilac underwear. She quickly looked away, hoping Rosa hadn't noticed. The situation was awkward enough without Rosa thinking that Elise was staring up her skirt.

'Any day now. Samuel thinks I should get it; there's no one else in the running anyway.'

He pushed his mashed potato around with a fork. Elise followed his gaze to his plate. He was shaping a face out of his mash with peas and carrots for eyes and a mouth.

'You'll get it; they'd be mad not to give it to you,' Rosa said, leaning forwards and squeezing Luca's knee. 'They know it's not your fault Seventeen died.'

Luca winced, but Rosa didn't notice and carried on. Luca stared at his plate, as if it demanded all of his attention. He carefully nudged two runner beans into position, eyebrows sloping downwards to a carrot nose until it was transformed into a cross food-face.

'And you might even get a promotion, get out of the Companion Department eventually, maybe some sort of lower management role. That reminds me, do you remember Eric from Engineering?'

Rosa wrapped her coil of blonde hair onto the top of her head and then, changing her mind, let it fall around her face. Elise shook her head in response. Luca didn't even look up.

'Really? Everyone knows Eric. You two need to leave your pods occasionally and mix with the real world.'

'I don't have a pod any more,' Luca said.

'You know what I mean. It's like trying to have a conversation with one of the displays sometimes.' Rosa looked over at Luca and cupped his chin in her hand, pulling his face around towards her. 'Eric's the tall, blond one who was promoted to Assistant to the Head of Freestanding Construction last week. He came to find me straight away to tell me the news . . .'

Elise tried to listen but then zoned out. Besides the odd encouraging smile, no response was required. She was worried about Kit and considering whether she should ask Luca to visit him. Mid-nod, she glanced over at Luca again. She couldn't stop staring at him; his shaved head made him appear older and more intimidating. Looking at him, she wouldn't think he was someone who shaped faces out of his food.

Luca glanced at Elise and their eyes met for a second; he gave her a half-smile and rolled his eyes. Elise knew then that he wasn't listening to Rosa either. Not wanting to be part of this game, she started to eat more quickly.

'. . . And that's when he said that he'd always loved me and he's been wanting to tell me for *years*. It's just rude. He's knows I'm with Luca,' Rosa said, smiling at him. 'It's just rude and . . . and *disrespectful*, don't you think, Elise?'

Elise was about to say that she thought it was badly timed rather than rude when Luca said, 'I think Harriet's coming over.'

For the first time, Elise was pleased to see Harriet. She craned her neck around. Rosa slipped her legs off Luca's knee and sat up on her seat.

No one was moving aside for Harriet; they were too caught up in their conversations. Elise could see her head bobbing up and down. Each time it popped up over someone's shoulder, she looked even more cross as she glared at Elise and Luca.

Elise sighed, remembering what Georgina had told her, and glanced over at Luca. 'We'd better go over. She'll explode if we keep on ignoring her.'

Luca grinned and shrugged, but Elise wasn't playing; she didn't like the familiarities that he was slipping back into. Without looking at him again, she stood and abandoned her food. Waving goodbye to Rosa, she pushed her way through the museum employees, promising herself she would never come back at lunchtime again.

Elise had never been in Harriet's office before. Images of the leaders crowded the walls, battling for space; some of the posters even overlapped. Behind Harriet's oversized desk, in pride of place, was a portrait of the Premier. Its positioning made it seem as if he were sitting on Harriet's shoulders, overlooking everything she did.

In the corner of the room was another, smaller desk that could only be described as a shrine. Clusters of framed photographs and certificates were lined up neatly: Level 2 in Worker Profiling; a Commendation in Interview Techniques (Day Course); a black-and-white photograph of Harriet standing stiffly on the steps of the museum with other senior staff members; Harriet waiting in line to shake hands with a visiting Potior from Adenine Base. Elise wouldn't have been surprised if she'd found a lock of Fintorian's hair in a keepsake box as well.

'I've asked you both here because some changes are going to be made in regard to the Neanderthal Project.'

Harriet leant back in her large, leather-upholstered chair and placed her hands on the armrests. Elise's attention was drawn to Harriet's sleeves, white, lacy ruffs that hung over her knuckles, one of which must have been dipped into her coffee that morning, as it was stained brown on the underside.

'Of course, it is unfortunate that Seventeen is no longer with us, but that is not a direct result of your actions, Luca. The museum recognises that, despite our normally strict policy on removing a Companion following the death of a Neanderthal.'

Elise glanced over at Luca, who was clasping his hands on his lap; his knuckles were turning the same shade as Harriet's lacy ruffs from the force of staying quiet.

'However, saying that, some changes have to be made. Lines have been crossed and boundaries have become blurred. We are concerned about where your allegiances lie. That goes for *both* of you. Your attachment to your charges, although useful in some respects, is also misguided. Instead of celebrating with the rest of the museum, you mourned the loss of one individual, one individual display amongst thousands.'

Elise could feel her anger bubbling and she pushed it down; it was not the time. Harriet would dismiss her in a second if she had a reason, and Elise couldn't leave Kit, especially not now he had become so withdrawn.

She distracted herself by staring up at the portrait of the Premier. He resided in Adenine and never left his base, unlike the other Potiors. He was rumoured to be over 120 years old, which made him one of the first Potiors to be created. A man of formidable presence, Elise realised he was not looking down at Harriet but instead straight ahead, a distant gleam in his turquoise eyes. He was stepping forwards, his long dress coat fluttering in the breeze; everything about the two-dimensional print suggested movement. He was looking to the future.

'Because of our growing concerns, we have decided to advertise for a new Companion for Thirty-Two,' Harriet concluded.

Luca opened his mouth to respond and Elise quickly touched his arm, willing him not to say anything. She could feel him trembling. She glanced at him and he snapped his mouth shut.

'Is there something you want to *say*, Luca?' Harriet said, with a half-smile.

Luca paused and Elise increased the pressure on his arm before taking her hand away. 'No . . . no, nothing . . .' Luca forced out.

Harriet looked disappointed. 'Good, well, in that case, we would want you to stay in the department to train the new Companion. And then we will find you work elsewhere, maybe the Maintenance Department. A change of environment might do you some good.'

Luca had turned a healthy shade of red and was trembling with the effort of keeping everything in; it was too much.

'What the f—?' he exploded, but he was cut off by an insistent knocking at the door.

Harriet tried to ignore it and looked pointedly at Luca, her eyes never leaving his face. Elise turned and stared at him, willing him to shut up; she knew that Harriet was searching for any excuse to dismiss him.

Luca plunged ahead. 'What do you people—?'

The knocking came again and even Luca was distracted. Harriet glanced towards the corner of the room and Elise realised there was a camera with them. Elise's eyes bulged as she stared at Luca, flicking her eyes over to the camera and back to Luca's face again, hoping he would understand.

'Oh, for stars' sake . . .' Harriet mumbled. 'Yes, what is it?' she called out. 'I'm in the middle of a meeting. Can you come back, please!'

The door burst open and Samuel half fell inside, only just grabbing the door handle to steady himself.

'Ah, it is the right room!' he said, straightening. 'I was worried I was going to miss the meeting, didn't realise it had been rearranged to today.'

'Yes, well, I thought it best to hold it as soon as possible. No point keeping them in the dark,' Harriet said, pulling herself up in her seat.

'Yes, yes, very wise,' Samuel said, looking around him with interest.

He ambled up to the desk in the corner and picked up one of the frames.

'I was just telling Luca that he won't be Thirty-Two's new Companion. I think he had something to say in response,' Harriet said, resting her eyes on Luca. 'Or maybe Elise has something she wants to say,' she continued, shifting her gaze.

'Distinction in Refresher Course on Performance Review,' Samuel read out. 'Commendable, very commendable, such dedication to your calling.'

He smiled at Harriet and then up at the portrait of the Premier.

'Yes, well, we all have to keep our skills sharpened. If you don't mind me asking, though, Mr Adair, why are you here? I am sure that I can manage this by myself.'

'Oh, I just wanted to update you on a recent development. Fintorian has agreed to Luca becoming my new assistant. I'm so caught up with the Neanderthal Project, I fear I am neglecting the other displays.'

Elise's face remained still, but inside she was cheering Samuel. She wondered whether her nose had moved and given her away. Luca was not so guarded; his face broke out into a wide, tooth-showing grin.

'I have not been told of this. It is most irregular!' Harriet said, her hands darting up to her tightly curled hair and patting it, checking it was still in place.

'I do apologise. I came as quickly as I could, but without knowing where the meeting was taking place . . . it took me a few tries.' Samuel carefully placed a photograph of Harriet at her graduation, robes trailing on the ground, back down on the table. 'So, if you don't mind, I am going to have to whisk my new assistant away. Important Collections business to be getting on with. Elise, will you join us? I want to talk to you about training the new Companion when they arrive.'

Elise glanced over at Harriet, whose mouth was noiselessly opening and closing. Head down, she quickly followed Samuel and Luca out of the room, careful to close the door quietly behind her.

'He is honestly the worst assistant anyone could imagine,' Samuel said, making the sign for 'hungry' to Bay, who was sitting contentedly on Georgina's knee.

Luca had been Samuel's assistant for nearly two months and Elise would regularly catch them bickering in the corridors.

At over three months old, Bay could already sit with some help, but she had taken to howling with frustration when they didn't know what she wanted. Elise was kneeling on the floor, feeding her small spoonfuls of mashed carrot every time Samuel made the sign for 'hungry'. Repetition was the key, Samuel said, but Elise was sure Bay must be full of carrot.

'He has no interest in cataloguing or categorisation,' Samuel continued, the frustration clear in his voice. 'Do you know he mixed up oak bolete mushrooms with meadow waxcap mush-rooms? I mean, really, they look nothing alike!' Samuel sighed and shook his head. 'It's always the same with the assistants: "Can I pat the dire wolves? When will we name the koalas?" What I want to know is, why does no one care about the classification of fungi?'

Georgina tightened the bow around Bay's hair, which was growing thick like her mother's. The pineapple leaves were longer and bounced every time Bay moved her head.

'And then there's that Rosa girl who keeps on popping up everywhere,' Samuel said, oblivious to Georgina looking over to Elise. 'Whenever she gets overexcited, she tries to hug me.' He switched to the sign for 'thirsty'. 'I don't like it. I never hug people, so why does she think I want her to do it to *me*?'

Elise dutifully gave Bay a sip of milk; she scrunched her eyes shut in response.

'Annoying as that may be,' Georgina said, 'you did the right thing by keeping him with us. You know that.'

Samuel looked up and stopped making the sign for 'thirsty'. 'I know. And he is good with the animals. Last week, one of the barriers failed again and the entire dodo population would have been wiped out if he hadn't rounded them up so quickly. They were heading for the giant sloth display, would have been crushed in a second; they really are the stupidest of animals.'

Georgina bounced Bay on her knee more briskly. The baby scrunched her eyes up in delight.

'It's not really Luca I'm annoyed with, if I'm honest,' Samuel said. 'There's something going on that's making me uneasy. Try as I might, Fintorian won't tell me what he has planned. Top secret, he says. I know it must involve the Neanderthals, but he won't tell me a thing.'

Elise looked up, still holding the bottle of milk.

'What do you think it is?' she said, unable to keep the worry from her voice. 'Is it to do with Kit or Bay?'

Georgina pulled Bay closer to her. 'They don't want to move Bay, do they?'

Samuel stared at them both. 'I doubt it, but I just don't know. All Fintorian will tell me is that it's a new direction he wants to take the display in. He won't tell me any more.'

They all looked glumly at one another. They were just about recovering from the loss of Seventeen and Elise didn't think they could take another.

Bay peered at each of their faces, all of them lost in their thoughts and not paying her any attention. But instead of howling for some more milk she touched her throat. All three of them looked at her with surprise and applauded. Elise leant over and gave her another sip of milk. She may have just signed her first word.

'How many other Neanderthals are there?' Kit signed.

Elise had slipped into Kit's pod to tell him the news that Bay might have just signed her first word, hoping that it would interest him. He had barely spoken to Elise in a week and had started to pick at his food. The only thing he continued to take an interest in was practising with his spear, so Elise had cut down working on her sling and instead watched him and asked questions while he practised. She was careful not to actually spar with him, as she knew Fintorian would not approve; it always came down to the 40,000-year rule. Following her meeting with Harriet, she knew her hold on the job was tenuous.

Elise looked at Kit, trying to read his unchanging features. 'Are you sure you want to know? Would it not be easier if we didn't talk about what's outside the museum?'

She stared at him, waiting for his response.

He met her gaze. 'No. I need to know. It helps. When you told me about Seventeen, it made her passing more real, but I did not feel so alone.'

'If you're sure.' Elise waited for Kit to nod before she continued. 'As far as I know, there are fourteen altogether, including you and Bay.'

'Have you met them?'

'No, Sapiens don't get to move bases like the Medius and Potiors. I've never left Thymine. Samuel would've met them, as most are in Guanine, where you used to be.'

'Are they older or younger than me?'

'I think some are older but most are younger.'

'Why are there only fourteen left?'

'Are you sure you want to know?' He nodded. 'A lot of the older ones. They're not with us any more. They were too isolated, had no one, not even a Companion. It was too much for them. It would be too much for anyone. I'm so sorry.'

Kit stared up to the clear winter sky and didn't reply.

CHAPTER 16

Samuel had been right to be concerned. Only a week later, Elise and Kit were standing in the sunny patch of grass by the pod door when it unexpectedly opened. But it wasn't Samuel or Luca; instead, Fintorian stepped through the door. He had not been into the pod since Seventeen died, but sometimes Elise would catch him watching them from the viewing platform. She stopped mid-swing and the stone fell out of her sling. Kit pulled the spear to his side and stared blankly at their guest.

'Please, do carry on. I've had the pleasure of observing you these past few weeks and I thought it was about time I saw it at ground level,' Fintorian said, radiating his usual self-assurance.

Elise looked at her feet, not because he dazzled her any more, but because she didn't want him to suspect anything had changed. She fixed on the passive expression that had protected her in the past and glanced at Kit. He just stared back at her, his face uninterpretable as always. Silently, he began jabbing and blocking as he normally did, although perhaps with a little less gusto. Elise followed his cue, loaded her sling and took aim at the cans set up thirty metres away. She could barely see them but knew she could hit each one in a row. With a thundering crack, she released the sling and skimmed the top of a tin. Kit was used to the noise, but she thought Fintorian jumped a little.

She loaded the sling again and this time missed. The third time, she knocked the can over. Fintorian applauded, despite her poor show.

'Wonderful, wonderful . . . They are going to love this . . .' he said, nodding to them and closing the door behind him.

Without a word to Elise, Kit laid down his spear and went to his sleeping area, where he stayed for the rest of the day.

Fintorian kept popping in at random times during the next two weeks. It made Elise edgy, as she never knew when he was coming. Even when he wasn't there, she was careful to regularly miss her shots, aware that she was being watched. On the third visit, Fintorian asked her to show him how she made a fire. She brought all of the equipment over and set it up. The pressure of having him standing over her made her hands shake; it took her thirty strikes of the flint before she could get the spark to hit the dry grass. She leant and blew, and it promptly went out.

She had to start all over again and could feel Fintorian's eyes never leave her. The second time, she was able to kneel in time to blow on the little flame until it caught. She fed it more dried grass and then some small twigs until it was strong enough for her not to have to watch it. She glanced around at Fintorian, who tapped on his screen.

'Seven minutes, thirty-six seconds. We might have to aim for a bit quicker than that, Elise. Try and get it to under five minutes if you can.'

Her heart sank when he told her to stop practising with the sling and instead concentrate on her fire-making over the next week.

She spent the next day dutifully practising. It now took her just over five minutes. But that wasn't quick enough and she wasn't sure she could do it with Fintorian peering over her shoulder.

That evening, she and Kit sat by the riverbank beside the largest fire Elise had ever made. She tried to speak with Kit about his training, but he was subdued and barely responded except to sign that he was tired and going to sleep early. Elise could only watch as he padded over to his sleeping area. He hadn't bothered to eat the broth she had made him. Elise finally admitted to herself that Kit was in a worse condition than when she had first arrived at the museum. All her progress was unravelling.

Determined to find out why Fintorian was paying such close attention to them, Elise slipped through the corridors to Samuel's office. When she was about to round the final corner, she heard voices ahead.

'When will this take place?'

Elise froze and pressed herself against the wall, recognising Samuel's voice.

'Soon. I'm still working out the timings.' Fintorian's rich tones were unmistakable.

'And what if she says no?'

'Then we will find someone else who will say yes.' Fintorian was smiling as he spoke. 'Stars, Samuel, she is not indispensable . . . I have observed that you seem to take an unusual interest in her. Not another one of your projects, is she? Instead of the Neanderthal Project, is it now the Sapien Girl Project? Want to test how much they've developed in the last forty thousand years?'

Fintorian chuckled and Samuel did not respond. 'In that case, it is fortuitous that we are putting her on display with Twenty-One. You can publish your findings then.'

Elise felt sick as the thoughts tumbled through her mind. They wanted to put her on display in the main museum with Kit. Could they even do that? She would refuse. But then she would lose her job. She needed more information, but after what she had heard, she never wanted to give Samuel the satisfaction of asking him another question.

Elise's attention snapped back to the present.

'When can I tell them?' Samuel's voice was steady as always.

'Whenever you think is best. I have other matters to attend to now, so I will see you tomorrow.'

Still pressed against the wall, Elise's heart hammered when she heard steps coming down the corridor towards her. She was in the wrong section of the museum for this time of night – had no reason to be here. Her mind raced as she tried to think of a valid excuse.

'I thought I heard someone,' Samuel said.

Elise's shoulders slumped in relief that it wasn't Fintorian.

Samuel searched Elise's face; she avoided his gaze. 'I only found out today. I promise.'

'I've got no reason to believe you.'

'It may not be as bad as it sounds. You would still be Kit's Companion and continue the same as you have been for months now, but Fintorian wants to advertise it as Neanderthal and early Sapien . . . living side by side.'

Elise snorted, not wanting to hide her indignation.

'You can still leave at night, of course, sleep in your own room, visit your family on a Sunday. But during the day, Fintorian will want you and Kit to continue practising with your weapons, making meals and whatever else he thinks is reflective of the time.'

Elise glared at Samuel. 'And I suppose there will be a Midder in the pod next to us holding a screen and managing a small department. Maybe a Supe in the next pod along, running the water treatment facility.'

'It's unfair, I know that, but . . .'

Elise couldn't listen to any more. She turned away from him. 'Elise, wait.'

Samuel grabbed her hand and she stared down at it in shock. His eyes followed hers and he also looked confused. They were both silent as he gently released her hand. Without another word, Elise continued down the corridor without looking back.

'I've found out what's going on,' Elise signed, kneeling next to Kit's sleeping mat.

Kit took one look at her face and sat upright. 'What's wrong? You're not leaving, are you?'

'Fintorian wants to make the Neanderthal display open to the public. It will mean us moving to the main section of the museum. Both of us. He wants us to practise all of our training together in front of the visitors. I will still get to leave in the evenings.'

Elise waited for his response, unsure how he would react.

Kit took a moment to think before signing, 'You don't have to do it. They will find someone else.'

Elise thought for a moment. She could just walk away. Leave the museum tonight and go back to her parents' home. Begin a normal life and wait for this all to fade into a distant memory.

Shrugging, she tried to smile. 'We've come this far. I'm not leaving now.'

For the first time in weeks, Kit scrunched his eyes at Elise and she knew she had made the right decision; she couldn't let her friend down.

Elise had been sitting on the bench watching the chameleon for an hour. In all that time, one fly had been caught and it had made two readjustments of its legs on the branch. It still fascinated her, though.

'I thought I would find you here,' Samuel said. 'Well, I went to the canteen first, but this was my second guess. Can I sit?'

Elise just nodded and shifted on the bench to make room.

Samuel sat and rested his head in his hands, mirroring Elise, who was staring straight ahead at the display cabinet. 'I'm sorry this has happened; it might not be as bad as you think, though. I've had glimpses of the pod Fintorian has been working on and it makes Kit's current one look like a hovel.'

Elise didn't raise her head. 'We don't care about the pod.'

'I know, I know. I'm sorry. I just don't want you to leave.'

'So you can keep on testing how much my inferior Sapien brain can absorb? It must make you feel like the benevolent Midder having me hang on your every word,' Elise said calmly without turning her head.

'What?' Samuel said, staring at her. 'You don't believe that, do you?' When Elise didn't respond, he crouched at her side so that he was peering up at her face. 'I don't think of you as any different to me.'

Elise laughed. 'That can't be true. Every other Medius does. Our whole world is built on our differences. We're separate species, after all.'

Samuel closed his eyes, clearly listening for the hum of minute wings. He then took off his glasses and, still crouched next to Elise, looked up at her. Elise did not flinch from the intensity of his gaze, waiting for him to speak.

'A couple of months ago, in this room, you trusted me with something that you'd never told anyone outside of your family and closest friends. I want to do the same in return.' He lowered his voice. 'What I am about to say, though, is not something that would just have me transferred into the Protection Department. They would expel me from the base.'

Elise stared down at Samuel, allowing him to continue without interruption.

'I have never said this to anyone else in this museum and I trust you'll never repeat it to your family, Georgina, Luca. To anyone. Or it will mean both our downfalls.'

'I promise,' she said eventually.

'Neanderthals and Sapiens are not different species of humans; they are actually sub-species of human. The next branch down. They are more closely related than you are taught. As you've learnt from the time you've spent with Kit, belonging to another sub-species doesn't mean they are so different. In fact, when Sapiens and Neanderthals lived in close proximity, thousands of years ago, they had regular, ah . . . relations with each other. There is clear evidence of their DNA mixing with Sapiens.' Samuel looked flustered but Elise didn't attempt to make it easier for him. 'What I mean is, there were common incidents of them having children together. Sapien descendants in Zone 3 still have small amounts of Neanderthal DNA. If they were different species, they wouldn't be able to have children together. Sub-species means they can mate and have fertile children—'

'Okay, I understand.'

Elise didn't know where Samuel was going with this, but it was starting to sound like another instance of him imparting his invaluable knowledge. She decided she would give him two more minutes and then leave.

'There are some of us who've been fortunate enough to have the opportunity to learn about genetics and taxonomy at the universities in Guanine Base. This has enabled us to discredit what we've been taught. Discredit it in private, of course.

'Following the Pandemic, nearly as many people died from starvation as they did from the virus. Food production and distribution had ground to a halt. In the cities, there were too many people to survive on what they could scavenge. In the countryside, most people didn't have the necessary skills to forage or hunt. Generally, it was only the ones who already lived on the outskirts of society that survived. And also the very wealthy, who stored reserves of food and could afford to hire security to protect it.

'The ones who survived understood that they wouldn't last through another onslaught, so they started tweaking the DNA of the next generation. Just a little to begin with, to make them resistant to diseases, but then it snowballed. An elite group emerged who decided that genetic engineering should only be for the few. Another generation passed and the Medius and Potior came, so highly designed that they seemed impossibly removed. Beyond anyone's dreams. But that doesn't mean the Medius and Potior are separate human species or even sub-species.'

Elise stared at him, then allowed herself a question. 'Then what are they?'

'They're just Sapiens with a lot of selective tweaking. That doesn't make them a separate species. It's like saying someone with brown hair is a different species to someone with red hair. It's just a way of dividing the Sapiens and Medius, setting them against each other.'

Elise searched Samuel's face, unsure what to say.

Samuel smiled up at her. 'So you see, I don't think of you as a different species. Because I know that you're not.'

Samuel leant farther in; he was so close now that Elise could feel the warmth from his skin. 'But that doesn't mean there aren't more species of human to come. For the last ten years, they have been working on splicing animal DNA with human. All the most desirable qualities of nature's vast imagination mixed in with the Potiors. And if that happens – when that happens – they will not be simply another species. They will be an unknown quantity altogether.'

Elise walked around in a daze for the rest of the evening, weighed down by the new knowledge that she had promised not to share with anyone. Everything slid into place, as if she had been given the key to a coded message. Who had taught her who the separate species were? Who had come up with those classifications? Why was she not allowed to continue her education past sixteen?

The next morning, when she arrived at Kit's pod, she realised he was not in his usual place. It was definitely 6.30 a.m., so that meant he would have been up for at least half an hour. By now, he should have collected the mint for his breakfast tea; he would normally be sitting by the riverbank waiting for her to make a fire. His routine was like clockwork. Standing by the stream, she looked around and her heart thumped. She glanced up at the viewing platform; there was no one watching them for her to signal.

She pushed farther into the foliage until she reached the densest part, where the bushes covered her. She could barely see the sky. Uninvited images flashed through her mind; she should never have told Kit about the move to the main museum without Samuel there. In her eagerness to prove her loyalty to him, she had failed him, had given him the final slice of information that broke him.

Without warning, a hand grabbed at her from below, pulling her down. She was about to cry out when another hand circled around her mouth. Lying on the ground, she tried to reach for her sling, for anything, but she couldn't move. They were too strong. She was locked down. Struggling madly, all she could do was lurch from side to side, unable to free either her arms or legs.

The person moved around from behind her. To her horror, it was Kit.

Her eyes bulged as she tried to comprehend what he was doing.

One arm still holding her down, he signed, 'Shhh . . . I won't hurt you.' He then gently released her. Before she could sit up, his hands moved in a flurry as he started to sign. 'We have only two minutes before they realise we're not here and the cameras come and find us. Sorry, but I need us in cover.'

'What are you doing? You scared me to death,' Elise signed, her hands shaking.

Pulling herself up, she realised that she was literally sitting in a bush – thick leaves covered her on all sides. Kit was kneeling next to her, his face about an inch away from hers.

'It was the only way I could think of. Sorry, but I need your help. I want to get out of here.'

'What, out of the pod? They'll be moving you to a new one soon anyway.'

'No, out of Thymine. I want to find the other Neanderthals and see if I can help them. I thought that if I did what they wanted, stayed calm, never showed anger or annoyance, I would eventually live with others like me. I never met Seventeen. I will never meet Thirty-Two. I can't do this any more. They will never let me go.'

Elise just stared at him, unsure what to say.

Eventually, she signed, 'Do you have a plan?'

Kit stared at her. 'How can I have a plan? I don't even know what is past the pod door. That is why I need you.'

With that, he pushed himself up and left her sitting on the ground.

They tried to carry on as normal for the rest of the day, but Elise was terrified that someone would come in at any moment and ask what they had been doing at 6.37 a.m. No one did.

Before she left in the evening, she signed to Kit, 'I'll be back tomorrow morning.'

Lying on her sleeping platform, staring at her pod walls, Elise thought of what Kit had asked. She tried to be sensible. She weighed up the risk to herself and her family. If she were caught, the repercussions would be devastating. Believing she had made her decision, her mind drifted forwards to the next few days, weeks, months, to what Fintorian had planned for her and Kit. She realised that she was fooling herself if she thought she had any real choice. She might be able to walk around parts of Thymine Base, but in reality she just had a larger cage than Kit. One that was going to become increasingly smaller once Fintorian had his way. But Kit had given her the power to make a choice that Fintorian had no knowledge or control of. If she was careful, asked Samuel for his assistance straight away, then maybe she could help Kit without being caught.

At exactly 6.30 a.m., she crossed the stream. Kit wasn't there. Pushing her way through to his sleeping area, she paused and let her body go limp. A hand shot out and, without thinking, she batted it away, blocking the second attempt too. She stepped quickly to her right and sat in the bush.

'There will be no more of that; you'll give me a heart attack,' she signed to Kit, who was nursing his arm.

'Sorry,' he signed. 'Have you decided if you will help me?'

'Yes, I will help you get out of Thymine Base, but no farther. I'm sorry, but I can't leave my family. But we will need more than just me. It has to be Samuel as well. Do you agree?'

'Yes, I want him to know too, but I can't speak to him. He's never here this early. I don't know whether he will help, but I can't just leave without him knowing. It would be wrong.'

'Good. Give me a few days to think about what to do and I'll speak to Samuel. This is going to need a lot of planning.'

*

The next morning, Fintorian came into the pod. Elise took one look at him and fixed on her protective mask. He wasn't alone; there were two men with him from the viewing platform, both in long white coats. He knew. He must know. They shouldn't have met two days in a row; Elise felt so stupid for taking such a risk.

She stared at her feet and waited for him to speak. Her body buzzed with adrenaline, preparing for what would come next.

'Ah, my two star attractions. Come over here, if you will,' Fintorian said, leaning against the pod door. 'I expect that Samuel has told you by now that you will be moving over to the main museum shortly.'

They walked over to Fintorian, only lifting their heads briefly to nod.

'Well, we've had some most excellent news. My esteemed colleague, the Head of Guanine Base's Museum of Evolution, is coming to visit us next week. He has heard all about our plans and wants to see them in action.'

Elise did not like where this was going.

'I have, therefore, decided to move you both to the main museum in two days, so that you can settle in.'

Elise's heart sank. Two days wasn't enough time; she hadn't even spoken to Samuel. Once Kit was in the main museum, they would tag him. At least, in this pod, he could theoretically walk out of the door without being repelled backwards by an invisible barrier.

She willed them to leave so she could find Samuel straight away. She had to tell him what was happening, see if he could delay the move.

'To that end, there is a bit of housekeeping to attend to.'

Elise glanced up and froze as one of the men pulled out a syringe from the pocket of his white coat. He took two steps over to Kit and smoothly injected him in the neck.

'There, much better,' Fintorian said, looking at Kit. 'We don't want someone stealing you away now, do we?'

CHAPTER 17

Elise raced over to Kit, who had already sunk to the ground. She tried to barge the man in the white coat away from him, but he wouldn't budge. He glared at her. He was so oversized that he didn't seem to have a neck, just thick bands of muscled shoulders with a turnip-shaped head perched on top. He was still holding the needle, which he pointed at Elise, glancing towards Fintorian for approval.

Elise felt in her back pocket for her sling and started to pull it out. She paused, though, when she heard Fintorian call out.

'No need to fuss, Elise. He'll be fine in the morning. It just takes some time to work its way into the right spot and the sedative in the injection helps with that.' Fintorian looked amused, still leaning against the pod door. 'Come with me, Benjamin. We are needed elsewhere; lots to do before next week.'

Benjamin appeared disappointed. He mouthed, 'Soon,' at Elise. Then, with a smirk, he sauntered over to Fintorian, who patted him on the back as he passed. Elise swung around and positioned herself so she was between them and Kit, not moving until the pod door shut.

Bending, she pulled at Kit's tunic so she could inspect his neck. There was a trickle of blood from a large puncture wound. Whatever the tracker contained, it was clear Kit's body didn't want it inside him; his neck was already swelling and inflamed. She pulled his head around and his eyes rolled over to meet hers. They had lost all of their usual alertness.

'Come on, Kit,' she signed. 'I want to get you back to your sleeping mat, but you're going to have to help me by standing.'

Kit rolled his eyes over to the far end of the pod in response.

Elise tucked his arm over her shoulders and Kit squeezed his eyes shut. She could only hope that he had understood her; there was no way she could lift him by herself. He grimaced and started to push himself up with his other arm, his fist digging into the grass. Elise took the strain as well and heaved upwards with everything she had. Her legs were shaking with the effort – she thought she was going to collapse under his weight at one point – but she managed to get him to a standing position. He took a tentative step, his arm still around Elise's shoulder. At first, he couldn't remember how to lock his leg when it was straight and Elise felt him buckling next to her. She knew that if he fell, she would have no other choice but to bring the mat to him. As if reading her thoughts, Kit surged forwards and together they stumbled through the pod. Elise understood his sense of urgency; he wanted to be in his own sleeping area, where he felt safer, rather than exposed in the open grass.

It took them half an hour, and they nearly toppled into the stream, but they made it. Dripping in sweat, Elise found a reserve of energy when she saw his shelves with the carvings. She tried to lower him to his sleeping mat, but halfway down the effort was too much – they collapsed.

Kit rolled his eyes round at Elise and then over to his shelf. Elise smiled and pulled back the covers from his sleeping mat. She heaved his legs around and under the end of the furs. Leaving his arms out, she drew the covers over him and tucked them around his body like her mum would do for her when she was ill. She then took one of Kit's giant hands in hers and held it until he fell asleep.

As she watched his shallow breathing, her mind whirred with what to do next. She didn't want to leave him to wake up alone, but she was desperate to find Samuel. Torn, she felt alone and overwhelmed. Giving herself a mental shake, she decided to take it step by step; she would start with a fire.

Once it was crackling, she ran around the pod picking vegetables for a broth. Without any preparation, she just threw them all into the pan of treated water and hung it over the fire. When it had been bubbling for half an hour, she poured it into a bowl and placed it on Kit's shelf, hoping he would see it. She then put a cup of treated water next to his mat, checked on him one last time and sprinted through the pod to the steel door, pleading to the stars that Fintorian hadn't locked her in.

She was about to pull the door open when she realised she was making a mistake. She couldn't go out into the museum flustered, her chest pounding. Cameras would be drawn to her. Resting her head against the door, she willed her body to calm; she thought again of how much she needed Samuel. He would know what to do; she just had to get to him in a way that didn't draw any attention. She concentrated on the coolness of the metal door against her forehead and let her body calm itself.

Once she felt in control, she pulled at the door, grimacing as she prepared herself to find it locked. It swung open, but it was too early to celebrate; Shauna Thinckle, her mouth-breathing neighbour, was leaning against the wall on the other side.

'Where you goin'?' Shauna said, pushing herself away from the wall.

'What are you doing *here*?'

'New security detail. They've hired more of us to watch the place. I asked for this post,' Shauna said, smirking.

'Congratulations. I'm sure you're very pleased with yourself.' Elise stepped around her.

Shauna stepped sideways and blocked Elise's path. 'I said . . . *where you going*?'

Looking directly at Shauna, Elise could see right into her mouth; a brown film of coffee coated her tongue.

Elise sighed; she did not have time for this. 'I'm going to the canteen for lunch, so move out of my way.'

'Maybe I won't let you go. Maybe you'd better get back into your little cage with your *Ned friend*.'

Elise had no idea what Shauna's instructions were, but she was going to have to take a gamble.

She looked Shauna in the eye and kept her voice calm and low. 'You haven't been here for even one day, and I'm betting you've at least a week's probation. You've no idea how things work around here. The Potiors have big plans for me and Twenty-One and they won't like it if you get in my way.' Elise pulled herself up. 'They would have hired ten of you this week, but there's only one Companion, so *get out of my way.*'

Shauna hesitated and Elise knew she had been right: she had no mandate to keep her in the pod. Before Shauna had time to think, Elise pushed past her and casually strolled down the corridor without turning around. She listened for footsteps, but none came.

Once Elise turned the corner, she leant up against the wall. She couldn't go running around the museum searching for Samuel; he could be anywhere. It was lunchtime; she knew where Luca would be.

Pushing her way through the throngs queuing for their free food, for the first time, she was grateful there were so many. Their loud chatter and collection of heartbeats would distract following cameras. She scanned the canteen and stopped. Samuel was sitting at a table with Luca and Rosa. As soon as he saw her, he jumped up, leaving his tray, and pushed his way over.

'I thought you might come here to find Luca. I've just heard they're moving you in two days and they've brought more security in. It's not safe in my office or Kit's pod. Are you okay?'

Elise had to stop herself from hugging him; she knew he would hate that. 'I'm fine. Where can we go?'

Standing by herself in the nocturnal exhibit, Elise listened to the squeals of fear mixed with delight coming from the Medius school children. They were clustered around the different glass windows, peering at the collection of snakes, lizards and spiders. She could only just make out the round shadow of their heads; the corridors were pitch-black, with little windows of artificial moonlight to allow the visitors to see the night-time habits of each creature. It was still the middle of the day outside, but to this collection, it was the early hours of the morning, unaware of the trick that had been played on them.

It was the perfect place to meet. Outside, there were teeth and claws that could kill any one of the children in a second. But it was in here, in the dark, that their fluttering pulses were really raised.

She felt someone next to her and peered into the gloom to make out their shape, even their height.

They leant in closer. 'It's me. Don't worry. Calm thoughts, remember?'

She smiled. In hushed tones, she explained what had happened that morning, how they had already injected Kit with the tracker.

Samuel waited patiently. 'It was wrong of them to do it in that way, but you knew it was going to happen. They would have tagged him once he moved into the main museum anyway.'

'That's not the problem, though; well, it is the problem really. You see, there's more.' Elise took a deep breath. 'It's Kit; he wants to leave. I said I'd help and now I can't get him out. He needs you.'

Elise could hear Samuel's sharp intake of breath. The silence was excruciating. She couldn't see his face to decipher his thoughts.

'Is that what he really wants? Are you sure it wasn't just a passing comment?' Samuel finally said; Elise could hear the desperation in his voice.

'He lay in wait for me in the undergrowth. Pulled me down, covered my mouth so I couldn't move or breathe, just so that we wouldn't be seen by the cameras. I think he's given it some thought.'

'Yes, well, it would seem that is the case. Look, of course I'll help, if that's what he really wants. I suspected this might happen. But it's going to take weeks, if not months, of careful planning. I've not only got to think about how to get us out of the museum, but also decide where to take him afterwards. Tell him to hold on. For the moment, you have to carry on as normal, both of you.'

Elise knew he was right. 'Could you do one thing for me now?'

'Of course, anything.'

Elise sensed Samuel take a step closer to her. He was so near, they were almost touching.

'Can you put in a request to move the new guard to another area of the museum and swap her for another one? I know her from back home and she hates me, tried to lock me back in the pod.'

'It's done. I'll get her moved to the dinosaur display at the other end of the museum – you'll never have to see her again.'

Samuel left first and Elise waited half an hour before emerging from a different exit. When she got back to Kit's pod, Shauna had already gone and a six-foot bone-breaker was in her place. Elise nodded at the new guard, who eyed her suspiciously then nodded back once her identification worked on the pod door. Elise hoped for the cordial relationship to continue.

Back in the pod, she found Kit was still asleep. She nudged him gently, but his eyes didn't flicker; he was going to be out for the rest of the day. Her sling would shatter any peace he might get, so she sat next to him quietly until it went dark.

Over the next two days, Elise only left Kit's side to bring him food and tea. The first day he was still groggy, but by the second his strength had returned. He was quieter, though, if that was possible, and started absent-mindedly touching his neck at the site of the injection.

On the morning of the second day, Elise had used Kit's sleeping mat to roll up his few possessions; the carvings were wrapped in a hide for additional protection. She tied the roll with strong reeds and placed it by the door. She was determined it was coming with them. She then set off to find Kit, who had wandered off an hour ago.

Elise faltered when she first saw him; he was standing in the middle of the stream on one of the stepping stones, gazing into the water. Her mind flicked back to the first Neanderthals to be revived. It was only a few feet deep, but Elise knew she wouldn't have the strength to pull him out if he didn't want her to. She crossed the stepping stones and held firmly on to Kit's hand, something she had only done once before. He turned to her and his normally blank face revealed something; he looked defeated. Gently tugging his hand, she guided him over the stepping stones and they sat next to the stream, where they had spent the most time in each other's company.

Still gazing at the water, Kit signed, 'I don't remember coming here. I only remember my pod in Guanine Base. It was the same as this one. I don't know what is outside the door.'

Elise looked up at Kit thoughtfully. 'First, you'll step out into the corridors. Most of them feel dark and confined; they're all grey. Once we get through those, we'll arrive at the main museum, which is the opposite of the gloom of the corridors. It's full of light and filled with plants and trees like your pod. There are so many different animal calls, you'd think it would be overwhelming, but it's not. They work in harmony and that makes it peaceful. You can smell all of the flowers and pine trees. The ceiling is made of glass, so at night you can see the stars. I think you'll like it; you might not feel so contained.'

Elise stopped when she heard the pod door open. They glanced at each other and, without a word, stood and walked over to the door. Her heart sank when she saw Benjamin come in first, then another white-coat, followed by Fintorian. Elise bent and picked up Kit's hand-tied roll of possessions; it was so light she could carry it under one arm.

She raised her head to look up at Fintorian. 'We're ready.'

'Good. I think you will like your new home. It's exceeded even what I thought possible,' Fintorian said, smiling pleasantly. 'I trust that no further sedation is required?' Kit nodded his response. 'Good. I want you in peak condition for the opening.'

Elise hung back and watched as Kit stepped forwards. But when she tried to move to his side, she was blocked by Benjamin and the other white-coat, who positioned themselves to either side of him. Elise was forced to walk behind them. She stuck close, though, determined that Kit would know she was there.

When they stepped out of the pod door, Kit stopped and looked around him. Twenty white-coats lined the walls and a team of eight security guards were waiting at either end of the corridor. Elise kept her face still, trying to convey that this was normal. As they moved down the corridor, with Fintorian leading the way, the white-coats peeled away from the walls to follow. The security guards book-ended the front and rear of the procession.

They turned the first corner. Elise tried not to smile when she caught a glimpse of Samuel, Luca and Georgina standing by the only window, framed by the light. Georgina gave them a little wave and Luca grinned at them. They were not alone after all.

No one spoke as they moved through the vast lengths of corridor; the only sound was of forty pairs of feet hitting the concrete floor. Fintorian would stop at seemingly random points and press the walls. A hidden door would then swing open and they would traipse after him; he wanted to avoid moving through the main museum.

Fintorian finally stopped outside a steel door and the procession shuffled to a standstill. One of the white-coats skirted round him and pulled back the three bars across the door. He held up his security tag and the door swung open.

'I think it would be fitting if Twenty-One and Elise entered their new home first,' Fintorian announced to everyone gathered at the end of the corridor.

He stepped aside and beckoned them over. Kit turned to Elise and she nodded at him. They pushed past the white-coats, who barely stood aside for them, and made their way to the front. Elise felt one of them jab her in the side, but she didn't flinch. When they reached the door, Kit faltered. A bead of sweat trickled down his forehead. Sensing his panic, Elise stepped around him and took the lead.

Walking through the door, she prepared for the onslaught on her numbed senses. But there was nothing, no dazzling light or animal calls. Instead, she was met by darkness. When she tentatively stepped forwards, her foot caught on the uneven rock flooring and Kit grabbed her arm to stop her falling. One of the white-coats sniggered. She held her arm out to her side and her palm traced the cool rock face. She swung her arm overhead and her fingertips were met by the same rough, cold surface. Her eyes adjusted; she could pick out a faint beam at the far end of their new home. Tugging at Kit's sleeve, she made her way towards it.

Trying to remain calm, she prayed to the stars that this wasn't all there was. As they made their way towards the light, the rock floor gradually evened out. There was a light dusting of sand in places. The sound of running water got louder as they moved towards the strengthening light, until she realised it wasn't just running water; it was cascading.

When they turned the next corner, they stopped in their tracks. Sheets of water fell from the top of the ceiling to the lip. Elise had never seen anything like it; they were behind a waterfall. Kit edged his way to the corner of the cave mouth; there was a path down the side of the cliff face. Cautiously following, Elise bent to place his sleeping roll by the wall of the cave. Stepping onto the path, she breathed in sharply as she surveyed their new home.

Her eyes followed the waterfall's descent as it plunged into a deep pool. The gentle banks led up to a meadow, dotted with blue and yellow flowers. Two pathways had been chiselled into the rock wall either side of the cave mouth; they sloped down to the grass. All around the cave mouth were impossibly high cliffs that made Elise dizzy when she tried to peer up at them. Leaning against the rock wall, she looked out past the sparkling pool, past the meadow, to a small pine woodland. Birds flew overhead and Elise could see a hare springing into a bush. High above the tops of the pine trees was an enclosed glass walkway, empty of the visitors who would soon peer down at them. For the moment, they were alone.

Kit had already made his way down the pathway and Elise followed cautiously; even though it wasn't narrow, she was always uncomfortable being so close to water. When her feet hit the grassy meadow, she turned her face to the warming sun. She stared up at the cliff face and admired the waterfall tumbling down the mouth of the cave into the basin. The sunlight picked out every drop and it was as if a curtain of molten silver were covering the cave mouth. She couldn't help but smile.

Elise glanced over at Kit. 'What do you think?'

Kit looked around him. 'It's just another cage . . .'

He had been about to go on, but he dropped his hands to his sides when he saw Fintorian striding down the pathway.

'So. Pretty special, eh?' he shouted to them. They nodded and Elise smiled tentatively. 'Well, you have a few days to get settled in. We don't want to rush; you should feel at home by the time the first visitors turn up in five days. I envisage that you will try to stay in the meadow most of the time, as we want people to have the best view. Don't hide away in the cave; it's just for sleeping in.'

Fintorian glanced at them and his smile started to fade. 'This project has come so far that it can't falter now or some readjustments will have to take place. Understood?'

Elise nodded. She stared down at her feet and tried to look suitably chastened.

Fintorian brightened his voice. 'Enough of that for now, though. I don't think you've met our new Companion yet. Elise, you two will be working closely together over the next few weeks. Hand-picked this one myself; I thought we needed a slight change in direction. I do so hope that you make every effort to impart your valuable knowledge and make him welcome.'

Elise glanced up at the mouth of the cave, ready to greet the new Companion. Nothing could have prepared her for when Lewis Thetter emerged from the cave mouth.

CHAPTER 18

'Well, I'll let you two get acquainted. I'm certain there is a lot you want to talk about.' Fintorian beamed at them.

'Oh, yes, indeed, sir. I'll make sure I'm available later, though, if you need me,' Lewis said, dropping his head.

'Thank you, Lewis. Maybe spend some time with Elise and Twenty-One once they get settled in. When Thirty-Two is an adult, we might consider putting everyone together in this pod if things go well. The possibilities are thrilling, aren't they?'

Fintorian waved goodbye to them, humming as he picked his way up the path.

Elise stared after him, lost as to how Lewis had managed to wangle his way into working at the museum. Kit took a good look at Lewis and, without saying anything, walked towards the middle of the meadow and sat pulling at tufts of grass. Elise remained where she was, her eyes fixed on Lewis.

As soon as Fintorian's footsteps had died away into the cave, Lewis raised his head slowly and smiled.

'Is everyone from the Outer Circle getting a job here now?' Elise said, not taking her gaze from his.

'You wouldn't join us, so I had to come here myself.'

'What? What are you talking about? Is Holly alright?'

'She's fine, really well. Blossoming, in fact. I've Holly to thank for teaching me a few choice phrases in sign language.'

Elise took a step towards him. 'Stay away from us. Don't think you're fooling anyone here.'

Lewis stared at her. 'I'm not done with you yet, Elise. I want this to be a harmonious relationship, if possible. Don't make life difficult for me; I won't be pushed around or threatened.' He then switched to signing and said the words at the same time. 'So you'd better be careful.'

Elise laughed; she had been pushed too far to care. 'You just signed "You'd better be kitchen."'

But Lewis's self-assurance didn't falter. 'Don't get too confident; Holly also told me a thing or two about you that no one else here'll know.'

Elise's smiled faded. Holly knew everything about her, had always kept her secrets. Elise could only assume that Lewis knew what she had spent her life trying to conceal.

'So if you're still not interested, we should come to an agreement. I'll stay out of your way if you stay out of mine. Agreed?' Lewis raised an eyebrow.

'Agreed. Now get out and don't come back.'

Lewis shrugged and waved goodbye to Kit, who stared blankly at him.

Once Lewis had disappeared into the cave, Elise sat next to Kit.

He tapped Elise on the knee. 'His body says things differently to his words.' Kit paused. 'And why does he want you to be a kitchen?'

Elise smiled. 'He's just someone I know from back home. Don't worry, though. He's not going to be around much.' She looked towards the woodland. 'Shall we see what this pod has to offer? I'm starving.'

Kit shook his head, before going back to pulling up tufts of grass. 'You explore if you want. I am tired.'

That evening, after they'd had dinner, Elise decided on what she had to do. She waited until Kit was settled in the cave and then signed to him that she would be back first thing in the morning.

Elise looked around anxiously and quietly tapped at the door again. The corridor was deserted but someone could turn the corner any second. It was ten in the evening and she was in part of the museum she had never entered before.

She couldn't wait any longer. Pushing the door open, she smiled apologetically. Samuel's wet hair was scraped back from his face and she guessed that he had just got out of the shower. He had even shaved, his handsome features clearly visible. He looked at Elise with surprise and pulled out a chair, which Elise ignored as she gazed around the room.

There was a large mahogany dining table with eight chairs around it, each with an upholstered seat. Intricately patterned rugs drew her eye to the other end of the room where two squishy sofas faced each other, an elegant glass coffee table in the middle. Two doors led off to other rooms, richly woven tapestries hanging at either side of their frames. Elise glanced at the three-tiered chandelier hanging over the table, the crystals still silently twinkling from the draft of the door closing.

'This is your pod?' she asked, trying not to laugh.

'Well, yes. I didn't decorate it like this; it just came this way,' Samuel said, blushing.

Elise picked up an engraved silver disc from the table; there was an identical one placed in front of every seat. It was the same size as the palm of her hand and only a few millimetres thick.

'What's this?' she asked, turning it over in her hand.

'It's a coaster,' Samuel said, glancing at Elise's blank face. 'You put it under glasses so any liquid that drips over the side doesn't mark the table.'

Elise put the coaster back on the table. 'It's a good job you don't have to stick to Reparations; this place is brimming with pointless chaff.'

Samuel laughed. 'These last few days, I've tried to, ah . . . wean myself off the good life.' He gestured towards one of the doors.

Elise wandered over and peeked through the doorway. Thick scarlet carpet covered the floor surrounding the largest bed she had ever seen; it was so wide she could have comfortably slept stretched across it. The majestic frame had petals and leaves carved into the posts at each corner. Heavy brocade curtains were artfully draped around it, hanging from a peaked canopy. Rows of pillows, gradually decreasing in size, advanced down the mattress; Elise counted ten. In stark contrast, at the foot of the bed, were several wooden crates with a sleeping mat laid over the top.

'Do you still pull the pillows down when you can't sleep?' she asked, smiling at him as she moved back to the table.

Samuel laughed. 'Yes, but not last night. I've still got a way to go until I'll survive out there, though.'

Elise's smile faltered, but she decided to press on. 'That's why I'm here. We might have to shift everything forwards a bit.

Something's come up; well, someone actually.' She glanced at Samuel, who had sat opposite her. 'It's the new Companion. I know him from back home. I think he's here for another reason.'

Samuel looked at Elise with a bemused expression. 'Do you mean the one who looks like he could be a Medius? I thought he was rather harmless. Can't sign properly, though. Told me his favourite animal was a bread knife. Fintorian chose him, not me.'

Elise rolled her eyes. 'It's all an act; he's part of this group that wants Sapiens to live separately from the Medius. He asked me to join and wanted me to do something for him at the museum. I refused. Now he's threatened me. I don't know what he's up to, but it's nothing good.'

Samuel breathed out slowly. 'Well, I'll have to tell Fintorian, get him out of the museum right away.'

'It's not as simple as that. My friend's in his group and I can't get her into that level of trouble. He also knows what I can do. He threatened that, if I got in his way, he'd tell everyone.'

Elise glanced up at Samuel, waiting for his response, waiting to see if she had been right to trust him. Samuel stood and started pacing. He was frowning with concentration and it was a few minutes before he spoke.

'And you're sure that they have something planned, that he doesn't just want a new job?'

'He made my friend leave her job at the school because he didn't like her working around the Medius. He definitely wouldn't want to work here unless there was a reason; he hates them.' Elise glanced up. 'I think they're going to stage something, I don't know what, but I bet it's to do with the other

Potior visiting. And I think that whatever they've planned will ruin any attempt to get Kit out. As soon as they do anything, the museum will triple security, dismiss me, replace both Companions with Medius and we'll never get Kit out.'

Samuel stopped pacing. 'But that's in five days, Elise.'

'I know, but we have to get Kit away from here. You've seen what's happening to him. He's losing the hope that has kept him going all these years. It's hard enough with the added security at the moment and it's only going to get worse.'

'What do you think they have planned?'

'I think it has to do with living separately from the Medius. Maybe they'll take a Potior captive and demand some land in exchange for his release. I don't know; I'm guessing.' She clenched her fists, frustrated she hadn't tried to find out more when she had the chance. 'Whatever happens, though, we have to find a way to get Kit out before it does. The longer we wait, the harder it's going to get.'

Samuel crossed the room to a chest of drawers with smooth opal handles. Pulling each drawer out, he rummaged around until he finally brought out a cardboard tube.

'I knew I kept one here as well as in my office,' he said, brandishing it at Elise.

He snapped the lid off the tube and there was a satisfying pop as the pressure was released from inside. He dug his hand in and, for a moment, he looked like he had one freakishly long arm. Pulling out an enormous scroll of paper, he tried to flatten it on the table, but it kept rolling in on itself. Elise placed a coaster on each corner to hold it down; they did have a use after all.

'It's a map of the museum,' Samuel said. 'See here,' he pointed to hatch markings across a wall. 'That indicates a concealed doorway. If we can trace a route through the museum, we might be able get Kit out without having to go through any of the pods.'

They spent the next hour poring over the map, trying to find and then memorise a route. They couldn't risk marking it on the map, in case it was found, so they had to repeatedly trace the route with their fingers. By midnight, they nearly had a clear path, except for two areas they couldn't get around without entering or exiting a pod.

They were so engrossed in their task that they didn't notice the footsteps advancing down the corridor. Two raps at the door and they swung round. Elise tried unsuccessfully to push the map off the table.

Without a pause, the door opened and Luca stepped in. 'Sorry for coming this late. I just needed to check . . .' He closed the door with one hand. 'What're you doing here?' Luca glanced between Elise and Samuel before recognition crossed his face. 'You know it's illegal, right? That you'll get caught?'

'What . . . ? How did you know? We've only just started!' Elise said, looking around for cameras.

'It's been obvious for ages,' Luca said dismissively.

Elise's eyes widened and she turned to Samuel. 'If Luca knows what we're planning, others in the museum will as well.'

'What?' Luca said, alert. 'Wait. What do you mean, planning? What are you planning?' He stepped around Elise and pulled at the map that was dangling over the side of the table. 'This is the museum. What are you up to and why aren't you including me?'

'I think there's been some confusion,' Samuel said, looking slightly embarrassed, before taking control of the situation. 'But honestly, I think we probably do need his help,' he said to Elise.

Mortified, Elise could only nod as she realised not only what Luca had wrongly suspected was happening, but also that she had so easily given away their plans.

Luca looked at them both. 'Go on ... .'

'I don't really know how to start. You might want to sit down for this,' Samuel said, taking a seat himself. 'We want to help Kit leave the museum. And I think we're going to need your help.'

Elise was expecting Luca to look shocked, to try and talk them out of it, but instead he banged his palms on the table, grinning. 'Finally! I was beginning to think I'd die of old age before we got around to it! I've been practising building shelters for months. When do we go?'

Elise laughed, pleased she didn't have to convince him. 'In the next few days.'

She filled Luca in on her dealings with Lewis Thetter. After she had told him about Lewis threatening her, she had to hold on to his sleeve to stop him from finding Lewis to haul him out of the museum himself. She felt a twinge of guilt for leaving out what Lewis knew about her; she would deal with that later.

'We have to find Georgina and Bay, take them with us,' Luca said. 'We can't just leave them here with Lewis; he's half-baked.'

Samuel, who had been listening quietly, interjected. 'As much as I want to, we can't take Georgina and Bay with us. Bay's just a baby; we have to be realistic. The more of us that try to leave, the more likely it is that we will be caught. And if we get caught, they won't just expel us – it's hardly a worthy punishment for people trying to escape. They'll imprison us for the rest of our lives.'

'Well, that's cheery,' Luca said, rolling his eyes. 'So once we get Kit out, where are we going to take him?'

'We're going to sneak into one of the other bases; he wants to find some way to help the other Neanderthals.' Elise tried to sound as if this was a perfectly reasonable mission.

'All of the bases have Neanderthals in their own museums,' Samuel said. 'From what Fintorian has said, they want to work towards a similar project to ours. They admire the ingenuity of having Neanderthals and Sapiens living side by side so, naturally, they want to copy it.'

Luca grinned. 'You can count me in. I've always wanted to visit the other bases.'

'What about Rosa?' Elise asked, before she could stop herself.

'She is *not* coming with us,' Samuel spluttered.

Luca glared at Samuel. 'No need to worry, Samuel. Rosa won't be coming. I realised that I'd made a mistake. I ended it a few days ago.'

Elise tried not to look shocked as she processed this new information.

Realising this was not the time to go into it, she said, 'What are we going to tell Georgina?'

'We can't tell her anything, in case we are caught. She has to be completely innocent or they will take Bay from her,' Samuel said, leaning over the map. 'We have to get Kit past the barriers. We could use the second chip the engineers have been working on to temporarily override the tracker, but the injection includes a sedative that results in complete syncope.' Samuel looked at their blank faces. 'If Kit were injected with the second chip, it's very likely he would pass out and we'd have to carry him, which is hardly ideal.'

'So this is how far we've got,' Elise said, tracing her finger along their passage through the museum. 'As you can see, there are two points we can't cross. The first one is Kit's pod and the second is at the end of the museum in the orangutan display; there are no corridors around it.'

Luca peered over Elise's shoulder; he was closer than he had been in months. She hadn't forgiven him, but she had to admit it was better when he was working with them.

'I can see where the problem is,' Luca said. 'But have you thought about going up?'

'Of course! Why didn't I think of that?' Samuel exclaimed.

'Because, despite your spiced-up IQ, you lack my lateral thinking capabilities,' Luca retorted.

'There are so many fallacies in that sentence, one wonders where to begin.'

'Stars, could you actually sound any more Pre-Pandemic? No one would think you were only four years older than me,' Luca said, looking at Samuel pointedly.

Samuel was opening his mouth to respond when Elise cut him off. 'How're you going to survive out there if you keep bickering like this? Soon, you'll only have each other and Kit, so you have to find a way to get along. Now, will someone please explain to me what you mean by *up*?'

'He means we climb over the barriers,' Samuel said, pushing back his now-dry hair. 'They are only around fifteen feet, which allows some of the less precious birds to fly overhead throughout the museum. To get Kit out of his pod, we'll have to climb the rock face. The barriers only repel from the sides, not the top. It prevents the tree dwellers from being shocked to the ground if they climb too high. They can't escape from the tops of the trees, but we should be able to. We might have to go on a recce to the orangutan pod, though, as I've got no idea how we'll get over that one.'

'You mean I'll have to climb up the cliff in our pod?' Elise said, alarmed.

'No, I'll make the climb with Kit,' Samuel said.

'Good, because I'm still working on my upper-body strength. It's taken me months to pull myself up ten times on the branch in the mornings.'

'What are you going to tell your folks before you leave?' Luca asked.

'Nothing. I'm not leaving. I'm going to get Kit out, but that's as far as I go.'

Luca looked shocked and seemed about to protest, when Samuel stopped him. 'Her mind's made up, Luca. She has family here and we don't. She's made her decision.' He rounded on Elise. 'And when all of this happens, you have to be safely asleep in your room. If they even think you're involved, you'll be tried for treason. You must stay away and keep your thoughts hidden. I've observed that you are quite skilled at that, which is good – we can't risk anyone finding out that you're involved.'

Elise knew he was right.

They carried on discussing their plans until nearly 3 a.m. By then, they were going around in circles about how to get through the orangutan display. Elise suggested they might as well visit it. Surprisingly, Samuel agreed.

Despite their lack of sleep, they became alert when they entered the last pod in the eastern wing. The moon was nearly at its fullest and in the silvery light, they surveyed the last hurdle the museum could present. It was different to any of the other pods Elise had been in before, a small rainforest teeming with life. Strange calls and rustlings came from every side. Besides the orangutans, there were hundreds of other creatures in there.

'The orangutans are asleep,' Samuel whispered as they pushed through the rainforest, 'and we don't want to wake them.'

A fine mist fell through the trees and Elise thought she could hear a gentle snore above. 'Why? Are they dangerous?'

'No, they're the most passive of the great apes. I just don't want to attract any cameras.' Samuel gestured upwards. 'They make nests out of leaves high up in the branches. The mother shares the nest with her infant until she has another, which is around every seven years. It really is a remarkable bond.'

Elise peered through the leaves, wishing it were light so she could catch a glimpse of one of the shaggy-haired apes. 'When you hear their little snores and imagine a mother curled up there with her baby, it seems very probable we share ninety-seven per cent of our DNA with them.'

Samuel looked at her with surprise.

'What? You're not the only one who can retain information, you know,' she said, smiling at him.

Luca was surveying the tops of the trees with his hands on his hips. 'How high up do you think the barriers go?'

'The same as Kit's pod, around fifteen feet.'

'So we need to pass through the tops of the trees then,' Luca said. 'We could use a zip wire maybe. Attach each end to the highest trees at either end of the pod.'

'That might work.' Samuel glanced over at Luca. 'We could set it up the night before. The wire would be hidden in the tree-tops; no one would see it there.'

'When will we do it?' Elise said.

Luca came over and they huddled, the hum of the rainforest masking Samuel's words.

'We've got to give ourselves the most time, so the night before the opening, which gives us just three days.'

Instead of going back to her room, Elise went straight to Kit's pod and slept for the two hours left before dawn. When the first light broke through the waterfall, she pulled herself out of her bedroll and prodded Kit awake.

She knelt next to him. 'You've got to get up. We've only got three days to get ready for our opening.'

Kit rolled over and leant up on his elbow for support as he sleepily signed with one hand, 'I thought it was in four days.'

'I was sure it's happening in three days,' Elise signed. 'Either way, I know that Luca will help us.'

Kit stared at Elise's face and she knew he understood.

CHAPTER 19

Fintorian had ordered Elise to go home. The opening was the next day, and following that she would have to stay in the museum for at least two weeks. She had spent every moment of the last two days with her friends, knowing that once Kit, Samuel and Luca left Thymine Base, she would never see them again. They would be unable to return, and she could never follow. It was this thought that had kept her awake the previous night.

That morning, she said her brief goodbyes to the three of them, unable to say anything of real meaning. Samuel gave her a new sling that he had woven. He told her that after visiting her parents, she had to go straight to her pod and not leave until the following morning. Kit had given her a small carving of a man with his hair tied back, holding a spear. For once, Luca was speechless and just folded her into his arms. He still didn't understand why she wasn't leaving with them, but Samuel had banned everyone from discussing it any further; they had to minimise all risk of discovery. Only Samuel knew where he was taking them. Even if Elise changed her mind, she would never be able to find them.

*

Her parents' front door was pulled open as soon as she reached the top of the neat pathway. Sofi beckoned Elise in; she looked strained and kept glancing over Elise's shoulder as she stood in the doorway.

Closing the door behind her, Elise surveyed her parents' kitchen. Knives and heavy pans covered every surface and the table was on its side in front of the stove.

'What's happened? Is Nathan okay?' Elise asked, her eyes flicking between Sofi and Aiden.

'She saw you, Elise,' Sofi said, walking over to hug her. 'Deeta saw us in the forest with the sling, and now she keeps on dropping hints about the Protection Department.'

Aiden was aligning the knives so each handle was the same distance from the next.

'Have they come?' Elise asked him.

'No, not yet,' he replied, still not looking up at her.

'So you think they will, then?'

'It's likely, and if they do, they might take Nathan before they come for you at the museum. He's your brother after all,' Aiden said, his voice devoid of emotion.

Sofi burst into tears. Elise was next to her in three steps, hugging her mum close to her chest. 'We don't know what to do,' Sofi sobbed. 'I will *never* forgive Deeta for this.'

'Shhh . . .' Elise said, trying to comfort her. 'First things first; we're going to put this kitchen back in order.' She looked around. Left to his own devices, her father had made the hub of their home into a fort. 'If anyone came in here, they'd know something was wrong straight away. Let's go back to how it was, with maybe just a couple of pans and knives out. Make it look as if you're in the middle of cooking, rather than the Rising.'

Sofi nodded, her smile at odds with the tears.

Aiden shrugged. 'I was just trying to keep them safe.'

Together, they moved the table back to an upright position and tidied some of the surfaces. Elise went out the back door and picked sweet peas, which she put into various-sized jugs, the vibrant colours bringing some warmth back to the room.

Once they were seated at the kitchen table, Elise busied herself making them tea.

'Where's Nathan?' she asked, trying to keep her voice level.

'He's at Jada's house. We're trying to get him to stay there as much as possible,' Sofi said, clasping her mug. The slight tremor of the liquid revealed that she was still shaking.

'Tell me what happened, from the beginning.'

'It only began a few days ago,' Sofi started, staring into her tea. 'Deeta visited and mentioned that she hadn't seen you come back that Sunday. She must have missed you, she said. Then she asked if you'd moved to your security position. I didn't know what she was talking about.' Sofi glanced up at Elise. 'For once, I decided to take Deeta seriously and I flattered and coaxed her until she told me. She'd been walking through the woods to pick mushrooms for her dinner when there was a loud noise. Having never heard anything like it before, she walked towards it. Spotting us in the distance, she was about to come over when, in front of her, a rabbit fell to the ground. There was some blood on its temple. She saw you had a rope and guessed that you'd used it somehow to kill the rabbit. She didn't know how, but she knew that it shouldn't be possible. Staying behind the tree trunk, she watched as Aiden collected the rabbit. She heard Aiden say that he'd never seen anything like it before . . . I think she'd just been waiting to bring it up. She enjoyed watching me squirm.'

Elise dropped her head into her hands. Holly, Lewis, now Deeta . . . and that meant Shauna as well. Too many people she didn't trust knew her secret.

'I should've wrung her neck in the forest. If only I'd seen her . . .' Aiden said.

Elise raised her head. 'No, you shouldn't have, Dad. She hasn't said anything yet, but we know that she probably will; she's never kept a secret in her life. I had a run-in with Shauna at the museum this week and if she knows, she'll either blackmail me or expose me. We must plan for the worst, and throttling Deeta Thinckle, as much as we'd all like to, isn't going to help.' Elise looked at her two exhausted parents. 'There's another problem as well. Even if Deeta decides to keep quiet, Holly hasn't. She told Lewis Thetter; he threatened me at the museum. Said that he'd tell everyone if I got in his way. It's going to come out.'

'Holly! Holly did that? All to get her paws on a Thetter?' Sofi looked incredulous. 'What can we do?' She started rocking on her chair.

'You have to talk to me; this is new territory. You know what the Potiors will do if they find out, but you've always tried to shield me from it. Tell me, what will they do first?'

Aiden stared at Sofi and she nodded.

When he spoke, Aiden's voice was flat, as if reciting something he had considered many times. 'First, two or three Midders will visit you at your home. They'll tell you that you're wasted in manual work, ask to move you out of this life and give you a future worth fighting for. They'll offer you more tickets, excitement, a place in the world. All you have to do in exchange is leave your family, devote yourself to your training and swear allegiance to the Protection Department. If that doesn't turn your head, they'll start following you. Turn up at your workplace, maybe your friend's house. Make you feel as if there's no escape from them, that they've eyes and ears everywhere. It's what happened to my brother and sister.'

Sofi fumbled for Aiden's hand. 'When Lisa and Toby refused to join, they followed them relentlessly. Midders would turn up everywhere they went, telling them they didn't have much more time to choose. It made the local Sapiens grow suspicious of them; people they'd known all their lives stopped speaking to them. I remember it clearly. Lisa was my closest friend; it was through her I met your father. She could do what you can, Elise. You were named after her. Quick as lightning, she was. She didn't even have to think about reacting to something; she just did. Aiden's father was the same, but he kept it hidden. And I kept Lisa's secret, not like Holly.

'The Potiors found out about Lisa and Toby because of the Rising. It took them a while, but once all the recordings of the fighting were viewed, the Potiors knew what they could do. How quick their reactions were, how many Midders they could fight and win against. The Potiors wanted them to become part of their Protection Department, to keep order in Thymine, make sure that those Sapiens who were expelled never make it to another base.'

Elise sat down abruptly. 'What do you mean, "make sure they never make it to another base"?'

Sofi and Aiden looked at each other.

'She needs to know,' Aiden said before turning to Elise. 'Most don't know this, or would refuse to believe it anyway, as it goes against everything the Potiors tell us they stand for. But there were a few of us who always questioned why no one was ever seen again when they were expelled. Or why we never saw anyone from another base make it to the edges of our boundaries. Lisa and Toby were able to confirm our suspicions when they had talks with the Midders from the Protection Department. When a person is expelled from a base and the crowds disperse, a couple of members of the Protection Department will slip off and track them. If the exile gets too far, or looks like they might make it to another base, then it's their job to make sure they get no further.'

'They kill them?' Elise said in disbelief.

Aiden nodded. 'So you can see why your aunt and uncle didn't want any part of it.'

'What happened to them?'

Sofi glanced at Aiden before letting him continue.

'The Protection Department came in the middle of the night and took them. They left me, though. I was big and could fight, but I wasn't as fast as Lisa and Toby, so I wasn't valuable enough to bother with. We never heard from them again.'

'I'm so sorry, Dad,' Elise said, leaning towards him. 'I didn't know how it happened. I thought they'd died in the riots.'

'And now it's going to happen again,' Aiden said, his eyes staring blankly. 'But this time it'll be both my children.'

Elise stood. 'No, it won't, not if we can just think of a way around it.'

'How can we stop them? I couldn't fight them off then and I can't now. There were too many.'

Elise stared down at Aiden. She felt almost detached from the discussion, as if it weren't her they were trying to save.

'Looking back, what would you have done differently? What would you have told Lisa and Toby if you'd known what was going to happen?'

Aiden stared at her. 'I would've told them to leave, take their chances outside of the base before anyone knew where to start tracking them. They'd have had a good head start. It's got to be better than killing Sapiens or dy—'

'Aiden, no!' Sofi interjected. 'Think about what you're saying!'

'He's right, Mum,' Elise said, keeping her face still, hiding her panic and fear. 'I have to leave. I can't be part of their security, get paid to protect people I loathe, maybe even having to kill someone I know. I'll refuse an order one time and they'll execute me. And if I stay, they'll take me anyway, Nathan as well.'

'But where will you go? You'll die out there too!' Sofi said, the panic rising in her voice.

Elise leant over and brushed the hair from her mother's face, the smallest streaks of grey smattering the chestnut curls. She thought about how much to tell them. It was best they knew as little as possible to keep them safe. But they had to know she was leaving the base or they would put themselves in danger trying to find her.

'Luca will come with me. He's desperate to leave, has been practising making shelters to help us survive out there. You like what you've heard about him, don't you?'

'Yes, he's kind. He gave you the clothes, didn't he?'

Elise just nodded.

'I'll come back and get you when it's safe, when we've found somewhere to go. I promise.' Elise looked over at her dad. 'But what we have to think about now is how we're going to protect

Nathan. How do we make sure that even if Deeta talks, Nathan will be safe?'

Elise willed them to move along and make a plan. She didn't want to discuss other ways to protect herself; it was futile. There was only Nathan to think about. And then she knew what they had to do.

Stumbling, Elise only just managed to stop herself falling. The rain had made the pathway slippery and her right foot had threatened to skid from underneath her. She turned her head towards the patchwork house and spat on the ground, looking at her mum and dad, who were both blocking the doorway.

'Get out. You're a disgrace!' Sofi screamed, hair plastered to her face from the rain.

Elise pulled herself up and started walking back towards them. Out the corner of her eye, she could see windows opening along the pathway. The rain was pelting against the glass and obscuring their neighbours' view; they needed a better one.

'*I'm* a disgrace?' she shouted back. 'None of you can do half of what I can; you're all pathetic! I'm ashamed to call you my parents.' Elise gestured at Aiden. 'Not that he even is.'

Sofi advanced down the pathway. Aiden tried to catch her arm but she tugged free.

'What did you say?' Sofi shouted, trembling.

'Everyone *knows*, Mum! Let's just say it out loud for once. He's not my father; he's my *uncle*. My real father died after the Rising.'

'Be quiet, Elise! Just be quiet! He raised you, didn't he? And that's the thanks he gets!'

'Thanks? You've just held me back. You're all useless; especially that half-brother of mine, couldn't fight his way out of a paper bag.'

'I said shut up.'

Elise's head cracked backwards as Sofi's fist punched her cheek. She tasted the blood in her mouth and for a moment was so dizzy she couldn't remember where she was.

'He might not be able to, but I still can,' Sofi said, clenching and unclenching her fist.

Elise took a step back and rested her hands on her knees, willing her head to clear. She looked up slowly at Sofi and sneered as she spat on the ground again; it was red this time.

Turning down the pathway, Elise touched her cheek – there was blood all over her hand.

'You'll regret that!' she shouted at her mum, halfway down the lane. 'You have *no* daughter!'

Clutching her cheek, she didn't look back.

Elise closed her pod door behind her. She tentatively touched her fingers to her face and winced. Looking at herself in the mirror, she knew that her cheekbone was fractured. Her eye had begun to close from the swelling and the blood had started to clot in lumps on her cheek. Sofi had done a good job.

The family had agreed that the blow was necessary to make the performance realistic. It was unlikely any of the neighbours would report the incident. They would think Elise had got what she deserved and they wouldn't want Sofi to be expelled from the base. Their neighbours might think Sofi was odd, but none of the Sapiens would want to be responsible for an expulsion, especially when she was always willing to help heal them if they were low on Medi-stamps. It was a small risk they would take to keep Nathan safe. Elise pushed the thought away; she knew if she started down that path she would curl up in a ball and not get up again.

Step by step. It was the only way.

Shrugging on her grey jacket, Elise pulled the hood high up over her head so her face was covered. She then made her way through the corridors, head down, to Georgina's room. Elise had to repair her cheek quickly. It would raise too many questions and she needed to remain in the periphery of the museum's concerns for the next few hours.

Knocking gently on the door, Elise waited to be called inside.

'Elise, I'm glad you've dropped by. Bay managed to . . .'

Georgina stopped mid-sentence as, wincing, Elise pulled her hood down from her face. Her left cheek was now twice the size of her right one and her eye was completely closed. The swelling had pulled the side of her mouth up so she looked as if she were giving a wry half-smile, as if she were amused at the irony of it all.

'Stars, Elise, your face!' Georgina hurried over and guided her to the hospital bed. 'Was it one of the animals? When the barrier came down today?'

Elise could only see out of her right eye, but concern was etched on Georgina's features.

She patted Georgina's arm. 'Not unless the spider monkeys have learnt how to produce a right hook.' Her voice sounded strange in her head. 'I know it's a lot to ask, but can you patch me up? It hurts to talk. I have enough tickets to pay the museum.'

After checking for cameras, Georgina refused to take payment. She was as efficient as always; she used a machine to knit the bone back together and, within half an hour, she was placing the bottle of Dermadew back into the cabinet. Elise lay back as instructed and tried to nap for an hour while the swelling reduced. She couldn't switch off, though; she turned over and examined what she had to do next. She didn't let her mind flit backwards, or too far forwards. Just to the next step.

'There, take a look,' Georgina said, holding out a small mirror to Elise.

'Umm . . . Georgina, did you put Dermadew all over my face?'

'Well, yes, you couldn't have one perfectly smooth cheek and the other . . . normal-looking. And, then, when I'd done both cheeks, I did your forehead, nose and chin – for continuity.'

Elise inspected her reflection again. Her cheek was still swollen but her eye had opened again and the corner of her mouth was back in its normal place. What was more noticeable was that her skin radiated health; she looked like a June bride and expectant mother rolled into one.

'Thanks. I can see why the Medius ladies hoard the Dermadew.' Elise glanced up at Georgina. 'When will it wear off, though? I look like I've spent all day grooming.'

'Don't worry. You'll be back to normal in around six to eight weeks, quicker if you exfoliate regularly.'

'I don't even know what that means,' Elise said, smiling.

'Never mind. You look great, though; amazing what a skin-care regime could do for you. You have all the necessary parts; you just need to bring them out a bit. And not get punched in the face . . . What happened with that anyway?'

'Ah, it was nothing. Something I had to take care of back home. It's all wrapped up now. I won't need any more repair work; don't worry,' Elise said, her face bleached of emotion.

'Well, if you're sure,' Georgina said, glancing up at Elise from her stool. 'You know I'm always here to talk to if you need me. Always here, not going anywhere.' Georgina sighed. 'But at least we have Bay; she keeps us going.'

Elise could only smile back. She walked over to Bay's crib and peered down. The baby was fast asleep, her sturdy little legs kicking out as she dreamt. Elise touched her soft hair and thought of Seventeen; how proud she would be if she only had the chance to see her baby.

With her back to Georgina, Elise signed, 'Bye, little one.'

She turned to Georgina and gave her a wave. 'Take care, Georgina. Thank you for . . . well, thank you for everything,' she said, closing the door quietly behind her.

Once her pod clock turned over to 1 a.m., Elise shrugged her backpack onto her shoulders. She had spent the last few hours stuffing it with everything she could lay her hands on that might be useful outside of the base; a bit of light thieving from the museum was nothing in comparison with what she was about to do.

She slipped through the corridors, stopping at each corner to check that the route was clear. She wanted to see as few people as possible.

'It's the grand opening tomorrow, Angus,' she said jovially to the guard who was walking towards her along the corridor to Kit's pod. She flipped round so she was walking backwards when she called out after him, 'I'm too excited to be able to sleep; I want everything to be perfect.' She even gave a little squeal and clapped her hands.

Angus gave a grunt and carried on walking to the end of the corridor. Still facing him, Elise held her identification to Kit's pod door. She had just closed it when Angus turned and began the second part of his patrol back down the corridor. He hadn't seen her backpack.

Creeping through the cave, she used the damp, moss-lined wall to guide her to its mouth. Standing behind the curtain of water, she relaxed her body and stepped away from the arm that came at her. She ducked the second time as well.

'Stop it. It's me,' she whispered.

'Elise, what are you doing here? I told you not to come,' Samuel whispered.

Elise leant towards his voice and felt him pull her sleeve as he guided her down the path. Her eyes adjusted to the dim light and, peering up, she could see two figures halfway up the cliff wall, Luca and Kit.

'I heard someone in the cave and came down to see who,' Samuel said, his mouth pressed up against her ear.

'There's been a change of plans. I can't explain now, but I have to come with you. Things are different at home; I have to leave,' Elise whispered.

There was silence. Elise started to feel nauseous; what if he didn't want her to come? Where would she go?

Eventually, Samuel spoke. 'Are you sure? You won't be able to come back.'

'I know what it means, Samuel, but I've no choice. I'll explain if we get out of here alive. That's if you want me to come with you?'

'Of course I do.'

Elise smiled into the darkness but she soon had other things to consider. She looked up at the sheer rock face. Samuel stuck close and guided her hands when necessary. Halfway up, Elise's foot slipped; he grabbed her arm and effortlessly pulled her up to the next ledge. Heart hammering, she tried not to look down.

'What if I fall into the water?' Elise whispered once she had resumed her climb.

'Then you'll get wet and have to start again,' Samuel replied.

'But the water – it could be dangerous.'

'It's all treated. There's a pump running up behind the rock wall that drags the water from the basin to the top of the cliff to create the waterfall. It's just one circular motion of treated water. You don't think Fintorian would risk his prize possession, do you?' Samuel guided her hand to another ridge and she strained to pull herself up. 'We're all carrying water from this pod in our backpacks – enough to keep us going for a while,' he explained.

Elise was too exhausted to respond, but she was grateful that Samuel had taken care of one of her main concerns; she only had a day's worth of water with her.

Luca and Kit pulled themselves over the ledge. Using her last reserves of energy, Elise climbed the final ten metres in silence. When she glanced down, the drop was so far she couldn't see the ground. She decided it was best not to look again.

Samuel was slightly behind, braced for if she fell. Her muscles were shaking with the strain when her hand finally felt the top of the cliff ledge. Two strong arms pulled her over and clean off her feet. She was staring straight into Kit's eyes, but they didn't have the scrunched-up smile she expected. Instead, they were fearful. Elise turned to Luca, who was fixed on something over her shoulder. She followed his gaze and caught her breath.

Fintorian was silently watching from the other end of the ledge – ten guards surrounding him.

CHAPTER 20

* *

'How good of you to finally join us,' Fintorian said, watching Samuel pull himself over the edge. 'I thought you'd be the first, but clearly you had other concerns.' Fintorian nodded at Elise.

Elise looked around her, trying to work out how their odds of escape had flipped so dramatically. They were on a flat plateau of rock that contrasted sharply with the scaffolding holding everything together. She felt as if she were backstage at a theatre performance and being exposed to the nuts and bolts of the piece had ruined the magic. Between Elise and the raw scaffolding were ten surly-looking guards. Benjamin, the white-coat who had injected Kit, was standing at the front, arms folded, smirking.

Fintorian was towards the back, clearly visible due to his height. He was leaning against the scaffolding, as casually as if they had just passed him in the corridor.

'How?' Samuel asked, glancing between the guards.

'Did you honestly believe I wouldn't notice what has been going on? Ever since Seventeen died, I've known that you have an unhealthy attachment to this project. All those "secretive" meetings. The trip to the orangutan pod . . .'

Elise's sharp intake of breath drew Luca to her. It was over. There were ten of them and a Potior.

'There are guards all over the museum, mainly stationed in the orangutan pod,' Fintorian said, smiling at Luca. 'I told Angus downstairs to let anyone in this evening; I wanted to see who exactly was involved in this little coup.'

Elise never took her eyes from Fintorian. Samuel stepped around Kit.

'And now I know.' Fintorian flicked his hand towards Elise and the others. 'Take them all, and don't worry about hurting them. Leave Twenty-One unharmed, though; we need him ready for the opening tomorrow.' Fintorian's voice carried over the tops of their heads.

Elise pulled out her sling. Before she could even load it, Kit had charged past Samuel, directly at two of the guards. Their confident looks slipped as Kit skidded to his knees in front of them. Without pausing, he swung his spear around at calf level and took them down in one clean sweep.

Samuel sprang into the air and took another two guards to the ground with him, both knocked out by the force.

Elise released her sling and the crack of the stone snapping through the air made all the guards stop for a second; they had never heard anything like it before. Luca took advantage of their brief distraction and barged one of them to the ground before pouncing on top of him. Another guard clutched his leg, his kneecap shattered by the stone from Elise's sling.

A guttural roar made Elise flinch. Benjamin had cleared a path and was sprinting towards her. A solid leg kicked at Elise's stomach and she only just managed to spring out of the way. Benjamin followed this up straightaway with two weaker punches to Elise's chest. She ducked out of the way of the first one, but the second knocked her to the ground – she only just managed to hold her head up to avoid it slamming onto the rocks. She quickly kicked herself back to her feet in one smooth motion, silently thanking her dad for his years of training.

Fintorian looked amused as he pushed away from the scaffolding to join in. Elise tried to focus on Benjamin but she knew they didn't stand a chance now Fintorian had tipped the balance further into the guards' favour.

Benjamin was too close for Elise to use her sling, so she circled him, blocking all of his punches while desperately wondering how she was going to knock out someone twice her size. Then she knew.

She circled around, still dodging and blocking. Waiting for an opportunity to open up.

'Getting tired yet?' Benjamin said, switching stances. 'I can do this all day; just one blow to your head is all that's needed.'

Elise moved to the left as another fist whistled past her ear. She then leant her weight on her right leg and turned to her side, kicking out with everything she had, straight into Benjamin's stomach.

Benjamin gasped for the breath that had been knocked out of him. A look of alarm crossed his face; he wasn't used to people fighting back. He took a step back from Elise, who followed it up with another hard kick that sent him over the edge of the cliff. She tried not to wince when she heard the crunch of his body smacking against the wall of rock on the way down.

Resisting the urge to peer over the edge, Elise loaded her sling as she spun around and shattered the elbow of the guard on top of Luca. Pushing the last of the guards off him, Luca grinned at her.

Elise caught her breath as Samuel hurtled in an arc over her head. Fintorian had punched him, sending him flying ten feet in the air. Laughing, Fintorian ran to where Samuel landed on the ground and raised his foot to stamp on his chest. Without hesitation, Samuel rolled out from underneath him and leapt to his feet. He sprang into the air and knocked Fintorian to the ground.

They were moving so fast that Elise could barely follow them. One would soar into the air, building up all their force to try and break the other. Blows and punches landed, sending each of them flying. Sometimes the strikes were dodged, balance was lost and an advantage was gained. But then they would flip up and start again. Luca and Kit were circling around them, unsure where to aim.

Fintorian landed on his back and skidded along the ground. Wiping the blood from his mouth, he stared up at Samuel, who was racing towards him. A look of realisation crossed Fintorian's face.

'Of course,' he muttered as he rolled out of the way and kicked himself back onto his feet.

Without a pause, he ran up the side of the scaffolding and flipped himself backwards, landing behind Samuel.

Samuel had tracked him, though, and switched round. With a sideways kick, he knocked Fintorian high up into the air. For a second, he looked like a rag doll tossed away by a child. Time slowed for Elise as she took aim.

With a crack of her sling, she released a stone. It hit Fintorian clean on the temple – a shot in a thousand.

Fintorian dropped to the ground. No one spoke as they all stared at him, waiting to see if he would get up. He didn't stir and his eyes remained closed.

Kit tucked his spear behind him so it was held in place by his backpack.

'Shall we go?' he signed.

His blasé manner broke the tension and Elise had to grin; but they still had to get Kit past the barriers and out of the museum.

Samuel bent over to grab his bag. 'We need to get out of this room without the cameras following us so, firstly, everyone has to calm down.'

They stood in awkward silence for a few minutes. Samuel felt each of their wrists and nodded.

'Let's go, before the cameras decide we're more interesting,' Luca signed.

Elise could see the little black dots circling around the pile of groaning guards on the ground. They were unintentionally assisting the escape.

After scaling the cliff front, climbing down the scaffolding was easier. When they reached the ground, Samuel held up his hand and they silently waited as he scanned the area for cameras.

'No more vocal discussion of our plans while we pass through the corridors. I know where we need to go, but we can't let anyone know where we're moving next; it's the only lead we have,' Samuel signed, looking around him. 'There's still a hundred guards placed throughout the museum. Fintorian was over-confident to only bring ten with him. The odds won't be in our favour next time. We have to move now.'

'Where, though?' Luca signed. 'The plan's in tatters; they know we were going to move Kit through the orangutan display. They know everything.'

'No, they don't,' Samuel signed. 'Why do you think I never talked about what we were doing after we got out of here? There was a strong possibility that we were being watched. We just have to get out of the museum and then we'll be relatively safe.'

'And since when could you fight like that?' Luca signed, turning on Samuel.

The question hung in the air for a moment before Kit stamped his foot to get their attention. 'Can we please form a new plan. All of this means nothing. Where do we go now?'

'We can't go through the last pod so we're going to have to go to the control room. The only option we have left is to use the chip the engineers have been developing that will override the original tracker.' Samuel turned to Kit. 'I'm sorry; but you'll pass out. Luca and I will carry you the rest of the way. We'll get you out, I promise. We have to; there's no way back now.'

Samuel led the way through the corridors. Twice they heard feet traipsing along the corridor they wanted to use, but Samuel would double back or press open a doorway for them to dart through.

In less than ten minutes, they were circling the outside of a pod, using the shadows to hide them as they climbed the steel stairs of the control room.

Pushing open the door, Samuel went in first. The two guards in the control room were tied up and locked in a cupboard in less than three minutes.

'Everyone spread out. We're looking for the prototype chip that blocks the transmission to the barriers; I'm going to look at the barriers themselves.' Samuel walked over to the ceiling-high display of screens.

Elise systematically pulled out drawers – she didn't know what she was searching for and found herself peering at every item. After ten minutes, everyone was frantic, throwing things to the ground as they sorted through rows of shelves and cupboards. Samuel was tapping at different screens and sighing as he waited for each response.

Elise jumped when the door to the control room opened. Pulling out her sling, she turned to face the rows of guards as she backed away from the entrance.

She faltered; only two people slipped through the door.

Lewis Thetter, followed by Georgina.

Everyone stood still and stared at one another, the shock registering on their faces, even Kit's for once.

'I see we have company already, Georgina,' Lewis said, the brief look of concern swept cleanly off his face as he regained composure.

'Oh stars, I can explain . . .' Georgina started.

It was Kit who moved first. In four steps, he was by Georgina, tugging Bay out of the wrap that secured her to Georgina's chest.

'No!' Georgina shouted, but Lewis held her back when she struggled to get to Kit.

Elise, Samuel and Luca stepped forwards in front of Kit. He cradled Bay, who was asleep, unaware of the unfolding drama. The first Neanderthal he had met. Kit's eyes locked onto Bay. He stared at her without blinking, his heavy brow ridge casting a shadow across his cheek, the only feature of his face that was distinctively un-Sapien.

'That's enough, sister. We've got more pressing matters,' Lewis said, his strong arms encircling Georgina as she struggled to get free.

CHAPTER 21

'*Sister!*' Elise exclaimed, forgetting to sign.

'Yes, sister,' Lewis said.

'But how?' Elise said. 'She's a Medius and you're a Sapien.'

Georgina looked up slowly; her eyes dulled as she stopped struggling. 'I would've been a Sapien, if it weren't for the lottery.'

'You're a lottery baby?' Luca said.

'Yes, she is,' Lewis said, squeezing his arms tighter around Georgina even though she had stopped struggling. 'Perhaps now we're all on the same side, we can work together on this one.' He glanced around the room. 'I believe that you may have hit a wall, so to speak.'

'Samuel, don't,' Elise said, glancing up at him. 'We can't trust him.'

'I don't think we can trust many people,' Samuel said, his eyes not leaving Georgina.

'I'm so sorry,' Georgina said. 'When Elise got hurt, I tried to stop, but he wouldn't let me. Told me I had to keep making sure the codes were working. I changed the type of animal that was released, though, made sure it was the harmless ones so no one got hurt, possums and dodos. I'm so sorry, Elise. I never wanted to hurt you.'

'It was you!' Samuel glared at her. 'It was you deactivating the barriers. But how? You don't even have a code and you would need two anyway.'

'That's where my sister's tweaked genes came into play,' Lewis said, looking down at Georgina, who was half his size. 'Very attractive, isn't she? Not hard for her to coax and seduce the codes out of a few one-track Overseers. I believe you were one of them, Samuel,' he said with a half-smile.

Georgina moaned and bowed her head. Thick tears fell down her cheeks.

Elise looked between them. 'Samuel! You seduced Samuel?'

Luca snorted and rolled his eyes, enjoying himself for a moment.

Georgina's head snapped up. 'No, no, I didn't. He wasn't interested in me; it's hard to entice someone who doesn't like to be touched. I had to drug him in the end.' She turned to him. 'I'm so sorry, Samuel. We weren't friends then; I just needed your code. I tried to stop, but he wouldn't let me.'

'You're a disgrace,' Samuel said, turning away from her and glaring at Lewis.

'Oh, that's easy for you to say,' Georgina said. A look of resignation settled on her perfect features. 'I never asked to be a Midder, to go to a different school, live in a separate circle to my family. I had no one until Lewis found me a year ago. I thought I was helping rebel against a system I despise, but when Elise was hurt I told him I couldn't continue. And that's when he started blackmailing me . . . He said he'd tell the museum that I'd released the other animals.'

'The Dermadew . . . . That's why you insisted on using it even though you knew you weren't allowed. Why you didn't want the shirt I bought you. You felt guilty all the time,' Elise said.

Lewis clamped his hand over Georgina's mouth. Luca stepped forwards and Lewis shook his head. 'Back up now. Let's not do anything we'll all regret.'

'What do you want, Lewis?' Luca asked, inching towards Georgina.

'I want a lot of things. But right now I want to release all the animals in this stars-forsaken place and get out blameless. That should prove that the Midders and Potiors aren't in complete control. Show the Sapiens there's still hope. And that's where my pretty sister comes in. All those codes locked up in her head—'

'But you don't have to hurt her,' Luca said, stepping towards Georgina.

'I don't have to, but I will if any of you get in my way. So here is what I want; I want my sister to release everything she can and then I want to escape the museum, or I will throw her to the saltwater crocodiles.'

Georgina's eyes bulged over Lewis's hand, still covering half her face.

'But she's your sister!' Luca said.

'She would've been my sister, but she's just another Midder. A necessary sacrifice for the greater good. I have to look at what's best for my species; I can't let personal ties get in the way.'

'No,' Samuel said. 'You will not release all of my animals. It would be a massacre. If Georgina dies, so be it.'

'Samuel!' Luca said, shaking his head.

Samuel was unmoved. 'What?'

'That's just plain cold.'

'Do you think her life is more valuable than the hundreds of animals that could die?'

Worried that this was going to get out of control, Elise decided to take the lead.

She turned to Lewis. 'What if we release only the herbivores? It'll still be mayhem, just not as bloody.'

'Think about it, Lewis,' Luca said, warming up to her idea. 'Elephants, mammoths, giraffes, giant sloths, bush-antlered deer. It'll take days for them to be rounded up. Everyone in the base will hear about it.'

Lewis looked around at them as he considered. 'I'm guessing that you're all trying to break Twenty-One out.' No one responded. 'They didn't confide in you about that, did they, sister?'

'Good job as well,' Samuel muttered.

'It's actually in my interest for your mission to be successful. It's an even bigger blow to the museum's reputation if they can't hold on to their precious Neanderthal display. They might start listening to our demands if pressure is applied in the right places.'

Elise and Samuel looked at each other.

'We agree,' Kit signed. 'Samuel, take Bay.' He placed her in Samuel's arms before he could object. 'She is coming with us. She needs to be with the strongest one and separate from me.'

Elise was about to protest when she realised Kit was right.

'What? What did he say?' Lewis asked. 'I only caught half of it.'

'He said that we agree. And that he'll personally decapitate you if you betray us,' Luca said, no hint of his usual sarcasm in his voice.

'Good,' Lewis said. 'Now we all know the rules. No one hurts me or Georgina dies. I don't betray you or it's decapitation with a blunt spear.'

He slowly removed his hand from Georgina's mouth, pinning both of her arms with his.

Kit gestured for the wrap around Georgina's chest and she shrugged it off over her backpack, Lewis only allowing one of her arms to go free at a time. Kit turned to Samuel and carefully strapped the still-sleeping Bay tightly to his back, pulling to make sure that she was secure. Georgina glanced over at Bay as Lewis led her to the wall of controls.

'How many codes do you have?' Samuel asked.

'Five, including yours,' Georgina said, not looking at him.

'Mine won't be working now that Fintorian knows I can't be trusted,' Samuel said. 'But we can take down the cameras as well as the barriers with four codes.'

They all watched as Georgina plugged each of the sixteen-digit codes into the large screen, all from memory.

'One of the three gifts of genetic engineering from my father,' Lewis said conversationally. 'He was never really a true anti-Midder – he was a hypocrite. He wanted their gifts for his family just as much as everyone else does. He wanted Georgina to have an excellent memory so she would never forget what she was able to learn – what I'd never have the chance to learn.'

'The only sensible one he chose,' Georgina said. 'He had three choices to make and the other two were the selections of a half-baked drunk.'

Lewis cracked his elbow into the middle of Georgina's back and she doubled over under the force. They all rushed forwards, even Samuel.

'Stop there, please,' Lewis said calmly. He shook Georgina. 'And you, you had better remember who you're talking about, Midder.'

Straightening, Georgina shook her head and her features settled into their own protective mask. When the final code was plugged in, they all looked around at one another.

'Well, there's only one way to test this,' Luca said. 'I'll take us through the herbivores' pods to the exit.'

Silently, they left the control room, Kit and Samuel in the middle, followed by Elise. Lewis was at the rear, still holding on to Georgina. Elise didn't like having her back to Lewis, but he refused to leave until she was in front.

It was three in the morning and they only had two hours before the sun would start to rise. Two hours to clear the museum and get to the edge of Thymine Base.

Following Luca, they ran, bent low, as quietly as possible, snaking through the first pod. Nothing stirred in the long grass as they crossed to the other side. At the edge of the pod, Kit stopped and tentatively inched forwards, his body braced for the shock that might send him flying backwards. They stood watching him, also bracing, prepared for failure. But nothing happened.

'It worked,' he signed, moving into the next pod.

This one was harder to run across. The cold air caught in Elise's throat as her feet skidded on the frosted tundra. She gasped as she passed six woolly mammoths eyeing the intruders. Their tusks were huge, mobile weapons; one had a set so long it was as if they were reaching round to shake hands with each other.

'Elise, your sling,' Samuel shouted back at her. 'We have to get them moving. They don't know they can leave.'

Still running, Elise loaded her sling and shot a few stones at them, careful not to hit their skulls, their shaggy hair dulling the force. Trumpeting in alarm, the oldest matriarch of the herd roused her daughters.

'Agghh!' Luca shouted as the herd stampeded after them, chasing the humans out of their territory.

After the stillness of the last pod, the noise created by the roused mammoths was terrifying; they found they could all run faster.

Lewis had to let go of Georgina as they sprinted to the other side. A younger female mammoth overtook the grandmother as she blazed after them, forgetting about the boundary wall. Seeing that she hadn't been repelled by the electric fence, the other mammoths followed, blaring their low calls to one another across the pod.

It was a domino effect. Once the mammoths entered the impalas' pod, the small antelopes scarpered, overtaking the humans. Pod after pod, the inhabitants ran from the mammoths or circled in panic. Elise dodged around a glyptodont that lumbered in front of her, his armadillo-like body nearly as tall as her and twice as long. The largest deer Elise had ever seen leapt over the glyptodont's shell and she only just ducked in time to avoid being hit by one of his twelve-foot antlers. A quagga – half-horse, half-zebra – skittered around Elise, his hooves making the dust fly before pounding off in the opposite direction to the antlered deer.

Elise skidded to a halt when a giant sloth, resting on his back legs, turned from picking the leaves from the highest branches of a tree. With a force that made the ground shake, he dropped onto all fours. Instead of moving away from the mammoths, he started to lumber towards Elise. He was nearly the same size as the mammoths and had no fear of them. Elise realised that she was cut off from Samuel, Luca and Kit, who had managed to circle around the other side of the tree. She was trapped between the mammoths behind and the sloth ahead.

'This way,' Georgina shouted, veering to her right into another pod. 'Into the Tasmanian devil's pod; it's a carnivore, so there's still a barrier.'

Elise ran after Georgina and Lewis, her heart pounding as she moved farther from Kit and Samuel. She was by the edge of the museum and there was an exit to her right. Elise didn't want to take it, though; she couldn't lose sight of Luca, who she knew was leading them to the northeast exit. If they didn't leave the museum together, she might not find them.

Spotting the doorway, Lewis shoved Georgina out of his way.

'This is where I leave you, big sister,' he shouted as he sprinted to the southeast exit. 'Don't follow. You're not welcome where I'm going.'

Elise grabbed for Georgina's backpack, but didn't catch her in time. She fell heavily to the ground. Elise glanced over at her three friends in the far corner by the northeast exit. She could just pick out that they were waving at her; she waved back. All three of their waves grew more frantic and Elise turned around to help Georgina up.

There was no time to react. Fintorian slammed her into the ground.

Flying back, she held her head up, trying to soften her fall. She had thought she had knocked him out or even killed him; he was stronger than she had imagined. Landing on her back, she felt all the air leave her lungs. Gasping, no relief would come. She willed her body to work again.

'You didn't think I would let you get away that easily? My life was nearly taken by you. That is unforgivable,' Fintorian said, standing over her.

Placing a foot on Elise's neck, he started to push his boot down.

'When the dogs forget who their masters are, they must be reminded. Order must be preserved or the whole pack turns.'

Elise felt the slow pressure increase on her neck, taking her breath. Choking her. She froze at the realisation that she was nothing to him.

'No one will be sorry when they hear you were trampled in the pandemonium you created. A fitting end, I believe,' Fintorian said, not a trace of emotion in his voice.

Elise clawed at Fintorian's leg, but he didn't flinch. Instead, boot still on her throat, he reached down to Elise's right hand and took her index finger between his hands. Before she even realised what he was doing, he snapped her finger backwards and twisted it, making sure the fracture was displaced.

Elise opened her mouth to scream, pain flooding her hand as hot tears squeezed out of her eyes, but no sound came out; she was choking. Her eyes bulged as Fintorian's boot pressed deeper into her throat and he reached for her thumb.

She desperately gasped for the breath that couldn't get past her crushed airway. Her eyes began to close as she weakened, consciousness resurfacing briefly as Fintorian snapped her thumb at the knuckle.

Black spots flooded her vision when the foot moved and instinct kicked in. Her body took over and she automatically gasped as the pressure was released. Elise glanced up; Georgina's tiny frame was clinging to Fintorian's back with a syringe in her hand.

Enraged at her intrusion, Fintorian pulled Georgina from behind him with both hands. With no effort, he threw her away from him. Her cheek scraped along the ground as she landed heavily.

'Go, Elise! *Go!*' Georgina shouted, panic making her voice rise.

Fintorian cocked his head to one side as he examined her. 'Those sedatives won't work on us, nurse. We only stock the ones Potiors are immune to.' Then, with a sickening thud, he kicked Georgina in the side and knelt down next to her. 'Such gifts you were given, which you've decided to squander. A fitting punishment would be to take those aesthetic qualities away.' He picked up a rock and held her face still with the other hand.

Both Elise and Georgina cried out in matching terror, but it was Elise's scream that drew Fintorian's attention. He dropped Georgina's head and turned his focus back on Elise. He stood and smiled as he walked over. Elise moaned. Her broken fingers dug into the earth as she desperately scrabbled backwards. She felt the tears on her face; she hadn't realised she was crying. She glanced over her shoulder. Luca, Samuel and Kit were running towards her, but they were still too far away to help.

Elise tried to stand as she edged backwards. Fintorian was nearly on top of her, taking his time, savouring her fear. He stretched out his hand. Elise turned her face away, willing him to be quick, not to toy with her.

Sparks flew and a faint sizzling hung in the air. Fintorian was repelled backwards by the pod fence. He landed next to Georgina with a thud. Realising it wasn't a sedative Georgina had injected into Fintorian, Elise pushed herself unsteadily back to her feet.

'*Run!*' Georgina screamed.

She raised her head from the ground, blood pumping out of the gash to her cheek. Without pausing, Fintorian grabbed Georgina from behind. Towering above her, his arm snaked around her neck, preparing to snap it, as he would have done with the sabre-tooth. With a roar, his arm locked into place and Georgina squeezed her eyes shut.

Samuel's spear whistled past Elise's ear, making her flinch. It lodged deep into Fintorian's throat, bursting an artery. Confusion flitted across his face as he reached for it with both hands before slumping to the ground, his eyes rolling up in his head.

Elise ran towards Georgina and looked down at her blood-streaked face. 'Can you run?'

'I think so,' Georgina said.

'Do you want to come with us? Or do you want to stay here and repair your cheek?'

'I can stitch it up with your help when we get to the woods. The scar will have to stay.'

'Come on then,' Elise said, hauling Georgina to her feet with one arm, careful to hold her own useless right hand close to her chest.

Taking Georgina's hand, she tugged her along as they pelted towards Samuel, Kit and Luca, who were only halfway across the last pod. Elise could see guards in the distance, but they were preoccupied with the escaping menagerie of animals stampeding across the vista.

Elise ran past her friends, still holding Georgina's hand. 'She's coming with us. No time for discussion.'

The three men sprinted after them to the northeast doorway, Bay nuzzled into Samuel's back, her pineapple hair bobbing behind them. None of the museum guards saw the five dots in the distance slipping out through the exit.

EPILOGUE

. . . .

3 Days later

Elise looked around the small campfire at her companions. No one spoke. They had unwillingly come together for the warmth only.

After hiking for three days with no idea of where Samuel was taking them, the atmosphere in the camp was strained. Luca had tried to speak to Georgina a few times, but had given up after she had pulled her hood across her face and turned away. Despite saving her life by throwing the spear that killed Fintorian, Samuel had not spoken to Georgina at all, still furious at her betrayal. Similarly, Kit ignored Georgina; Elise guessed out of loyalty to Samuel. Kit would only approach her in the afternoon to take Bay from her, an unspoken arrangement, but one that worked. Georgina wore a glazed expression most of the time; and the only person who could jolt her out of her thoughts was Bay. Elise, meanwhile, had found herself avoiding Luca whenever possible, unable to slip back into an amiable friendship with him. The multiple betrayals had splintered the group.

Staring down at her hand, Elise winced as she examined her index finger and thumb under the flickering light of the fire. Georgina had used all her skill to try and align the broken bones

Fintorian had so casually destroyed, but it would take weeks before she knew whether they had set properly. And there was nothing Georgina could do for the thick band of purple bruises around Elise's neck; they would just need to time to heal.

Elise quickly pushed the thought aside, not wanting to remember the first day they had spent out of Thymine Base. The only positive memory had been when she'd stood at the lip of the valley and watched as Kit made his way up the final winding path that led them out of the only base she had known. Every few seconds he had glanced around, the wonder on his face clear for everyone to see. After walking non-stop for twelve hours, setting false trails and doubling back on themselves several times, they had decided that they had put enough distance between themselves and Thymine for the day. That evening, Georgina had tended to Elise first. With no anaesthetics, they had to put a cloth in Elise's mouth for her to bite down on while Georgina pulled and twisted the two bones back into place. Even then, Samuel had had to clamp his hand over Elise's mouth to muffle her screams as he held her still. Luca had had to do the same for Georgina when Samuel sutured the cut on her cheek.

Despite all this, Elise had treasured the last two days and the new experiences they had provided outside Thymine's small valley. They had walked from sunrise to sunset, tracing their way through the woodland, her attention caught by every bird that flew overhead, every rustle below her feet. She had only ever seen the forest in the distance and never entered it before. They had followed Samuel, Elise and Kit straggling at the back of the line, pointing out new plants and animals to each other.

She smiled to herself, remembering Kit's expression when it had first begun to rain. He had worn a look of confusion as the drips slowly snaked their way down the channels of the leaves. The rain had grown heavier and the noise as it pummelled against the foliage high above their heads had made him jump. Within minutes they had been soaked, Elise grinning at Kit while pushing the hair from her forehead, Kit scrunching his eyes and then tilting his head up to the sky to catch the rainwater in his mouth.

That evening, they had emerged from the edge of the woodland, blinking even in the fading light. Kit had gasped as the wind whipped around their heads, unused to the elements after his endlessly still pod. They had stood at the top of a rock ledge and peered down at the expanse of moorland, the purple heather running for miles in every direction.

They had stood next to each other, shivering in the cold but still enjoying the view, and Samuel had brought over his backpack and offered them some of his clothes. After consideration, Kit had pulled one of Samuel's jumpers on over his tunic; it was the first time he had worn something he had chosen for himself.

He had then settled on the ground, propping Bay on his knee, and taken in his first full sunset.

Elise watched the loose sparks from the fire jet upwards before abruptly disappearing. It was the first fire they had lit, despite the cold, as Samuel hadn't wanted to risk attracting attention. However, this evening they had found a small cave underneath the rock face that offered them shelter for the night, so Samuel had grudgingly allowed it.

Elise gazed around the campfire at her silent friends. Kit was dressed in a jacket zipped up to his chin, cotton trousers and sturdy boots; she thought he could be mistaken for a Sapien. It was only his heavy brow ridge and non-existent chin that would make someone look more closely. Luca was checking their water supplies; Elise didn't know why, but he had become quieter in the last day. Samuel looked strained. His left eye had started to tic slightly; he had barely slept in three days. He insisted on watching over them each night, arguing that he had the best hearing. Elise couldn't see Georgina's face, as she had pulled her hood up over her bandaged cheek.

Kit leant over to Elise and handed her a sheet of paper.

'I tore it from the outside of the museum. What does it say?' he signed, before idly playing with the zip on his jacket.

Elise unfolded the paper and glanced over it.

'It's a notice about the cost of engineering increasing in price. See here,' she signed, tracing her hand over the writing. 'Empathy: 2,000 tickets; Height: 5,000 tickets; IQ: 8,000 tickets. It goes on to list them all; I'd say there's at least a hundred. Shall we use it for kindling?'

Kit stared at Elise, his thoughts hidden as always. Taking the notice from her hand, he folded it and tucked it into his backpack. 'It has no other use now. When we're settled, can you teach me to read and write?'

'I always wanted to but the Potiors wouldn't let me. No forty-thousand-year rule now, though.' Elise leant over. 'How're you finding it, being out of the museum?'

Kit thought for a moment before responding. 'I think I will get used to the setting and I am looking forward to seeing a house like you grew up in one day. The weather will take longer to get used to, but I want to watch a thunderstorm. It is the freedom and choices that are hard to adapt to. Yesterday, I nearly refused the sandwich Samuel had brought with him as I thought it was not for people like me. All that is going to take a while to change.'

'It will, but you've time now to decide what you want. No one's making choices for you any more.' Elise turned to Samuel. 'You should say where you're taking us.'

Samuel was roused from his thoughts; he studied each of their faces. 'I said it before; it's not safe yet.'

'We need to know; you can't make all the decisions.'

'Elise is right,' Georgina said. They stared at her; it was the first thing she had said in two days.

Samuel rubbed his eyes. 'There's more at stake than just our safety.'

Luca was massaging his temples. 'Cryptic as always, Samuel. Why don't you leave us a trail of clues that we can puzzle over? Maybe there can be a leader board; it'll help keep track of who gets closest to guessing where you're taking us.'

Elise glared at Luca before turning her attention back to Samuel. 'You're not thinking straight; you're exhausted. There are no cameras; they would've followed us into the cave and you would've heard them in here. It's safe.'

Samuel rubbed the nape of his neck. They watched him as he stared up at the roof of the cave.

'You're right,' he said wearily. 'I was hoping to do this when we got closer, but I see now that it can't wait. There are a few things you need to know.' He turned to Kit and gave him a half-smile. 'Although the others have never been con-fined to a pod like you have, in some ways, they know as little about the outside as you do. Less actually, because first they have to unravel what they've been taught before starting again. I hope you take some comfort from knowing that you're not alone in this.'

Kit nodded and leant back on his hands.

'I want you all to know that I don't intend to sound as if I am speaking from some lofty, omniscient height. I'm aware that I sometimes appear to be lecturing, or maybe even looking down on you. But please understand that is never my intention. I find people difficult to understand and relate to, but that doesn't mean that I don't appreciate them, or enjoy their company.'

Samuel paused. 'It is correct that there are four bases, each with their own distinct specialism. But there is also another place, Uracil, which is unknown to the leaders of Zone 3. It's located in the remotest region, far from the other bases and also inland so it cannot be found from the coast. It has existed for nearly fifty years and is made up of those who were able to escape their bases and locate it.'

'I thought you were born in Adenine?' Luca said, unable to hold back any longer.

'Yes, I was. I grew up there before going to university in Guanine, where I first met Kit. But my mother was brought up in Uracil. Twenty-five years ago, they decided to send some of their residents back into the bases. Some would call them spies, I suppose. They wanted to know what further advancements had been made. They fear the hold the Potior have and where the next scientific discoveries will take them. My mother volunteered, then I did as well. There are a few of us located in each base, observing and gathering information before returning to report our findings. I was asked to watch over the Neanderthal Project.' Samuel glanced at Kit.

'Something I've never regretted. I was supposed to return seven years following my eighteenth birthday. But it seems I will be six months early.'

Elise tried to swallow, her mouth dry. 'Show me your wrist, Samuel.'

He pulled back the sleeve of his jumper and displayed his wrist to Elise. The distinctive tattoo – the one they all had except Kit – was where it was supposed to be: Samuel Adair, 20 May 2244, Adenine Base, Medius.

'Mine is real,' he said. 'Marked on my fourteenth birthday, the same as all the other Sapiens and Medius. My mother's is not, though; she had it forged before entering Adenine Base and her details were slipped into the system by one of her associates at the data offices.

'So that is where I am taking you, to Uracil. And from there you can decide what you want to do. I have given the matter some considerable thought over these past few months. I know that each of you wanted to leave the world you were brought up in, and that you'll be of use and benefit to our small community. You as well, Georgina; Elise was right to bring you with us. There are a lot of changes taking place in Uracil and they will want our help.'

A few hours later, Elise was the only one awake. She had managed to persuade Samuel to let her guard the group for a few hours so he could finally have the sleep that he needed. Once he had told them where they were going, the five of them had chatted together for the first time in weeks, relaxing at last in one another's company. The tension had lifted.

Sitting beside the dancing flames, she thought of how much had changed in the last year. Where would she be in a year's time?

Watching over her companions, she thanked the stars that – regardless where she ended up – she had been given the opportunity to view the world through her own lens.

AUTHOR'S NOTE

Much has changed in the world of paleoanthropology since I first began reading about Neanderthals. When I drafted the first book in this series the consensus was that Neanderthals died out around 30,000 years ago, but in recent years this has been revised to 40,000. Similarly, Homo floresiensis was thought to have existed until 12,000 years ago, which was almost touching distance for us when the whole of human evolution is considered. However, this has now been revised and it is believed that they died out 50,000 years ago. Archaeologists are constantly developing their theories on the basis of new discoveries or new dating techniques applied to older samples. This fascinating area of science is constantly evolving and therefore the research that has gone into this book is a snapshot of what was available at the time of publication.

I have tried to be as faithful as possible to the information I have been able to gather, but have taken some artistic licence when discussing Neanderthals' speech and possibly their cognitive abilities. Both are uncertain areas, where behaviour can largely only be inferred, and consequently there is a wide range of opinions. Also, as the series is set in the future there will be more discoveries to come and the current trajectory is that Neanderthals were far more advanced than what was believed even ten or twenty years ago.

Perhaps, in five years time we will have newly revised dates for extinction, or further discoveries that confirm, rather than merely hint at, Neanderthals participating in burials and art. I am looking forward to finding out.

A. E. Warren, 2021

ACKNOWLEDGMENTS

I had always believed that writing a book is a solitary endeavour, but I am happy to confirm that it is not. When I began writing, I was incredibly grateful that several people around me became interested in this new path I had taken. My thanks therefore begin with Lee, Jo, Darryl, Julie, Lorraine, Mike, Yash, Lindsay, Kat, and Richard for the hours of your time you willingly gave, your much needed advice and most of all your encouragement. I'd also like to thank my original editors, Rowan Fortune and Sara Litchfield, for encouraging me at a time when I was considering giving up writing.

I also need to say a big thank you to my agent, Bev James, who championed the series and secured my publishing deal. At Del Rey my gratitude continues to the whole team. I have only met a fraction of them, but every one of them has contributed to this publication. In particular, I would like to thank Sam Bradbury, Ben Brusey, Kasim Mohammed, Rachel Kennedy and Roisin O'Shea for their expert guidance and support.

Lastly, but never least, I would like to thank everyone who has bought, read, or reviewed my books. Your support and encouragement has driven me on, picked me up and safely delivered me to where I am today.

ABOUT THE AUTHOR

After spending eight years working as a lawyer, A.E. Warren began to write in the evenings and early mornings as a form of escapism from life in a very small cubicle with lots of files. She self-published her first novels in her spare time, which were picked up by Del Rey UK which is the science fiction/fantasy imprint of Penguin Random House. She is an avid reader, occasional gamer and fair-weather runner. Subject Twenty-One is her debut novel and there will be four books in the Tomorrow's Ancestors series. She lives in the UK with her husband, daughter and hopefully, one day, a wise border terrier named Austen.

You can find her at aewarren.com or one of the following:
  Instagram: @amauthoring
  Facebook: @amauthoring
  Twitter: @amauthoring
  Pinterest: @amauthoring